Paper Alley

William A. Wright
Dale Ann Edmiston

Brave Knight
Writers

Paper Alley
By William A. Wright and Dale Ann Edmiston

Brave Knight Writers
www.braveknightwriters.com

Editor: Deb Hall (thewriteinsight.com)
Cover Design: Jennifer Fleming
Cover Images: William A. Wright

Paper Alley/ Wright & Edmiston. —1st ed.
ISBN: 978-1-7357522-7-3
ISBN (e-book): 978-1-7357522-9-7

OTHER TITLES BY THE AUTHORS:

Havasupai

St. Croix: the novel

Instead, by Grace

St. Croix: through the wall

For the unborn

So, it becomes the devil's business to keep the Christian's spirit imprisoned. He knows that the believing and justified Christian has been raised up out of the grave of his sins and trespasses. From that point on, Satan works that much harder to keep us bound and gagged, actually imprisoned in our own grave clothes. He knows that if we continue in this kind of bondage... we are not much better off than when we were spiritually dead.

—A.W. Tozer

PROLOGUE

There are two people in every small town who know everything about everyone: the bartender and the pastor. The people in these pages felt at ease confiding their innermost thoughts and feelings to me, part of my job. Being third generation in my profession provides an additional advantage of knowing the history of this insignificant speck on the map. Is the story I tell based in truth? Of Irish descent, I am equipped with a natural storytelling gift accompanied by a tendency toward embellishment. Rest assured, any dalliance on my part contributes an entertaining element to the text and in no way distorts the underlying truths.

Pull up a stool. Where should I begin? To set the stage, first let me paint the picture of eternal war. Acute for some, chronic for others, denied by fools, but for all humankind a war truly exists, acknowledged or not.

Second, if statement one is true, can we assume war emanates from unseen elements? Consider good versus evil, God versus Satan. If these terms are bothersome, surely you will concede there is a war at the very least between entropy and intelligence, or chaos and order. So, let me begin in an era before my time.

ONE

Harry saw him first. A smooth, flat stone skipped from his hand, bounced errantly, and smacked against the boot. Lee's ears, then his eyes, followed the sound. John was slow to focus on the scene. Too young to grasp the reality of their find, none spoke. None of the three had ever seen a real dead man. The body floated face down. Long hair flowed in the current. He bobbed leisurely, no hint of struggle. Spellbound, they watched as the current lifted then sank the torso, only to lift it again. The youngest of the three dropped his crawfish bucket and backed away from the others. The body had a familiar look to it, even face down in Stony Creek.

Like a starter pistol, the crashing bucket triggered a race. Barefoot boys made up for their pause by sprinting the mile back to town. They scaled the tumble of rocks along the falls. Speechless, they leapt over logs on an ever-uphill journey away from the rapids. Through the hemlock grove they fled, along the marsh at the edge of town until their feet slapped on the only paved street, Main Street. They didn't stop until they burst through old Doc Boggs's front door, hurtling past the receptionist. Without a word they hunkered, gasping for breath.

Doc Boggs stood frozen in front of his medicine cabinet. He dropped his hand from his mouth, almost losing his grip on the glass he had just emptied with a gulp. His other hand rested on a clear bottle perched on the counter, contents unlabeled. "You boys gave me a start." The old doctor wiped his mouth with his sleeve. "Do you have an appointment?"

The tallest boy caught his breath. "There's a body in Stony Creek down below the rapids!"

"Ya don't say?" Doc rubbed his chin as his heart slowed. "Have you told anyone else?"

"No, sir. We came straight here. Ya gotta go, Doc."

"Is he underwater, boy? I mean face down, you know."

"Yes, sir."

"Well, I doubt there's much I can do for him. Besides, this old body would never make it down below those rapids. We best fetch some volunteers to go down and bring him up to me."

The youngest of the boys slumped into Doc's worn red leather chair. "It's my dad."

Doc rested a hand on his shoulder. "You sure about that, son?"

Doc knew everyone in the county and knew the boy's father better than most. He had tended to him after many a fight. Seems the boy's father had a way of ruffling the feathers of the town's establishment. He worked hard, spoke straight, and had ambition, a threat to some. Doc thought highly of the man; his attributes were rare in this town. Doc knew him as a young man returning from Europe in the summer of 1919. A survivor of Meuse-Argonne, the front lines of hell and "the war to end all wars." A million American souls wallowing in the mud and blood in a shattered landscape. Haunting images of men racked in fear unable to move even their bulging eyes. A man who led the charge of fellow soldiers toward an enemy trench. A group of soldiers equally frightened, scrambling on their bellies and eating mud for a hundred yards, hot lead inches overhead, only to drop into a shattered trench of frightened enemy, where so many succumbed to a German bayonet. This man now lay floating face down in Stony Creek? Doc shivered; he had always envied McKenzie's courage. Unfathomable.

Squeezing the boy's shoulder, Doc whispered, "Sorry, John, I hope you're mistaken."

John began to sob.

Doc refilled the glass, swallowing with a look of a man who had just consumed hot lava. "Well, what's done is done."

While the boys struggled to decipher what Doc had muttered, he shouted, "Emma, come in here!"

Emma popped her head around the door.

"We're closed for the day. See to it these boys get home to their mommas."

"Yes, sir." Emma reached out and hugged all three boys together, then led them from the room.

###

The body had a lot to say. Doc made a conscious choice to ignore the shouts made by the lacerations and bruises. He discarded the shred of cloth clutched in the man's hand. The obituary repeated the official report:

A tragic accident has taken the life of a local businessman, Jim McKenzie. He is survived by his widow, Louise, and young son, John.

Jim McKenzie's widow never officially challenged the report. She knew it was no accident. She never again went to see Doc, nor did she ever send the boy to him. The McKenzies toughed out their ailments using home remedies. As the years passed, the town saw less and less of the widow McKenzie. Eventually, she never ventured out of the house. John ran all the errands and took care of her as best he could.

During the first year after Jim's body was found, it was all the talk—at the barbershop, in the market, and around the woodstove at the hardware. Few believed it was an accident. A few speculated it was a suicide, spawned by a bad debt. With the stock market crash and all, suicides were the headlines of the day, never mind that the crash might just as well have been on the moon as in this backwater town. Others said it was murder. A word which, when spoken, usually brought silence and downcast eyes. Jim was a good-looking man. Possibly it was a jealous husband. But Jim always acted the gentleman. Even so, there were many who were jealous of widow McKenzie before she bore the title. If he had been murdered for those reasons, it would have been the murder of an innocent man.

Widow McKenzie's cousins tried to talk her into petitioning the state for an investigation, but she refused. She wanted peace and safety for John. She knew who killed her husband. She knew why he was killed. She knew all she had to do was outlive the murderer, stand her ground, and let him stew. Her vengeance would be served on a cold platter. She silently waited, praying—and remaining faithful to her Jim. The guilty ones knew she held all the cards. Most of the town chose not to speculate on the truth; instead, they dallied in fantasies. After a while, talk of Jim just faded away.

As for old Doc's drinking, it took a bad turn when the report got filed. He had a conscience, and he tried to drown it. His drink went from a like to a need. He doubled down the first month and doubled down again the next. He began to keep irregular office hours, and Emma ran low on excuses. Eventually, Doc took on a young assistant for the sake of his patients. Ironically, by the third autumn after Jim was found in the Stony, Doc's body was also found. He had finally made it down below the falls. His body floated in the same pool as Jim's. Another tragic accident was logged in the record books.

Widow McKenzie showed no emotion upon hearing of Doc's demise, but she knew it, too, was no accident. Doc had called on her the night before he was found. He wasn't drunk, and he spoke of his plan and how he finally had gained the courage to right a few wrongs.

###

Time marched on. The war in Europe became all the talk. The town looked outward for the first time since World War I. Most of the men joined the service or were drafted. Widow McKenzie took in a boarder, a young female college student who agreed to look out for her so John could enlist. When John returned at the end of the war, he married the girl. The fifties came and went. Vietnam snatched several of the town's boys.

###

Louise lay dying. John held her hand in the house Jim had built. It was 1973 and Louise needed a promise, but first she needed to explain to her son just what had happened to his father. There wasn't much time; her eyes kept slipping shut. Her breathing was shallow. She motioned for John to lean near. When she was done, John closed his eyes, squeezing her hand. A knot formed in his throat. As she spoke once again, he saw himself standing on the shore of the Stony, a small boy, crawfish bucket in hand. When the bucket dropped, his last shreds of innocence had gone with it. Finally, it all made sense to him. His eyes caught her last gasp for breath, her lungs rattling.

"I promise, Momma, I promise . . ." His voice trailed off into a whisper as Louise let out her last breath.

"Momma . . ." John's eyes welled. *I'm done with this town, the small-minded lunatics*. John would keep his promise. A promise and a curse would go with the house if ever he sold it. He could no longer live in the house or the town or even the county. But for as long as he lived, he would make sure his promise to his mother would live on. Taking up her Bible, he scratched a few words and placed it in her secret place, to rest in the house forever. He wanted to avenge his father, even if the guilty were long dead. Now the town belonged to the murderers' descendants, and they could have most of it... but not Jim's part. Never.

Truth, like the Stony Creek, coursed into time.

TWO

A thick oak crown obscured the second story of the old McKenzie house on Elm Street, and if that wasn't enough, heavy drapes smothered any hope of a peek beyond its filmy windows. One drape, however, shifted ever so slightly.

"Here it is, Mrs. Winslow, your final duty station. What do you think?" Harold McDonath, realtor, placed his car in park with his one good hand. His cosmetic prosthesis rested on his lap.

"Were you in the war, Mr. McDonath?" All week Julie had wondered how he lost his arm, but she didn't want to be rude by asking him directly. Their recent conversation had McDonath asking her about her military service, so the urge coupled with opportunity could not be constrained any longer, and the words blurted out with a blush and regret.

"In the military... no... but isn't life war? My arm represents a battle won, Mrs. Winslow, don't be troubled." Seasoned by life, McDonath long ago realized a sense of injury is dependent on assuming a legitimate claim has been denied. Turning his battle into a win required him to refuse claim to his missing arm; the move had reduced his youthful ill-tempered rage. "But to the point, I thought you might like this house. Let's just say, no commissions involved, I'm doing this gratis for dear friends."

Mr. McDonath gently stroked his prosthetic arm. Most men of his age had long retired. His spirit would have none of it. His fear consisted of dying in a costly nursing home amid lying doctors and nurses promising life and encouragement while wallowing in a belief that sickness offers excuses for self-indulgence. Instead, this man, with a watchful eye, sought knowledge of the true condition of the vessel containing his spirit and remained afloat in the surf.

"You're friends with the owners?" Julie's eyes focused on the house, which had a captivating style, and she felt an instant connection to its need for renewal, after all—the next phase of her own life.

"Not just the owners but also an interested party." Mr. McDonath paused, taking time to read Julie. "You said you're tired of moving every two years, want the children to have a stable high school experience and a sanctuary for Mr. Winslow. Well, I can put you in this house well below market. A contact through the bank can provide additional perks. Your military pensions will qualify you without question. I suggest we stay away from involving the VA."

"Why would you do this?" Julie's eyes expressed concern.

McDonath took a deep breath. His eyes never blinked; his tone exuded both confidence and sincerity.

"Let's just say, you fit certain criteria. We like helping veterans." McDonath appreciated the fact that Julie and her husband stepped forward to volunteer, sacrificing to protect others, regardless of the fact many of those others exercised protected rights with contempt and mockery.

"My friends would love having a couple of warriors resting here. I think you'll contribute much love where it is most needed. Love... isn't it what makes life sweet?"

Julie crossed her arms across her chest in a hugging fashion

"Look at the setting. It's just as you described your dream to me, isn't it? These old oaks look glorious in the fall."

Julie and McDonath separately toyed with the adage "You never know when you are in the presence of an angel."

"This is it! It's perfect, just as I imagined." Julie opened the car door without getting out.

Harold McDonath leaned forward looking through the windshield at a second-floor window. "All you've told me is your husband is currently deployed. Where might he be?" McDonath's question possessed a threat of pain as had her question about his missing arm.

Julie hesitated, her fantasy on hold in a burst of reality, and her eyes grew distant. Her pulse quickened, and her throat choked a bit, but she offered her best answer. McDonath felt remorse for asking as he read her face.

"He couldn't tell me. He just said he would have sand in his boots, code for desert duty. He said he'd just be doing the same thing I'm doing, checking out real estate."

A tear welled in her eye. She refused it and sent it home. Even with Julie's long military background, she couldn't imagine Dan's fate, but her thoughts were with him. Dan never discussed his missions with anyone; he compartmentalized his life and shielded his family from the horrors he faced.

At that very moment Dan faced grave danger.

###

The desiccated riverbank gave way under Dan's boot. No surprise—men of his stature are accustomed to the world giving way to them. His muscle-wrapped frame had willfully taken on the challenge of unaccommodating terrain. The crunch of sand and gravel beneath registered normal. His ears tuned for resonances of danger generated by hostiles. With a knee dropped, automatically catching the shifting weight of his body armor and weapon, such reflexes freed him to concentrate on more serious business. Dan paused to take note of the position of each member of his team, spread across the wash. Three bodies first, then the severed heads perched on sticks a distance away; he allowed only fleeting shock. His conscience quickly subdued the unconscionable horror, and he released a grimace. Dan, completely aware a blink could result in his own demise, intensified his vision rather than taking to retreat. Senses sharpened, he scanned for hostiles and IEDs. To his men, his raised hand signaled caution and concern for their welfare. Dead friendlies, rotting in a hot sun, possibly a result of meeting him outside the village last evening. It had been a meeting during the onset of dusk. The enemy found advantage in the absence of light and the dulling of senses. These bodies offer a display of terror, a warning to others about the consequences of sharing a truth. The stillness played on his nerves, for outside of time, there is no change. This land could surely attest today was no different than a Tuesday two thousand years ago. Here, only two conditions occur: intense light and absence of light. Dan, a courageous man operating in the light of day, saw the bodies only as a statement by a weak and tarnished enemy. Acts of terror work best on the self-focused. Dan focused on his men.

Confident in his body armor and a full pack, Dan surveyed the sameness of the brown terrain, wondering how or why life could be possible in these circumstances. Ideology, religion, ethnic and tribal issues all involved reasons for choking progress, but few mentioned greed. Greed? At first glance, greed appeared a ludicrous word, until reflected upon in terms of survival. Survival sows the seed of greed early, fertilizes its deepest root to flourish even in barren terrain. These corpses bore witness to the harvest. Hot wind carried a blast of grit into his face, sand being all this forsaken land could offer. In his pack he carried the necessities to feed his flesh, unaware of his spirit's hunger. Patiently, with resolve, his spirit longed for sustenance; his lack of providing nourishment to his soul was its only threat. The world's mightiest military paled in comparison to this wasteland's harshness. It was a barren region no one in his squad dared to call "nowhere," as survival depended on pronouncing it "now-here" instead.

###

"This is the place I go while Dan is off getting sand in his boots." Regaining her composure, Julie stepped from the realtor's car. The shaded streets of Stony Grove, Tennessee, were inviting after two years of blistering sun at Fort Irwin while Dan trekked off into the unknown.

"I thought you might think so." McDonath turned off the ignition and sighed. "Since it's not on the market, officially, I can't take you inside. It's just a pocket listing."

"Pocket listing?"

"Unofficial, a gentleman's agreement, so to speak. We've exhausted my official inventory. This was my last shot. I'm showing it to you because I've come to think of you as a special client. So, you like it?"

Truth be known, McDonath was well aware of the need for an infusion of new blood, the right blood to carry on. While showing Julie prospective housing, McDonath had assessed her potential, as he had done with so many failed prospects before her. McDonath had a mission: to thwart off the potential temptations of a new generation. He felt Julie functioned quite well in the moment. She resisted losing herself in the unrealities of a future impossible to know. Although she was a planner, McDonath considered that a bonus. She understood the temporal aspect of time—not frozen in some obscure past, no longer able to flow, yet strong of will—and she had a presence of light. She had her weaknesses, everyone does, but her strengths lay in the right arena.

"Like it? I love it!" Julie eyes caught the porch swing and the branches of the beautiful shade trees swaying in the breeze. "This is just what Dan and I need after all we've been through."

McDonath studied her. "Listen, Mrs. Winslow, this is a special place, but take your time. Don't make a rash decision. I appreciate yours and your husband's service and want to make sure you two are happy. It has curb appeal, a right handsome look to it, and good bones." McDonath had lived long enough and buried enough friends to realize, putting a claim to property was a fool's game, laughed at in both heaven and hell. The fact of the matter was that he viewed Julie as merely a potential steward. McDonath firmly believed it foolish to believe in the words *my* or *mine*, even to the point of his own body, for all returns to dust. Julie's spirit had his attention, and his instinct told him the town needed her.

Julie was sold; she had seen every other listing in town. This house wasn't on the market, another bonus. She could take her time without the worry of someone else putting in a bid. Harold McDonath walked around to the passenger's side of the car.

"No pressure. If you have a change of heart, just tell me." McDonath had believed all of his life that all we ever possess is the moment we are in, and it is a gift.

"Not likely. When... can I look inside? And please, call me Julie." Her hand pushed the car door shut.

"I'm also an old friend of the owners, and, not wanting it on the open market, they asked me to screen potential buyers. I will discuss my selection with them privately. They're in no hurry to sell. I can't take you inside just yet, since this is an off-the-record showing, as I mentioned. You've become familiar with house values in these parts. Even so, I'll run off some comparables for you and show you your savings."

Julie paced the sidewalk viewing different angles of the house. She folded her arms across her chest, anxious to go inside.

"Looks like just what the doctor ordered. I know I'm going to want it, contingent on seeing the inside, of course." Julie spoke the words, but McDonath knew the inside was of no consequence, his mark made. His best approach was slow and easy, careful not to spook Julie. Harold McDonath was a good man, a good, loyal friend.

"Let's walk around a bit, maybe look at the backyard and such. Sometimes a good deal comes with concessions. Are you willing to work with me on those? I sincerely want the best for both parties." McDonath glanced up at the window from where the owner peered through hazy glass shielded by heavy drapes. His good arm close to his side, his hand offered a slight wave.

Throughout their house search, Harold McDonath had sprinkled tales of him being a fourth-generation townie and patriarch of the family's four-hundred-acre homestead. Real estate broker, farmer, township supervisor, soon-to-be eighty-two years old, lifelong member of Faith Community Church, and member of a barbershop quartet. Julie liked and trusted him within two minutes of their meeting; his stories were merely icing on the cake. His sincerity and kind smile had won her confidence and put her at ease to tell stories of her own.

She took a deep breath walking across the front lawn. "The shade and smell of oak possesses a healing quality. Don't you think?"

McDonath strolled with Julie, noting the landscaping—in dire need of attention—but he had to agree the two giant oaks shading the front lawn offered cool relief from the late-July sun.

Julie's thoughts bounced between fantasy and stark reality, with reality offering little competition to a long-held dream. "The place needs a little sprucing up. Maybe trim the hedges, pull a few weeds, and take out a few of the oversized shrubs, but otherwise... well, I hope it's priced right. To make a proper judgment, shouldn't I know more? This viewing is superficial to say the least. . . I do find it charming." Yet she needed to consider Dan; he deserved a say, and this created a hesitation in her.

"Julie, we're talking about falling in love. Don't worry, the price will be suitable. You are an adventurer. Your love will grow as you make this home your own."

The yard's neglect came into full focus as they strolled. Julie had witnessed the ravages of war. In the big scheme of things, this neglect was nothing. The world was filled with damaged people and goods, all in need. Julie switched her focus to potential, a potential she knew Dan could draw out.

"It needs love. Dan's the kind of guy who can turn flaws into gems; he can fix anything."

McDonath smiled, finding refreshment in Julie's spirit. Rarely did anyone move forward with the kind of passion he perceived in Julie. His fellow citizens embraced a comfortable existence based in novel pleasures, always subject to the law of diminishing returns. Lacking advancement, Stony Grove's population had developed a shallow sameness, which in turn had led to follies in counsel, infidelities, and inconsistency in friendships. McDonath, a man of great wisdom, possessed a natural ability to read folks and cut to the chase.

"You're right. There is hidden value in this property. It's not a professional thing to say, but I have a bit of an emotional stake in it. It needs a woman like you. Yes, a good woman's touch can work magic, even on the condemned."

Julie cast an inquiring look.

"It goes back to my childhood. My best friend grew up in the house. I guess I'm just a sentimental old fool. I placed many of the residents currently living in this town. I've come to know the magic of a fit. When a client belongs in a house, I sense it, and I think you belong here."

Julie was charmed by Mr. McDonath's lapse, but she felt compelled to find a business resolve. "Price—you haven't told me how much they're asking." Julie quickened her pace down the driveway, outpacing McDonath.

"I still have to firm it up with the owners; they both work. It's tough to pin them down. I'll work up some comparables to show them, just like I'm doing for you. It'll be below fair market price, I can tell you this. If you forgo a home inspection, they will let it go even further below market value. I do recommend you purchase a home warranty, though."

"Comparables won't be easy. I've viewed your inventory. What's their fear of a home inspection?"

"They don't want to haggle over fixing anything. This sale will be 'as is.' They'll have to give you a full disclosure, though. Well, let me nail it down. I assure you, it will be fair to both parties."

Julie stood looking at the garage as McDonath closed the gap. Her eyes were not as glossed over as at first. Reality began to settle in. She walked to where the back lawn touched the driveway. The backyard stretched level until it reached a distant stand of old trees.

"Are they moving because of his work?"

"No, he's the principal of the high school, and his wife teaches. Nice family. They have two boys who just left for college. I think they just want a change, to downsize. They're tired of yard work." He kept stride with Julie, his age not showing a bit.

"Yard work?" Julie smirked as she noted the overgrown lawn tangled in dead branches shed by trees two to three years past.

McDonath shrugged his shoulders in agreement.

"Their boys aren't going to college here?" The college is one of the reasons Dan and Julie wanted to move to this town, along with the drive to his potential new job being convenient. She had read small-town living is all the trend, particularly college towns. They could use the college facilities and capture a little of the college experience, something Dan and Julie never had. They were nontraditional, did school at night and on the weekends. Julie had confidence the town was going to see a real estate boom, due to the university and population trends.

All McDonath could offer was another shrug.

Julie looked toward the neighboring house. It dawned on her the driveway leading to the garage and backyard also led to the garage of the neighboring house. She glanced between the garages and the street, assessing the implications. The neighbor's house appeared neatly kept, with a well-manicured lawn. The well-kept lawn was a positive, but what of this shared driveway?

"Sounds like a great business trend, Mrs. Winslow. If I were younger, it might even excite me. You know, I've been here since the days when the college was called a normal school, so I kind of take it for granted. I'll be retiring soon, long overdue. My daughter, Tricia, wants me to help her with researching our genealogy. My grandson wants me to help him start up an organic orchard. Real estate doesn't offer the thrills it once did, too much computer stuff and government oversight... I'm a romantic. As for the owners' sons, they're bright boys. They're going to private schools."

Julie's attention was elsewhere. "This is a shared driveway; I don't know if my husband will like this. The garage looks weathered, bet the roof leaks. It even has a bit of sag to it."

"You aren't trying to talk yourself out of it, are you? Think price—accepting concessions drives pricing."

"You know, Mr. McDonath, I've never done anything like this before. I feel a little overwhelmed."

"Oh, Julie, relax, everything will be fine. There will be concessions to consider but also a solid guarantee for return on investment, with just a wee bit of sweat. Search your heart—you know best, how to sort through your affairs."

Julie's thoughts were on Dan, unable to accompany her, on his latest last-minute deployment before processing out and awaiting those final discharge orders. Julie had processed out a month earlier in order to embark on this reconnaissance mission in the hopes of finding a home before the start of the school year. Their two teenage sons were staying with her widowed mother for a few weeks, offering Gram comfort.

Time was closing in, and Julie felt the pressure as she mulled the positives and negatives. The decision fell on her. Living in a college town was her fantasy. Her boys could go straight from high school to college and stay right at home. The family had been uprooted at least every two years and dropped into different bases all over the world. An exotic life at first, but she now envisioned a new life—stable, living in one place. She wanted to watch her boys finish maturing into promising young men in a permanent home, keeping them close, even as college approached. Their extended families both lived within an hour. This place could offer much-needed tranquility for Dan and assorted projects to fill his spare time, as he wasn't the type to sit long on the couch. As she struggled to separate her fantasies from the realities, her heart ached. Maybe, because this was the last option, she was justifying the need and ignoring the issues, or perhaps her nurturing heart told her she could make a difference with this suffering home.

"It will all be reflected in the closing price, Julie. I must make sure you know, I represent both you and the sellers. Even though I've known them longer, I can assure you it doesn't give them an advantage; your welfare is of equal concern. The detractions will be considered. As far as the neighbors who share this driveway, they are of the utmost in good character and citizenship. Ed works at the college as a professor, and Mary teaches high school math. They have a daughter in high school, she's top of her class, and their son just left for college, a private school out East, I believe. Ed's a volunteer fireman, active in community affairs. You'll get along fine with them."

"This driveway seems like it could be a problem."

"This isn't a driveway... it's a paper alley. It means there's an encumbrance which exists between the properties, a right of way, that neither party owns nor has absolute control of. It was established on the initial grid layout, when the town was founded. The easement simply allows both parties access."

Julie nodded, then snapped photos of the house from every possible angle to send to Dan. The sun lit the shrubs and hedges, offering warmth to the images. Overgrown, they offered backyard privacy. The lot ended at a wooded area with no homes beyond. *Dan will love the backyard.* One of his fears about town living was to be crowded in on all sides by neighbors—he's country at heart. She knew he would be striking off for walks into those woods. He might even want to get a dog. These things might balance the negatives, such as this paper alley.

"As soon as we settle in, my husband will probably want to walk back there." Julie smiled. "He'll love those woods."

"Ah, yes, I used to hunt back there. Does your husband hunt or fish?"

"No, but he loves the outdoors and open country."

"Out beyond those trees he'll find Stony Creek; it kind of meanders as it flows through town, then it runs fast and furious, good bit of white water as it drops toward the Gorge." Harold's eyes were fired by memories of past adventures. His right hand reached over and grasped his prosthetic left forearm. "We used to hunt crawdads," he murmured.

"What?"

"Nothing, dear, just another long-lost memory, nothing of importance to you," McDonath answered, but Julie's thoughts had already moved beyond her question. So much to grasp, she skipped over details.

"He'll be able to cross-country ski right out the back door. I've got a good feeling about this." Julie glanced at the prosthetic arm, then looked away. They ambled back up the driveway toward the car. She tried to make mental notes for her report to Dan. The photos would fill in the blanks.

"Good, good. I can't wait to talk to the Goldmeadows. I pray they are ready to settle on a price so we can make your dream come true. Let's go back to my office."

McDonath peered over the roof of his car toward the parted drapes in the upstairs window just as the gap in the drapes closed. Julie's eyes were focused down the street. As they settled into the car, a herd of young athletes jogged past in formation. McDonath eased the car away from the curb.

"You're going to like living in Stony Grove; it's a great place for kids." McDonath let out a sigh.

"I understand the community is welcome to use the pool and exercise facilities at the university. I hear they even have a climbing wall."

"The university and the town try to work together."

Julie watched the houses and trees pass by as Mr. McDonath drifted the car down the street. He never seemed in a hurry or ruffled, probably one of the reasons he didn't show his age. Julie smiled. The pace gave her a sense of serenity. Other than McDonath, Julie had yet to get to know anyone in town, except for the clerk at the hotel, but the clerk wasn't a local, didn't even live in Stony Grove.

McDonath turned onto Main Street. The business district, for what it was, had twelve small shops. Stony Grove had a total of four red lights, three gas stations, one bar, a microbrewery, two restaurants, one tattoo parlor, and a resident population of about thirty-five hundred, supplemented by ten thousand students.

"You have a microbrewery? It looks interesting. Do they serve food?"

"We never had drinking establishments in this town until two years ago. Anytime liquor licenses came up on the ballot, we voted it down. Times are changing, I'm afraid. The brewery's an absolute madhouse; I haven't been in it since it was remodeled. It used to be the town doctor's office and morgue. Kind of ironic, it turned into a brewery. I hear the food's not bad."

"Ironic?"

"Like I've said, I live in the past. Don't mind me. You'll find people in small towns hold on to things, even things that happened on the grade school playground. Major events to those of us who haven't had the adventures of you military folks."

"I know we are going to like it here; it feels like home. Learning its history will be like reading a good book. I feel like I've met a stranger and fallen in love at first sight. Silly, isn't it?" Julie sighed.

"Attitude, life is driven by attitude. Your family may offer this town just what it needs. Where are you originally from?"

"We've lived all over the world. I was an Air Force brat who signed up as soon as I turned eighteen. My mom's and dad's families live near Brookston. My husband grew up in farm country near there. My heart aches to be settled, Mr. McDonath. I want to be part of a town like Stony Grove."

"I know Brookston well. I can't wait to meet Dan."

"He's a wonderful guy. He has a job offer at the regional airport in air traffic control. He cross-trained in logistics a couple of years ago. He came up the hard way, a bootstrap officer."

"Pretty exciting work but too stressful for me. I like taking it slow and easy."

Julie refrained from commenting but offered a smile instead.

"Been going to church regular for almost eighty-two years. We have some lovely churches. Do you have a preference? I can show you one if you do. Myself, I go to a nondenominational church."

"We don't belong to an organized religion. I do read the Bible every morning to start my day. I pray my husband will find a desire to go to church. We're believers."

"Satan himself is a believer. Reading is a good start, but you should seek fellowship. It might be interesting to visit some of the churches, and you can pick one that suits you. It's a good social activity." McDonath looked concerned.

"Nice thought. We may just do it, but one step at a time." Julie smiled, pleased with the idea.

"Prayer is key, you know. Sometimes our needs are filled without it. It kind of leaves you wondering whose hand might have been involved in the outcome. When you pray, you know the hand at work."

THREE

Dan Wilson pushed through the crowd in the airport terminal in a struggle to reach Julie. She waited in her Explorer at the curb. He hadn't seen Julie in nearly four months. Now free of military obligation, a new job awaited him—and word was she had found them a dream home. He looked at his watch. The closing was scheduled in about an hour, but first he needed a hug. At the sight of Julie, he dropped his luggage. She had barely cleared the door of the car when he swept her up in his arms, kissing her.

"Oh, how I've missed you." Dan could have stood there for hours kissing his wife.

But Julie had other ideas. "We'd better load up and get to the closing. It's going to be tight." She grabbed Dan's hand and pulled him toward his luggage.

Even so, Dan paused and looked around. "This is my new base. I can't believe we're going to be civilians."

She chuckled. "I've already gotten used to it."

Four lanes traversed the entire route from the airport toward Stony Grove, all but the last three miles. It would make Dan's commute to work easy. During the drive, Julie and Dan caught up on events since they had last been together—most importantly, details of the house Julie had found. Dan was sold. Julie's enthusiasm and the tone of her voice said it all; she was happy, and even if it didn't hold up to his expectation, he would not say anything to dampen her joy.

Dan's gaze was riveted on Julie as she talked. Her eyes danced. She rested her right hand on his thigh, and he covered her hand with his. The highway cut through farmland with wooded hills sloping above them. He felt like he was coming home for the first time in his life.

Julie pulled into a bank parking lot about five miles from Stony Grove. "I'll finally get to meet the Goldmeadows. They sure are mysterious people," Julie said as she shut off the engine.

"You mean we're buying a house, and you haven't met the owners yet?"

"The day Mr. McDonath took me through it, they were at work. They moved out yesterday, God bless them. I wouldn't have wanted to be them." Julie let out a sigh. "The place was packed with stuff. It's all I can call it. The house just had too much stuff packed into it. It almost made me tell Mr. McDonath to forget it, but I could see the potential once they were gone, along with all their stuff."

"You've got me a little worried."

"It'll be fine, Dan, you'll see... for the price, we need to be willing to accept some concessions."

Standing at the entrance to the bank, Dan searched her lovely, trusting face and broke into a smile. After all they had been through over the years, he knew nothing could stop them now. He would overcome anything to keep her happy. He put his arms around her. "I love you, and I trust your judgment."

The moment was broken by the sound of another's voice.

"Julie, so good to see you, and you must be Dan."

Dan let go of Julie to grasp the proffered hand. He wasn't expecting quite such an ironfisted grip from a real estate broker in his eighties.

"Mr. McDonath, it's a pleasure to meet you. Julie has spoken highly of you."

"Thank you. Julie tells me you grew up near Brookston. I used to date a girl from the area."

"Small world. What was her name?"

"Oh, it was a long time ago, well before you were born. But yes, it is a small world." Mr. McDonath ushered them through to the bank's conference room, gesturing toward a woman seated at the table. "This is Lou Ann Peters. She'll be handling your closing for the mortgage company."

Julie looked about the room, then smiled at Lou Ann. Lou Ann rose and offered her hand to both Julie and Dan.

"The Goldmeadows aren't here yet?"

"Well, no," Mr. McDonath stammered. "There's no need for them to attend; all their signatures have been secured, and you know what a big moving job they had. They hauled a lot out yesterday but still had some more to take out this morning."

Dan looked at Julie and then at Mr. McDonath.

"What about a final walk-through? Julie, did you inspect the place after they moved their stuff out?"

"No, I didn't realize it was something I needed to do." Julie and Dan turned toward McDonath.

"The Goldmeadows are good people; I assure you the property will be in the same condition it was in when we toured it, Julie. We'll head there directly after the closing."

"Once we close, it's ours, Mr. McDonath. Then it's a little late, don't you think? My concern is not about damage; my concern is, Julie said they are hoarders."

"Mr. Winslow, I give you my word; I will make things right for you if there are any infractions."

"Dan, let's just go ahead with the closing. It'll be all right." She put her arm around him.

For the next twenty minutes, they signed stacks of papers committing themselves for the next thirty years. One paper caught Dan's attention. He had never heard of such a document. It was titled "First Right of Purchase."

"What's this about? Who is Mr. McKenzie?" Dan looked at Mr. McDonath and Ms. Peters for answers.

"It's just a formality. It has no impact on the value of the property or your right to ownership. It states, you agree to give Mr. McKenzie an opportunity to purchase the land from you at fair market value before you offer it for public sale. Trust me, Mr. McKenzie will pay you above market value if you decide to sell.

This document is more of a guarantee on the value of the property."

"I don't know this guy; why should I do him any favors?"

"Well . . ." Mr. McDonath started to speak, then paused. His good hand rubbed his prosthesis. "Dan, you don't have to sign the paper—no one can force you, but if you don't, this closing is voided, Mr. McKenzie will pay the Goldmeadows their asking price, and the property will become his. It's simple. I cannot offer you any more insight. Except to tell you Mr. McKenzie and I were boyhood friends. He's a good man."

Julie sighed. "Dan, let's sign it. What can it hurt?"

After a pause, Dan scrawled his name across the bottom of the page.

"It's an adventure! We just encountered another unknown."

###

The Explorer rolled to a stop on Elm Street in front of the brick two-story. McDonath parked right behind them. Everything looked the same as it did the first day Julie had seen it. She stepped out and stared at the house. Mr. McDonath approached the couple.

"Those dirty heavy drapes are still hanging in the windows." Julie's voice cracked.

"I'm sure Mrs. Goldmeadow thought she was doing you a favor by leaving them. Draperies can be quite expensive, you know, and drapery rods are fixtures—they must stay with the property. Trust me, she had kind thoughts." McDonath's tone seemed unconvincing.

The trio approached the front door. Julie unlocked it, and Dan gave it a push. It creaked open.

Before them stretched filthy yellowish-green shag carpeting, a style which died before disco. Julie felt a little relief when she saw the living room was devoid of the mounds of clutter and the furniture it had hidden. The trio ventured from room to room looking at stained carpets and dark, dirty drapes, but the debris was gone. The house had a lingering smell of stagnation.

"I'm embarrassed for them," Julie whispered. "They didn't even clean the place. Anytime I've moved out of a place, I made it spotless for the people who would follow us. It would mortify me to have people see I lived in such filth."

"I'm so sorry, Julie." McDonath dropped his shoulders. "I'll bring the missus to help clean."

"Forget it, we're responsible adults. We decided to close without a walk-through. It's on us, and we'll take care of it. It's an adventure, right?"

"But I gave you my word all would be well; I assured you."

"I'm sure you have enough to deal with, including the loss of faith in your friends," Dan said. "We'll be all right. Now let's see the basement apartment and furnace." Dan opened the basement door and descended the cellar steps.

The basement had an apartment; it was an uninhabitable shamble of moldy walls and damp carpeting, but even worse were the piles of stuff stacked chest high. When they entered the furnace room, clutter obscured the furnace from view. Stuff was piled to the ceiling. McDonath gasped and fell against the door frame.

"Been in real estate fifty-five years and never seen anything like this. I am so sorry. What can I do?"

"This guy is the high school principal?" Dan asked, not expecting an answer but not hiding his anger. "Julie, we can't move in here tomorrow."

"What are we going to do? The delivery truck is en route; it'll be here tomorrow afternoon."

"There's a garage, right? Let's see if we can stash our things there while we get this place cleaned out."

They all trooped out into the sunshine, and Dan pulled aside the sliding doors of the three-car garage. Julie's hand covered her mouth as she gasped. The sun offered the contents its first rays of light in years—trash, all trash, packed floor to ceiling, with not enough open space to step inside the door. Mr. McDonath dropped his jaw.

"Hard to believe they left so much stuff behind," a voice said from behind them. "I watched them haul five truckloads outta here in the last two days. Never knew they had so much, but then in thirty-some years I lived beside them, they never invited me in."

"Ed!" McDonath turned. "Good grief, man, I had no idea the Goldmeadows would leave such a mess. Knew they had a lot of stuff, but . . ."

"I think they tried their best, Harry. They were working their tails off, along with their boys."

"Well, these are your new neighbors, Dan and Julie Winslow," McDonath offered.

"Nice to meet you." Dan held out his hand, then let it drop when it received no greeting.

Julie's smile faded. The lack of enthusiasm on their new neighbor's face chilled her. Ed Knight avoided eye contact even with Harry McDonath, a man he had known for years.

"Well, you folks got a lot to do. Good luck. I just stopped home for lunch, and it's getting cold." Without making eye contact, Ed Knight turned his back on the new neighbors for a rapid retreat.

"Not a bad guy, a little strange—a Presbyterian, I think—but he's a volunteer at the fire department. I'll stick around and help you clean up," McDonath said.

"Well, if nothing else, he was right: I have a lot to do and little time to get it done." Dan heaved a sigh of impatience before he offered McDonath an out. "Thanks for your offer to help, but I'm sure you're a busy man. We have family backup."

"Matter of fact, I do have to get over to the borough building, but I'll stop back later. I'll make this right by you. I'll talk to my broker. No, I'm going to call McKenzie."

"We bought the place, and the responsibility is ours."

"I won't just let it go, Dan."

"Dan . . ." Julie watched a wounded man shuffle up the driveway. For the first time, McDonath looked his age and perhaps some, leaving them alone to deal with the mess. Dan held up his hand to stop her words. The two of them had been in tighter situations, including the mortar attack on their base during the first Gulf War.

"Don't say anything, my dear," Dan said. "We are in this together, and we'll be fine. Rough starts usually make for good memories. Someday we'll laugh at this moment and cherish our team effort. We may even find a hidden treasure among all this clutter."

"Where do we even start?" Based on her tone, Dan knew he had at least temporarily eased Julie's sense of guilt.

Dan looked at the garage and shook his head. "Not out here."

He leaned into the garage. The debris piles had a half inch of black soot all over them. It wasn't just dust but mouse and bat droppings.

"First thing I'm going to do is rip up carpets. Then I'll rip down those drapes so we get lots of sunshine. Everything goes on the front lawn. Tomorrow, I'll borrow my brother's pickup and haul this stuff to a dump. I'll tote. You clean." Dan wrapped his powerful arms around Julie and held her. "Our boys will help when they get here. It's going to be fine; they'll prove to be a real blessing."

They made their way into the house, knowing once they started working on this mess, they weren't going to stop for a long time. After a while of cleaning, Dan pulled up the corner of the living room shag. His eyes widened. Pristine oak, tongue and groove. He called Julie from the kitchen where she was trying her best to chip away a thirty-year buildup of grease and grime.

"Look at this! If the rest of the floors look like this, we're in business. Why on earth would anyone live with this funky carpet when this was underneath? See? Treasure!" He shook his head.

Julie clutched at Dan's arm. "Oh wow! It's beautiful. We won't have to buy new carpeting, just some area rugs. Some people's taste, you wonder. I never liked carpet anyway; it just holds dirt."

The carpets might have been 1970s tasteless and ugly, but they had provided protection for what lay beneath. Julie and Dan were thankful; the hardwood retained a pristine look. As if he were unwrapping a much-desired Christmas present, Dan took to the task of ripping up the carpeting and dragging it onto the front yard. Julie vacuumed the debris from the cracks of the boards with a rented machine from the hardware store. She had anticipated the need for some cleaning, but not to the extent they were finding necessary.

In an almost joyous frenzy, Dan clutched at one drape after another, tearing them from the windows to let the light shine in. The windows themselves had apparently not been cleaned in decades, leaving them translucent. Some even appeared etched with a mineral crush. The bright sun penetrated and illuminated the rooms. Dan, inches from the glass window, strained his eyes but saw only distorted images and shadows out on the lawn. Curiously, he found a couple of windows with clean spots, which allowed for limited visibility.

The front yard was filling up as he carried out piles of trash from the basement. In the clutter, not one piece carried intrinsic value nor could there be found any reason for a possible sentimental attachment. It was just trash. Dan sensed it as a symptom of a diseased mind. Yet the owners were people entrusted to educate the youth. These people functioned in the public arena?

Taking a short break, Julie strolled through the piles of trash in the yard. Occasionally, she paused to pick up curious items. Items which made her wonder what attachment they could possibly have held for anyone. She opened a cardboard box the size of a beer case. In it she found old letters in yellowed envelopes tied with ribbons and several old books, one an old Bible. It might be fun to read this stuff sometime. Then again, why should she care? She walked away and went to the porch where Dan was, her eyes reddened with regret.

"We can do this, Julie." Dan paused as he returned from the yard. He kissed her and went back to the basement for another load.

After a silent prayer for strength, wisdom, and guidance, she found herself staring at the old box, the one with the Bible and letters. The thought of hoarding repulsed her; she should just let it all go. But it was a Bible, and the letters might be of interest when all was done. She tried to distract herself with other thoughts and pulled her feet up onto the porch chair. Hugging her knees, she rested a cheek against her arm. In the end, she walked back out into the yard to retrieve the letters—and especially the Bible.

FOUR

Dan and Julie worked long into the night. They finally sat down for a break, but rather than commence work again, they collapsed to the floor on a pile of clothes dragged out of Dan's suitcase. Curled in each other's arms, they slept. Julie woke as the night air cooled the house. Dan's overworked muscles twitched as he tried to sleep. Crackles and moans filled the air as the old house relaxed from the stresses imposed by the heat of the day. Dan's chest rose and fell in healthy rhythms, as Julie's hands massaged his back. As much as she had traveled, she still had trouble sleeping in unfamiliar places. Her fatigue won out, and she faded into a quiet sleep, just as Dan opened one eye to check on her.

The sun strained to penetrate an opaque window, but it managed to awaken Dan—either the sun or the blasted knocking on the front door. His watch indicated seven o'clock. He staggered to the door in just his jeans while Julie ran to start coffee. Through the glass, he made out blurred movement on the front porch before he popped open the door.

"Good morning."

"We have codes in this town we enforce. With the town full of college kids, we can't give any slack. Your yard is in violation, and the fine is two hundred dollars a day. I am serving you notice, the clock is ticking."

"Who are you? Maybe you should start by introducing yourself." Dan repositioned the door to half-closed.

"Oh, well yes, I'm the mayor of this town, A. Whipple. I've had a lot of calls about this residence, complaints saying you are trashing our town. What's your plan? This mess must be out of here by sundown. You should have ordered a roll-off dumpster, but to just throw it in the grass is a violation."

"Look, we just bought this house. The people who sold it to us left a lot of trash. Our furniture arrives today, and I needed to clear this stuff out in a hurry. There wasn't time to order a dumpster. Do you know Mr. McDonath? He'll verify what I'm telling you."

"Harold McDonath? Yes, I know him. He used to be the supervisor, but he doesn't have any authority now. There's no excuse. There's always time to do things the proper way. You have until sundown." The mayor rose on his tiptoes and cocked his head to see into the house over Dan's shoulder. "Don't be doing any remodeling without a permit. Any structural, wiring, or plumbing changes require permits, approvals, and inspections. I suggest you check in to the motel. I wouldn't give you an occupancy permit when a place is in a condition like this."

"Occupancy permit? People were already living here."

"Yes, yes, I know. A permit isn't required unless you are turning it into a rental. I'm just warning you."

"Where's the nearest dump? I'll have the yard cleared out by sundown. My brother's coming with my sons and a truck in an hour or so." Dan ran his fingers through his hair and rolled his stiff shoulders. "You know, my dad built our entire house after World War Two without needing any inspections or permits."

"Nearest dump is seven miles down Route 103, can't miss it. Sundown, sir." The mayor stepped off the front porch. "Times have changed since your dad's day. We do it right now, so don't think you can get away with it. Here's a little advice, mister. You ain't local. So just watch your step."

Dan closed the door. "Welcome to Stony Grove."

"Who was it?" Julie yelled from the kitchen.

He joined her. "Welcome wagon. No, it was the mayor. He wants the yard emptied by sundown. We aren't voting for him next election."

She handed him a cup of coffee. He held it with both hands, savoring the aroma.

He found a polo shirt and sandals, gulped his coffee, then headed into the yard to survey the debris pile. The angle of the sun allowed its warmth to caress him, even under the old oak. The long grass tickled his feet. He couldn't wait to see the boys, and then to coordinate a team effort. He'd need to organize the loads for the most efficient hauling. Out of the corner of his eye he caught movement near the curb. For an instant he saw a tuft of hair—possibly some vermin crawling through the trash. It popped up with the delightful grin of a young treasure hunter, gripping an old movie camera. Then another head popped up from behind the debris. A long-haired blond angel of about seven stood with eyes wide.

"Are you the guy who bought this house?"

"Why, yes, I am."

The boy looked down, fumbling the camera from one hand to the other.

"What are you going to do with all these things you've put out in the yard?"

"We're taking it all to the dump, why?"

"Could I buy this camera off you? I want to see if I can fix it. I want to make movies." The boy held up the old video camera, which was almost as big as his little companion.

"What's your name?"

"I'm Victor and this is my little sister, Casey. We live across the street."

"Well, Victor, for all I know you could become a great Hollywood producer. I'm going to take a chance on it and hope you remember where you got your start. I'll tell you what. You can have anything in this yard for free, maybe something you can use as a prop in a movie. Help yourself, and it goes for you too, Casey. You would be helping me by taking it."

"Thanks, mister. We only want the camera. Why'd you want to buy an old, haunted house?" The boy held the camera lens to his eye. It was so heavy he had to rest his elbows on his diaphragm to support it.

"Haunted house? Where did you hear such a thing?" Dan scrunched his eyebrows.

"Haunted house on Elm Street, everybody knows 'bout it. Hope you like Halloween. The Halloween parade always ends here on Elm Street. You'll see hundreds of kids. The Goldmeadows always left town on Halloween, but all the kids would walk by and hope to see a ghost looking out a window."

Dan paused, hands on his hips, sizing up Victor's story when a sudden swoosh and thud sounded from the second floor of the house. Dan spun toward the noise. A window had been opened to ventilate the upstairs, and on its own it had slammed shut.

"See, I told you this place is haunted."

Dan turned back in time to see the two children's backs as they broke for home. So an old window fell. It didn't mean anything. He returned to the house and found Julie on the back porch. "Did you happen to close the upstairs window?"

"I heard a noise. No, I've been here, wiping down these railings and ledges so we can sit out here to eat if we want to."

He climbed the stairs to the suspect hallway window, lifting it with much effort. It was old, with layers of rough paint on it. Once opened, he tried to close it. It was harder to close than it was to open. He tried to jiggle it, shake it, and bump, it but it would not slide shut. Only a hefty downward pressure would budge it. It must have been in just the right position, a position which he could not now duplicate.

Nothing supernatural.

He stood in the hallway and looked around. The day had already begun to heat up, but he could feel a cold spot, a draft maybe, but from where? He returned to the kitchen, poured another cup of coffee, and said nothing more about it to Julie. After all, there was no such thing as ghosts.

Dan went to the porch and leaned on the door frame, surveying the work waiting for him in the yard. A new blue four-door pickup truck slowed to a stop in front of the house. Dan was off the porch in two steps and yelled for Julie. "They're here!" The passenger doors flew open, and out stepped two handsome young men. He grabbed them, one in each arm, and pulled them in tight to a group hug. Tim shut off the engine and danced his way around the truck. "Tim, many thanks for bringing the best kids in the world to me," Dan choked out. He felt rather than saw Julie approaching from behind him. She squeezed into the hug.

"Welcome to our new home, guys." She stepped back a little to get a good look at them.

As the boys and Tim drew their gaze away from Dan and Julie, they stared at the debris pile in disbelief. "Um, Dad?" Zane ventured.

"Not to worry. This is our project today—we're going to haul all this stuff out of here." "All this was inside the house?" Tim shook his head in disbelief.

"The owners had even removed truckloads of additional stuff," Julie answered.

"Julie, congratulations on stealing Dan from his first love, the military, to begin a glamourous job like this," Tim joked.

After a two-cent tour of the interior of the house, the men jumped to the task of loading the truck.

The trash pile dwindled with several trips to the dump. Zane and Trent split their energy between working and sparring with each other. On the last dump run Dan and Tim went alone. The boys stayed behind to help their mother clean. The furniture delivery would arrive soon. It should have arrived an hour ago. Dan slumped in the front seat, his head against the window, glad the unloading of furniture would be done by the moving company. His thoughts were of his soon-to-be-delivered bed and the good night's sleep it would provide.

Tim turned his gaze from the road toward Dan. "You know, you bit off a lot with this house. It needs a lot more than cleaned up. I hope you don't run short on passion before the job is done."

"I've got it covered, inch by inch, step by step. If I don't look at the big picture, I won't get overwhelmed, but I know you're right. This is Julie's big adventure. She stuck by me and held our family together all the times I deployed. I'll stick by her for this."

"I'll help when I can, but you know I'm out of town a lot."

"I'll be fine. Julie will be a tremendous help. The boys will learn a lot too." Dan assessed Tim's serious side, unsure if he should bring up the question. In the end, he couldn't resist putting it out there. "Do you believe in ghosts?"

Tim drove on in silence for a moment. "Are you serious? My heart is haunted by lots of women. Ghosts exist if you have a conscience, and it may not seem like it, but I do."

Dan rolled his eyes. "No, I'm talking ghosts of dead people. You know, like the kinds who haunt houses. Do you think it's possible?"

"Are we talking about your house? Do you think it's haunted?"

"A neighbor kid said the rest of the town thinks so and have thought so for years."

"From what we've been doing all day, my bet is yeah, your house has been haunted for a long time but not by a ghost, more like flesh-and-blood human hoarder-type weirdos. These people would have contributed to the ghostly legend. You've got a lot of reality on the old plate without getting bogged down in hocus pocus."

"These folks did live like the Addams family."

"Dan, I think ghosts happen in periods of stress and distress. Are they real? I think the effect and impact can become real. You know, when I'm feeling lonely, the past creeps up on me. When things are right with the world, there aren't any ghosts. When people talk about ghosts, where do they show up? In broken-down houses, around stressed-out people, in weak emotional periods. I think if you're strong and focused, you won't encounter any ghosts."

"Thanks." Dan held out his fist, and Tim bumped it with his.

Julie had planned a delicious lunch to be served on the front porch where they could view the unobscured and unblemished front lawn while sipping iced tea. They waited for the furniture truck. The tree-lined street offered a peaceful setting, and the food Julie had prepared was ample reward for a couple of garbage men. Tim rested the soles of his feet on the porch rail. Zane and Trent decided to go explore the town on foot. Julie rubbed Dan's shoulders.

"Well, I'd say you made your mayor happy. It looks right respectable out there." Tim slid his feet to the porch floor.

"No, I think I just removed a couple of bullets from the mayor's guns. He didn't look like the type you can make happy, unless he's got you backed into a corner. I read him as the type to enjoy putting the squeeze on people."

"Crooked mayors, haunted houses? Dan, it's not like you. I think you're stressed."

"Haunted house? What are you talking about?" Julie stopped rubbing Dan's shoulders.

"Nothing, we were just talking earlier—about if we believed in ghosts—generalities." Dan stood to give his brother a farewell hug.

"I need to get on the road if I'm going to catch my flight to Houston. I hope you two can squeeze in a little bit of exploring the area before I get back."

Julie took her turn hugging Tim. Dan doubted Julie had bought into his attempt to brush off the haunted house subject. If he knew her, she'd decided it could wait until after they had said his good-byes.

"This town has a lot of potential, Tim. I think it's at its lowest market value. I think we made a good move. This town is going to grow and prosper. It's a close enough commute to large population centers, and I hear a couple more of the restaurants are trying to get liquor licenses. We're only a block off Main." Dan was doing his best to reaffirm his belief in Julie's choice and hoped his words sealed his commitment to backing her up.

"Hope you're right, brother. With a little luck and a lot of hard work, who knows, this may pay off. It ain't Houston, but we all have to find our place. You're just the man to make it all happen."

"Thanks. You take care. Leave the flight attendants alone."

"They'll probably be guys, my man. Julie, you take care and don't let this guy overwork you. I love your place. It's got a lot of potential, and I know you'll take it to the limit. Love you all, tell the boys."

Tim pulled away with hand waving and head out the window. Watching his brother disappear down Elm Street gave Dan a sinking feeling.

"I wish Tim could stick around and help," Julie mused. "So nice to have him around."

"He loves us, Julie, but this isn't his style. We'll be fine—we just need to formulate a plan and go about it one step at a time. First thing is to stabilize the foundation and put a new roof on. Both of those will be done by contractors. I'll handle the interior work. The apartment in the basement needs to be gutted. I'll redo the bathrooms. Maybe we can convert two of the bedrooms into a master bedroom suite." His voice reassured Julie she had made the right choice and he was engaged.

"It all sounds wonderful, when do we start?"

"We already did. I want the foundation dug out as soon as we find an excavator. I'll start calling contractors tomorrow. We need new French drains, and we'll have the block sealed."

Julie put her arms around Dan, her head resting on his chest. She whispered a prayer, asking for strength for their little family.

Dan's eyes wandered. He noticed Ed Knight standing on the sidewalk staring down and shaking his head from side to side. *What in the world?*

"Excuse me a minute." Dan nudged Julie away and walked over to Ed, who stood with his hands on his hips, a scowl etched on his face. "What's up, Ed? You don't look happy."

"Look at the sidewalk. I think your moving truck cracked it. This is on my side of the driveway."

Dan looked up and down the entire length of sidewalk. Most of the concrete squares were cracked, with several sections in upheaval. It was a pitted, faded old sidewalk. This particular square appeared to be the only previously undamaged part of the sidewalk, though it too was faded and brittle looking. Dan kneeled for a closer inspection. It did appear to be a newer crack since there wasn't any dirt or debris in it. Dan looked up at Ed.

"Okay, Ed, I accept responsibility for it. What do you want me to do about it?"

"I want it replaced. I think you should make it right. It's what a good neighbor would do."

"I will, Ed. First thing. I sure don't want any trouble with my neighbors. Yep, first order of business."

Ed walked back toward his house without another word.

Dan lived up to his word and within two days he had removed the old concrete, formed in a new pad and hand mixed a batch of concrete. The new pad's appearance looked just like the old pad it replaced. Ed never commented on it or acknowledged Dan for his effort.

FIVE

The aroma of freshly brewed morning coffee wafted up the stairs. It filled the bedroom and Dan's nose until he stirred. He stretched his arm onto Julie's side of the bed and found himself alone. Exhausted from the stress of training for his new air traffic logistics position, he wanted to just stay put. The training alone was bad enough, but combined with the remodeling efforts on the house, he had pushed himself into burnout. He watched the whirl of the revolving paddle fan over the bed, savoring its gentle draft. Julie had let him sleep. A little piece of him felt guilty about sleeping in, but he decided it had been healthy.

The breeze tickled his bare chest. He thought about how hot the days had been. The aroma of coffee overwhelmed him. It inspired his only desire to get up, to satisfy his craving for caffeine. The breeze stopped. His eyes had never diverted from the rotating blades. He held his hand up toward the fan, its blades still revolving. Impossible, physically impossible—the fan had never stopped, yet the breeze was gone.

He stood, balancing on the bed. Holding his hand above the whirling blades, he felt the air movement upward toward the ceiling. For such a thing to happen, the fan would have had to have stopped and reversed—and it had not. It was absurd. He doubted himself for a moment, questioning whether he had felt the breeze in the first place, but he knew he had. He dropped, sitting on the edge of the bed trying to rationalize what had happened, but couldn't. The breeze started again, and he felt its tickle on his back. Jumping to his feet, he looked around the room, holding his hand toward the fan. He needed the coffee Julie had brewed. He walked to the doorway, then glanced back into the room... nothing amiss. *Ghosts appear when we're stressed or distressed.* Tim's words echoed in his head.

"Yeah, that's what it is," Dan whispered in reply.

Dan entered the kitchen, deciding not to mention the fan. "Good morning—coffee smells great."

"Dan, I wanted you to sleep until noon. You need a break. You've been working too hard."

"I'd hate myself if I wasted half the day sleeping." He sipped his coffee.

"Why don't you do something relaxing? Take a walk down back. Go explore the woods. You've been talking about it. I think you need an adventure. We've been here for weeks, and you have yet to go exploring."

"If you go with me, we might find a place to skinny dip in the creek back there. Now we're talking adventure."

"Tell you what, you go find a spot and then we'll talk about it. I need to take the boys school shopping; then we'll visit my mom so the boys can do her yard work while she and I see her lawyer about the power of attorney she wants for me. You have the entire day to yourself."

"You've convinced me, my dear. I love you." He wrapped his arms around her in a great bear hug and lifted her off the ground. "I'm going exploring, adventuring."

By the time he showered and dressed, Julie and the boys were gone. He walked into the backyard and looked toward the woods, a scrubby stand of junk vegetation offering little inspiration of adventure other than what was hidden beyond. He strolled across the lawn, then turned to look up at the rear of the house. Had anyone died in his house and how? Ghosts had never been his thing. He was a practical man with strong spiritual convictions, and he had often felt there was more to the world than met the eye. But ghosts?

There was no fear in his heart. He had confidence in his ability to handle any situation. He knew whatever he was experiencing, he would deal with it one encounter at a time. He moved into the brush, inhaling huge quantities of crisp air. He was more at home in the woods than anywhere. He was physically powerful and yet possessed a quiet spirit—traits acquired from a father of greater strength and spirit who had been tested in the Second World War.

For the first two hundred yards Dan weaved through tangles of brambles spiked with thorns, and dodged low-hanging branches. He followed a path of sorts, but it had not been traveled in some time. He pushed on in the hope the woods might open into older growth with an underlayment of leaves and pine needles. As he moved, he felt the tensions of life disperse. Julie knew him, the animal side of him. Her love of him encompassed both his animal and spiritual qualities.

The path ended at the edge of a field high with weeds and wild flowers. Beyond he saw evergreens, hemlocks. He could hear Stony Creek rushing through huge boulders. The boulders—dramatic and abrupt—spoke of a great primal upheaval. Here it was where the lazy meandering creek flowing through Stony Grove picked up the gumption to rage. He struggled to the top of a boulder. His vantage point gained a view of the edge of Stony Gorge. About a forty-foot plunge lay visible—impressive enough.

He sat and listened to the water tumbling off a rock ledge. The gush snaked over, under, and around bare stone formations, then disappeared beneath a dense hemlock canopy. The forest floor was padded with lush ferns and slick moss. His heart pounded. His wish to be surrounded by beauty was thwarted by the absence of Julie. The falls generated a cool mist, not subduing the summer heat but defying it. The Gorge beckoned. He checked his watch, then eased himself over the edge, testing his footing before he released his weight to each foot.

He thought about beauty, about how dangerous and intoxicating it can be. A misstep by the inexperienced and a life of regret could follow or end. Dan took every precaution to reach his goal. Moments later he was on the floor of the hemlock forest with a thick spread of needles smothering any undergrowth. He continued along the edge of the torrent. It descended at a more gradual decline yet careened through tumbles of rock. The terrain began to afford a more relaxed walk, better to appreciate the cool, dark forest.

Translucent waters pooled ten feet deep in pockets between the rocks, the pebbly bottom visible. Large trout rested with barely a wiggle to their tails. Ancient fallen trees now formed mysterious mounds beneath exquisite mats of moss. Their decomposition offered up food for the next generation. Earthy fragrances filled the air. Mushrooms, ferns, skunk cabbage, pine, and dampness all contributed to a mystical effect. *Enchantment,* Dan thought, *this is an enchanted place. How can it be so untouched? These woods were all but clear-cut in the last century—so how has this place survived? Time, I guess.* This place was of a different time, a time when life had grace and time kept pace. This was what God had intended for the world. This was His work, and Dan felt blessed to have stumbled into such a place.

The path appeared more worn now, but in truth, it had been the lack of sun preventing any undergrowth from thriving. This part of the trail could stay unchanged for eons. Dan passed through a crevice between two large stones—obviously cut. He entered an area of ancient ruin—of stone foundations, moss covered and abandoned. The blocks were of a size too large for one man to move. The layout was like one of a small village, perhaps twenty foundations of small dwellings. They circled two large foundations, large enough to be called grand. Trees grew from the bottoms of the footings with roots sprouting from crags in the crumbling walls. It offered a disconcerting sight. These compositions represented the dreams and hard labor of men. Something dashed those dreams, and now they lay neglected and forgotten. All for naught. Next to Stony Creek, now running in a white froth of rapids, Dan found what looked like an outlay of an old swimming pool. A cut stone water race entered it from the Stony, and another race ran downstream for an outflow, an engineering marvel. What was this place? And when was it built?

He rested on a large stone by the old pool, envisioning the possibilities, yet he couldn't fathom what he had found. It was an ideal location for a resort, but surely that was not the intended construction. Why would it have been abandoned? Two deer sauntered out of the hemlock and stood munching lush emerald grass, unaware of the human intruder. They flicked their ears, stood motionless, then bent to tear at the natural salad at their feet. They sauntered across the grounds, disappearing back into the forest. Birds fluttered about and butterflies danced, all unaware of these lost efforts of man. The world could not be more at peace, and Dan ached to have Julie with him to watch this show.

Dan whispered a prayer, giving thanks for all his blessings, starting with Julie and the boys. He acknowledged to himself that when he passed, their memory of him would be all they would have of him. The silence induced a twinge in him. His eyes welled, but he held back. Loss. Voices never to be heard again, thoughts and experiences never to be shared. He thought about his buddies lost in combat and a friend who had died of cancer. This place had been someone's dream, and the builders had laughed, joked, struggled, and shared the experience only to have it reclaimed by the forest. He plunged his hand into the icy water of Stony Creek. A surge of numbing coldness refocused his thoughts on the physical, the now. With a clear head he stood, got his bearings, and headed further downstream until he reached a bridge connecting a country road.

The iron of the bridge told its age, built sometime in the 1920s, the same vintage as his house. It probably had a plaque dedicated to some local politician. The base of huge cut stone supported a road bed about as wide as a car and a half, twentieth-century engineering overkill. Dan scrambled up the bank near one of the arches and heard the whinny of a horse. His curiosity got the best of him.

Across the road, he could see a building a hundred feet away. It was partially blocked from view by the underbrush hugging the edge of the neglected road. He wondered if anyone ever used the road, save a farm tractor or two. The building's exterior was weathered, unpainted clapboard. One story in height with an oversized roof extending out over a couple of nonfunctional ancient fuel pumps marked ESSO. A hand-painted sign tacked to the wooden roof support advertised BAIT. In the shadows of the roof Dan could make out the figure of a lone soul perched on a chair leaned back onto the front wall of the shack. The figure's face was obscured by the tilt of his head under a broad-brimmed felt hat, hands fumbling over some project in his lap. The scene had an illusionary look to it. Illusion or not, it did not fit the time frame of this century.

Dan crossed the road for a reality check. In the shade of a huge white oak grazed an old mare. The dusty parking lot was devoid of motor vehicles. Had he stepped back in time? The figure leaning back in the chair was whittling. Dan could make out the movements of skilled hands, but the face was still hidden beneath the broad brim of his hat. Dan's feet crunched in the gravel. Surely the man could hear his approach, yet the whittler never looked up. Stepping onto the wooden porch, Dan cleared his throat. "Excuse me, sir."

"You're 'scused, but what for?" The man continued to whittle.

"For interrupting you on such a beautiful day."

"You ain't interrupting me. If you're looking for bait, it's inside. It's all marked—help yourself. Just put the money in the cash box. We operate on the honor system so as not to interrupt me. If you're looking to learn whittling or make talk, it becomes a whole different matter. Those things would be interrupting me on such a beautiful day." He kept at his whittling, the piece of wood emerging into a detailed mallard.

"Well, I don't need any bait. I'm just out for a walk, and I noticed your place."

"Ain't my place, it belongs to the Strattons. I just work for 'em. I work the way I get paid, a little bit once every two weeks."

"My name's Dan, Dan Winslow." Dan held out his hand.

The man straightened his chair and put down his whittling, wiped his hand on his pants and gripped Dan's hand. He tilted back his hat back to reveal steel blue eyes surrounded by age lines penetrating from beneath a solid brow. His heavy cheek bones were separated by a strong nose, and his jaw protruded beneath, covered in a three-day growth of gray whiskers.

"I accept your apology then. I didn't realize you would be so persistent in interrupting me. Most folks just help themselves and move on. They don't seem to care about introducing themselves to this old hillbilly."

"I'm new to the area, so I'd kind of like to get to know my neighbors."

"Well, I'm Lee McDaniels. Pleased to make your acquaintance. Now you've earned your apology, 'cause I'm truly interrupted."

"Sorry."

"No, never mind, my hands was a needin' a break."

"What are you reading?" Dan pointed to a large book propped on the wall next to the chair.

"Gettysburg. I plan to go one of these days. Thinkin' if I read up on it, I might make a difference in the outcome next time. You might as well know right off. I'm a passively aggressive Southern sympathizer." Lee chuckled to himself.

"You are? Why?"

"Don't like the feds—control freaks, they are. Let's not go to talkin' politics, too nice a day. So, you're hoofin' it?"

"Yeah, I came down through the Gorge along Stony Creek." Dan pointed toward the Gorge.

"Dang pretty back there, dangerous too."

"Dangerous?"

"Right so, 'em stones can be treacherous slippery along the creek."

"I can swim."

"Swim? Not in those waters. Worse thing you can do. My grandpappy told me don't never struggle or swim in wild water; just relax and let it take you. Watch for an opportunity along the shore. You know there's two Stony Creeks." Lee stood up and stretched, taller than Dan by a good five inches, and Dan was of considerable good height.

"Two Stony Creeks?"

"They run one on top of the other. One goes underground. It rages through the tunnels under the stone. Lots of people get sucked down and never come up. They end up in the lower channel, stuck under a boulder. It's dangerous, but right pretty. They shoulda named that run of water after a woman."

"Gotcha." Dan smiled.

"In my younger days, I used to coon hunt the Gorge. Us boys done a lot of crawfish gatherin' too." He crossed his arms in front of himself. "It's different at night, seems haunted. Plenty of people died in there."

The screen door slammed against the wall, causing Dan to jerk in response. A lanky hound bounded onto the porch through the doorway, toenails clicking on the porch planking, his tongue hanging as long as his ears. He shook off his nap with loose skin flapping around his bony frame. Dan decided this pair was a fine example of the tendency for dogs to resemble their owners.

"Buck, I'm just talking to this here gentleman." Lee lowered his voice. "When he hears the *H* word, he gets all beside himself."

"*H* word?"

"I can't say H-U-N-T within earshot, or he hounds me until I take him."

Dan reached down and scratched Buck behind his long ears.

"You just made a friend. He loves being scratched behind the ears. Dogs are lucky, my hind legs don't afford me the pleasure of doing such things for myself, but its ole Buck's second favorite pastime after sleepin'."

Dan chuckled, then changed the subject. "What are those old foundations in the hemlocks? I had a strange feeling when I passed through there."

"Stratton Beach, been a long time gone."

"It looks like it was quite a place in its day. I guessed it to be 1920s vintage."

"It was. Had a dance hall, skating rink, and a swimming pool fed by the creek. They rented cabins out. Roaring twenties, complete with ladies... you know, them ones called flappers."

"Yeah, I recall reading about the time period."

"This here building was a railway station, then a gas station, Old Man Stratton's first business. Right off, you might guess the Strattons got a sentimental streak for keeping this place open. When the environmental people turned these pumps off, they turned off any chance at profit. For some reason, the Strattons keep it open and, praise Jesus, me employed. Are you a believer, Mr. Winslow?" Lee tilted his head down to get a good vantage from which to read Dan's face.

"I am of sorts. Call me Dan, please."

"Truly? I hope you aren't one of them lukewarm churchgoers."

"I don't go to church. I've just always had a strong sense of belief in a creator God."

"I'll agree, strong sense overrides a goer any day, sir. I have been a believer all my life, but I did have a fall. When I hit bottom, Jesus and the wife picked me up. They forgave me. Now I'm living my second chance. Alcohol was the tool Satan used on me. Turned me Amish, so to speak, I'll never have a driver's license again. I ride the old mare now. Funny, demons haunted me into drinkin'. Then drinkin' weakened me, so the demons seemed stronger. They ain't, though. Truth is, they ain't got no power but what is granted 'em. But hell, I'm a know-nothing hillbilly a-talkin' to a man the likes of you."

"The likes of me?"

"Well, you look like a fella who has been places. You can't chase demons with drink, no sir."

Lee looked off toward the horse tied under the old oak tree.

"Gettin' back to Stratton Beach, in the Roaring Twenties they say it was the place to go. Then times changed, the train quit running. The soldiers returning in the forties went to the Jersey Shore instead of Stony Creek. The place had burned anyway. Nobody ever saw no reason to rebuild it. They say it was an awful sight. Ten people burned to death. It was arson—" Lee clamped his mouth shut.

"Arson, you're sure? Who did it and why?"

"It was afore my time. Like I said, I was too busy catching crawfish to worry 'bout adult travesties. Keeping this place open seems to be makin' some sort of statement, I've come to figure. The Strattons have long memories. People in these parts hold grudges if you cross 'em. I'm glad the Lord put 'em on my side, is all I can say—and enough said, I'm thinking."

"The Strattons must be well-heeled to keep a not-for-profit business open out of spite."

"The Strattons own the salvage yard, the strip mines, the golf course, a trucking company, and about fifteen hundred acres of prime farmland, along with the lower parts of the Gorge. Would that be well-heeled?"

"I suppose it would."

"Are you going back the way you come?"

"I suppose it's the shortest route... and the most scenic."

"Won't find a prettier place or more dangerous. Say, would you be the fella what bought the principal's house on Elm?" Lee's eyes locked on Dan's.

"How did you make that jump?" Dan felt as if he were being studied.

"Makes sense since the trail starts in the backyard of the old house, plus your being a stranger and all. You know you didn't make any friends buyin' that house." Lee sat down and pulled a harmonica from his shirt pocket. Buck perked his ears up and slowed his pacing of the porch, which he had been doing since banging the screen door open.

"What do you mean?"

"Nothing, just hillbilly speculation, what do I know? Grab yourself a bottle of water to take with you, it's on me. Being careful is on you. I'm gonna calm ole Buck down with a tune." Lee tilted his head forward. His face disappeared under the brim of his hat. His gnarled hands cupped the instrument to his mouth as he released a few eerie musical notes.

Dan patted Buck on the head, fetched a bottle of water from inside the store, then headed off into the woods without any further exchange with Lee. The eerie sound of the harmonica shrouded Lee's words of warning for quite a distance. Dan took it those words weren't about Stony Creek. Not being a local, Dan felt a hunger to pick old Lee's memory but knew he had to gain trust first. A curiosity now rose in him. Arson, ten nameless victims, and an unsolved crime fueled the intrigue of Stony Gorge. The feelings Dan had as he sat on the stone by the old swimming pool seemed more understandable now. He couldn't even speculate on who committed such a crime and why—the trail was decades cold. It only mattered now to satisfy his curiosity.

As Dan strolled into the backyard, exhausted but content, Julie met him with a huge glass of iced tea and a tray of cucumbers and dip. "I was watching for you from the kitchen window. Tell me about your adventure!"

They sat in the shade of the oaks to share their day. She laughed over his description of Lee and Buck, but her face soon became somber. "My mom wanted to sign over power of attorney to me, and today we all saw why she felt this is important to do now. Some of the tales the boys shared with me on the way home, from their two weeks staying with her last month, indicate she'll be moving to an assisted living facility sooner rather than later. I scheduled a doctor appointment next week for her. I'm thinking she has early-onset dementia."

Dan reached for her hand. He knew he'd never deal with these same issues, as his parents had died in a wreck on the interstate highway when he and his brother were young men.

Julie sighed. "Today she must have asked me five times why you weren't with us. I saw in her newspaper that a woman she had grown up with had died. I told her I would take her to the visiting hours, but she insisted she didn't want to go. I found a condolence card for her to send, and signing her name took a lot of effort on her part." Julie held Dan's arm and snuggled in closer. "I just thought there'd be more quality time with her once we moved here. I'm not even sure yet how much she has put away for assisted living."

For lack of anything more hopeful he could tell her, Dan simply responded, "We'll take it one day at a time."

SIX

Weeks passed with Dan absorbed by demands at work coupled with remodeling projects. The boys had a less than enthusiastic commencing of classes at their new school. Even though they'd moved several times, they had always had plenty of other military kids as their classmates. Julie signed up for two graduate courses at the university. She began researching genealogy since they were now living in the general area of their ancestors. She visited her mother each week to organize her meals and to take her to visit assisted living facilities. Life fell into a rhythm of normalcy.

Julie arrived home from her morning class one Tuesday just before lunchtime as Mary Knight walked onto the driveway. She carried a basket of laundry from the backyard. So far Mary had been cordial with Julie if not a little standoffish. Julie decided to use the encounter to extend warmth on her part at least. She stepped out of the car smiling, then strode toward Mary.

"Hey, Mary—what a beautiful day. How have you been? We're so busy. Time flies by. Would you like to come over for lunch?"

"Thank you, but I have a lot of housework to do before Ed gets home." Mary avoided eye contact with Julie as she walked toward her garage door.

"Come on, you have to take a lunch break anyway. I've got a chopped salad ready to go. You can come in and see what Dan's done to the place. Is Ed coming home for lunch today?" Julie stood her ground, and Mary stopped.

"No, Ed has a lunch meeting at the university today."

"Then come on."

"I've never been in the house. I wouldn't notice the difference." Mary turned to face Julie. Her face was pocked with scars from adolescent acne. She was slight in build with mousy hair. Julie sensed a lost and abused soul. It appeared she had endured a difficult life.

"What—in all the years you were neighbors with the Goldmeadows you never visited each other?"

"Ed's not sociable. He says a good neighbor lets it go at hello and good-bye."

Mary—so thin and having such an unfortunate face—made Julie want to offer her joy. *Does Ed abuse her, not physically but mentally?* It drew her to try to engage her, if for no other purpose than to understand her. Julie persisted with her invitation.

"Come on, Mary, drop the basket. Have a salad with me. Nobody needs to know. Do you drink coffee?"

"I prefer tea."

"I've got a basket full of assorted teas. Come on."

"Well . . ."

"The salad is made. I have homemade dressings to die for. Nothing I made; Dan's brother makes them."

Mary set the basket down inside her garage, then returned to Julie wearing a crooked little smile. She held her hands in an impish childlike manner. Julie touched Mary's shoulder to reassure her all was well. The two entered Julie's kitchen through the back door.

"Oh my! This kitchen is beautiful. I love the porcelain tile floor."

"Dan did it. We like the light color and the fact we can see dirt on it so we know if it needs cleaned."

Mary's hand skimmed the island work station Dan had built. "It's so bright in here."

"Oh, Mary, I wish you could have seen this place before. Dan's been a busy guy. I am beginning to love this house now." Julie fetched the salad and dressings as she talked. She filled the teakettle with fresh water.

"Ed's not handy. He hasn't done a thing to our house since we moved in. When something breaks, he calls a repairman. Nobody ever taught him how to do things around the house. He is rather particular about neatness and cleanliness, though."

"Really?" Julie paused to look at Mary. Mary had turned her back, gazing toward the dining room.

Julie pursed her lips as she continued to prep. "Dan and his brother just seem to be able to do everything—cook, clean, build, and repair. Dan says it's because they always admired the cowboy heroes they had when they were kids. He said those guys could stitch themselves up, cook, ride, mend fences, build barns, mine gold, whatever it took, and then get the prettiest gal. He can even sing."

"Well, you are pretty." Julie's face flushed at Mary's comment.

Mary stepped into the dining room. "You know, when the Goldmeadows lived here, their drapes were always closed. I don't think they ever washed the windows. What a difference the sunlight makes. Don't you think?"

"For sure. We used steel wool and vinegar on some of the windows. Why don't we sit on the screened back porch? It's too nice of day to be indoors. Clean windows are great, but nothing beats being outside." Julie led Mary out to the back porch. A wrought iron dining set with a ceiling fan over it invited them to sit, a cool lunch setting on a warm afternoon. Mary sat silently as Julie shuttled the lunch necessities out to the table.

"This is my favorite part of the house," Julie said as she sat down.

"Ed doesn't understand why you are spending so much money and time on this place," Mary said as she filled her salad bowl.

"It's our home. Dan has high standards." It's what Mary had said about Ed. "We could have never lived in this place the way it was."

"Then why did you buy it in the first place?"

"We had never bought a house before, since we moved so often with the military. Dan let me pick the house because he wasn't discharged yet. He trusted my judgment. I guess I looked at the potential rather than the reality of what it was going to take. I didn't even know I should have done a final walk-through. Maybe old Harry is slipping, because he never mentioned it." Julie's mood brightened as she continued, "But Dan thinks this town's real estate is going to rebound over the next ten years."

"Oh, Ed thinks the landlords are running things into the ground."

"Landlords?"

"Student rental landlords. They buy all the single-family houses and turn them into student flop houses. You'll catch on when you've lived here awhile. My Ed knows about these things. He knows the biggest landowners. He says they aren't friends; they just all hang out down at the fire department."

Julie didn't respond, and Mary offered no more on the subject. Julie felt too ill at ease to ask.

How bad can things be? So far it hadn't been too bad, other than the foul language she heard around campus or at the convenience mart service station on the corner where the college crowd gathered to buy instant cappuccino, coffee, and donuts. Julie wasn't impressed with the students she had met. The two professors she'd been assigned seemed set on pushing an agenda right from the start. She hoped that her understanding of the world from her military travels was what tainted her opinion of this new environment. Mary had just added a new element to the mix.

Her salad finished, Mary stood without giving Julie a chance to offer dessert or more tea. She made fleeting eye contact with Julie. "The salad was good, I liked the dressing. Thank you, but I must get back home. Ed calls about this time every day. He doesn't like it if I'm not there to answer."

Julie remained seated. "Maybe the four of us could go out to dinner some evening."

Julie was startled by the look that came over Mary's face. Mary's gaze, always avoiding direct eye contact, now locked onto Julie's.

"It seems so logical. It would be a normal second step, wouldn't it? But it won't happen. There is nothing I would like more than to have a friend, but Ed won't agree to a dinner out. I know... he won't."

"Then let's work on him. We can break him down."

Mary shifted toward the door, her expression one of panic.

"No, Ed would never go. He won't approve of me wasting time on such things. I have to go now, Julie. Your house is lovely. Dan must be a wonderful husband. I will pray for you. Hope all this turns out for you. Please sit... I know the way out." Mary held up her hand in a stop position.

"Mary... I'll be praying for you too."

Mary shook her head. In fact, she shook all over.

Julie stepped to the door and watched Mary walk away. *What an odd woman. How does she put up with Ed's demands?* In two months of living in Stony Grove, no one had made her feel welcomed, not even at the three churches she had visited. Julie walked to the side of the porch to view Mary entering the garage until the door closed. Again, she thought, *Is Ed abusing her?* Mary seemed like someone who had never known normal, even as a child.

The difference between Julie's years in the military and this new situation contrasted sharply. She had taken for granted the ease with which one could befriend people in the service. There had been the common ground of deployments, constant change, and mobility. There were likely few in Stony Grove who had ever experienced the immediacy and needs of a life disrupted so repeatedly by their employment. There seemed to be no common bond with newcomers offered in this town. A new arrival was an intrusion. The locals were entrenched, seemingly content with generations of sameness.

Julie gazed toward the woods behind the backyard. Dan's foray into the Gorge had probably been the first anyone had taken there in years. Deep in thought, she began to clear the table. This new town they were living in seemed so alien, devoid of spirit. She avoided depressive moods, yet she couldn't help herself. She performed a little self-analysis as she was prone to do. Her conclusion was sadness, not for herself—for the town, where people apparently chose to live a small life, including her fellow students, who seemed obsessed only with their next tattoo, and the professors, so caught up in their own notions, often ungrounded and unfounded. Everyone, for the most part, appeared lost in some distrust of anything new or different. Julie felt sad for them all. She carried the dirty dishes into the kitchen, confident in her ability to switch gears if this didn't work out.

Rinsing dishes one by one, she then placed them in the dishwasher. The sun through the kitchen window felt comforting. She daydreamed of a foreign country she had considered home for a time. A noise upstairs startled her. Then another, a thud overhead—then the creaking of floors made her heart race. She stopped, turned off the water to listen. She stepped toward the entryway to the living room. She tilted her head, straining to hear. Dan would have left for work just before she arrived home from the university. Zane and Trent were at school.

Julie and Dan had always kept a gun in their bedroom, and she knew how to use it. It wasn't an option with someone already upstairs. *The intruder might already have it in their possession.* Then came a muffled sound so faint it had to be from the spare bedroom in the attic. Julie grabbed her cell phone, slipping out the side door to call 911. With the call placed, time pacing in the driveway lasted an eternity. She wanted to run to Mary's house but stopped herself. Mary was not a person she felt confident with. Eternity ended. Five minutes later the police arrived. Five minutes wishing she had a gun.

"Are you the owner of this home, ma'am?" the first officer asked as he approached Julie. She glanced at his name tag: Pete Peterson.

"Yes, I called because there is someone in my house. I was in class all morning, and when I came home for lunch, I heard noises upstairs, in the attic, I think." She had a difficult time controlling her voice.

"I'm Officer Peterson, and this is my partner, Jack Monroe. In your attic, you say?"

"The attic is finished off as a bedroom."

"We'll look around. Stay out of the house. We'll report what we find. Are there guns in the house?"

"In the master bedroom on the second floor, locked in the nightstand."

"Good to know. We'll call you when we're satisfied it's safe. The college brings in a lot of transients. Some of them are strung out on whatever. It makes them do stupid things. They're of no danger other than to themselves." The officer spoke with a voice of authority and self-assuredness, comforting Julie.

"The gun is loaded, but it's secured in a locked drawer."

"Thanks, ma'am, we'll be extra cautious."

The two officers entered the house, guns drawn. Julie continued to pace in the driveway. Two minutes passed before Julie's cell phone rang.

"Police dispatch, is this Julie Winslow?"

"Yes, this is Julie Winslow." *Why is the dispatcher calling me?*

"Ma'am, the two officers responding to your call have detained a suspect in your attic. They have him restrained. Would you please enter the house for ID verification?"

"They want me to go into the house?"

"Yes, ma'am, correct. The suspect is cuffed and on the floor. I am assured there is no danger to you, but the officers would like your assistance."

"I'll head right in." Julie clenched her phone in her fist as she entered the house. She dashed up the stairs toward the attic.

She cleared the last step and found herself staring into the suspect's flushed face, his hands bound behind his back. Officer Peterson's knees pressed hard into the small of his back, and his gun was drawn. Officer Monroe, his own gun still holstered, stood back, out of the suspect's reach. Every bit of Julie's energy washed from her. She couldn't catch her breath, let alone speak.

"He claims he's your son, ma'am, but he put up quite a fight. He was in the closet when we grabbed him."

"Mom! Tell them who I am! Why'd you call the cops on me?" Zane pleaded, but Julie just stared, shocked at the sight. "Mom! Say something."

Officer Peterson holstered his gun without Julie's spoken verification. The boy's pleas and Julie's body language said it all. Peterson let his suspect up. He released the cuffs as Julie took a deep breath. Peterson snickered. Monroe shook his head, indicating disapproval of Officer Peterson's overzealous police work. Monroe was the junior officer.

"Zane, what are you doing home? You should be in school. You could have been killed. What were you thinking?" Julie's final words were coated with tears. She felt a loss of trust. Neither of her sons had ever given her any reason to doubt their honesty or trustworthiness..

"I slept in and missed the bus."

"What?! The school's less than a mile from here. You could have walked."

The police officers backed away. Peterson secured his equipment. His grin had an evil glimmer to it. Julie caught enough of a glimpse of it to know Peterson had used the situation to amuse himself. She instantly disliked him.

"I was trying to get dressed when they grabbed me. I thought I was being attacked, so I fought back." Julie offered Peterson a hard stare. He returned it with a smirk. She was the one who had to break the eye contact. *What a real piece of work.*

"Zane, I'm speechless."

"Mom, I can't stand this school. The kids are weird. The teachers are lame."

"Zane, enough. Get dressed and go to school right now!"

"By the time I get there, my bus will be leaving to bring me home."

"Would you rather go with these gentlemen?" Julie looked at Officer Monroe, whose face offered compassion.

Zane grabbed his clothes and ran from the room. He hit every other step as he fled down the stairs. He emerged into the street a few moments later, heading toward the high school, but he turned to look back as Julie watched from the window. She saw a look of disbelief and anger on his face she would not soon forget.

"Sorry, ma'am, we have another call. Are you all right?" Officer Monroe's voice sounded sincere.

"Sure, I'm fine," she muttered. Officer Peterson had already started down the steps. Julie could hear his chuckling.

"We'll show ourselves out. You take care now." Officer Monroe gave Julie a little nod.

"Thank you, I'm so sorry about all this." Julie's voice was weak and trailed off as the officers descended the stairs. She walked to the stairs, collapsing onto the top step. She leaned her head against the wall. *This might turn into a long school year.*

SEVEN

The next morning Dan came home from work to find his boys sitting on the front porch steps waiting for the school bus. He rubbed their heads as he walked past them. He gave Zane a playful push. Zane didn't respond with his usual counterattack. Neither of the boys spoke when he said hello; they just returned with grunts. He went on into the house. Having just finished working an afternoon-to-midnight and midnight-to-morning double shift, he was transitioning into a couple of days off. Julie stood at the kitchen sink cleaning up after breakfast.

"What's up with Zane? He doesn't seem like himself."

"He's not adjusting to the new school very well, I think."

"He's always gotten along fine at other schools they've gone to. I wonder what the problem is."

"Dan, you have to be dead tired. Get some rest before we discuss him, and maybe we can talk with him... when, tomorrow?"

"Do you know, neither one of them even spoke when I said good morning to them."

"They're acting like teenagers, is all. How about you take another day off from house remodeling? You get to bed, and when you get up, go do whatever you want. You've been working too much. You enjoyed your hike down Stony Creek so much, why don't you go fishing, sit along the creek, and nap? Go talk to Lee, the fellow you met." She hadn't had the inclination to tell him about the police incident over the phone while he was at work.

"I feel guilty. There is so much to do on the house. I should finish some projects before I go fishing. You're always telling me to take a day off." Dan put his arms around her, giving her a squeeze.

"Yes, Dan, I need to tell you, or you will work yourself to death. There will always be projects. I also want to tell you before I forget, Mary was here for lunch yesterday."

"How did you manage to get her here?"

"It wasn't easy. She caved, after a lot of talk, but she didn't stay long. I'm concerned, I think Ed might abuse her."

"How so?"

"Mentally or emotionally, I'm not sure—I don't think it's anything physical. She just seems so meek and controlled. I don't think she can even speak her own mind. Most of what she said was just repeating Ed's thoughts."

"Too bad."

"Yes, and Ed has some thoughts about our remodeling."

"Like what?"

"Mary said he thinks we're wasting our time and money. He doesn't understand why you are working so hard on this place."

"I think it's a good investment. This whole town is going to start improving. Real estate prices are going to go up. I think Ed is wrong."

"I shouldn't have said anything. You should go to bed, and I should get ready for class."

"Julie, it doesn't bother me."

"I know. I'm just telling you what Mary said. Ed says the student rental landlords have too much influence on the housing market."

The doorbell rang. Dan let go of Julie. "I'll get it." He headed out of the kitchen for the front door. He didn't peek through the window to see who it might be. He just flung the door wide open. There stood a lovely young girl. Her auburn hair hung shoulder length, her skin milky white. Piercing blue eyes shifted downward as she introduced herself.

"Hello, I am Klaare Markov, a graduate exchange student at the university. I have been told, you may have an apartment to rent." She spoke perfect English with precise enunciation, yet she had a distinctive accent.

"Hello... well, yes, we have an apartment in the basement. We don't intend to rent it just yet, though. I still have a lot of work to do before it's ready to be rented." Dan looked back to see if Julie was coming from the kitchen. She wasn't.

"I am here from Estonia. The people who made my arrangements did not provide me with adequate living arrangements. I must leave where I am staying today. I will move into your apartment, unfinished."

"Not possible, we have to get an occupancy permit and an inspection."

"You must understand, where I am staying there are boys who will not leave me alone. They are making improper advances. I am frightened."

"Hold on. Please step in."

Dan walked backward holding up one finger. "I'm going to get my wife."

He stopped again and motioned toward the couch.

"Please, sit."

"I'll be right back. My wife is in the kitchen." Dan turned around to enter the kitchen, almost walking into the wall. He had missed the door opening by a foot. He glanced back at Klaare to catch her hiding a smile behind her hand.

"Julie, we have a visitor who needs our help. She's a university student from Estonia."

"She came all the way from Estonia and needs our help?"

"Come talk with her. She seems frightened of the place where her sponsors have lodged her. Somehow she heard about our apartment and wants to rent it. She said she will take it even unfinished."

"Dan, you said it won't be ready for weeks. You won't be able to work on it with her living in it."

"I know, but if her situation is as bad as she says, I'll put a push on it. I can have it done in a few days."

"Dan, that's crazy!"

They returned to the living room and their visitor. Before Julie could say a word, Klaare pleaded, "I am Klaare Markov. I am sorry to bother you, but I heard you have an apartment. I need a place to stay. My lodging is not safe. I cannot sleep there. I spend all of my free time at the library, but each evening when it closes, I must return to the place that is not safe."

"Klaare, have you told your sponsors about your unsafe situation?"

"Yes, they feel it is adequate because there are so many people living there that I am never alone. Maybe nothing bad will happen to me there, but I am very uncomfortable. The boys are always watching me."

Julie and Dan looked at each other and nodded in silent agreement.

"We can let you stay in the spare bedroom until the basement is completed. In the military, we learned what it's like to arrive at a strange place and be all alone."

Klaare expressed her gratitude a hundred times as she stepped off the porch to go collect her belongings at the house she shared with seven other students.

Dan hung his arm over Julie's shoulders, "I'm sure she will bring joy to this house. We're doing the right thing."

"There is not a doubt in my mind, not a doubt. It can be an ugly world. I'm glad we have an opportunity to make a difference. Now, you better get to bed, rest, and then you can make it happen."

He never heard Klaare return with her things. Julie showed her to her room, and then they walked together to the university.

###

Dan felt exhilarated even after a nap. The project now had a unique purpose. Feeling a surge of strength, he pulled new electrical feeds through the drop ceiling, ripped out seventy-year-old corroded galvanized piping, replaced it with PVC, and patched holes in the drywall. The bathroom had major issues. Dan tore out all the fixtures and scrapped the old linoleum floor to opt for porcelain. Julie ended his manic attack on the basement when she returned at five in the afternoon and insisted he stop for a dinner break.

Early the next morning Dan grabbed a cup of coffee and headed to the basement. Not wanting to lose any time, he refused Julie's offers to cook him breakfast. He would eat later. The basement had to be done by tonight. Tomorrow he had to transition to daylight shift, then short-swing back for midnight. At noon Julie and Klaare came downstairs with a lunch offering. They were shocked at the progress he had made. Klaare could not believe all this space was going to be hers. Julie wondered what living conditions she was used to in Estonia because the basement seemed small for a living space.

As they placed a tablecloth, paper plates, sandwiches, and a bowl of fruit salad on the floor, Julie and Klaare chatted. They seemed to have bonded in a mother-daughter manner, a relationship Julie needed.

Dan picked up one of the sandwiches and scanned his work while he ate. Julie grabbed his arm, pulling him toward her. The three of them perched around the tablecloth.

"How long have you been in the States, Klaare?" Dan asked.

"Four weeks. I arrived two days before classes commenced. It was most difficult after the long flight."

"Sorry you've had a bad experience so far," Dan commented.

"My sponsors thought they had done the right thing putting me with other Ukrainian students, but there is a cultural difference with them. The boys are not gentlemen. It is not Americans who have made it unpleasant." She shifted on the floor to sit up straighter. "What you are doing is beyond wonderful. I now have hopes my time here will be pleasant."

Julie touched Klaare's shoulder. "Did any of those boys hurt you?"

"No, I'm fine. I'm just happy to be here." She smiled.

"Klaare, you are a blessing to us. We consider it an honor to host you while you are here. If there is anything you want to do or places you want to go, please tell us." Julie relished the thought of exposing Klaare to new cultural experiences. Besides, they both could use a friend in this town. "We have a lot of museums and libraries within driving distance. There is a big flower show scheduled soon too."

Klaare took a bite of her sandwich, pausing before answering. "Can you take me to a tractor pull or a four-wheeler derby? The professors already have made cultural activity plans for me. I want to experience what other Americans do, all of the culture. I would also like to see Niagara Falls if it is possible."

"Those are the things you would like to see and do? Well, we will make it possible. Those things sound like fun."

"I like cowboys too. Is there somewhere I could see country-western dancing?"

"Oh, girl—you have landed in the right place. We'll have you dancing up a storm."

"Oh, no. I don't want to dance. I will watch and take photos."

"Why not? It will be fun."

"Fun to watch, yes." Klaare held her gaze.

"What about church? Do you go to church?" Julie had yet to find a church to suit her, but maybe she and Klaare could explore other possibilities. Dan's schedule had him working most Sundays.

"In Estonia I do not go to church. A professor here offered to take me. In Estonia we believe religion is all superstition. There is no God. I am not superstitious. Religion can undermine the harmony of a society. It is our purpose to have a well-regulated and stable population."

"God is not superstition. Ideas such as black cats bringing bad luck are superstitious."

"No, such things as black cats and broken mirrors are true, they bring bad luck. It is not superstition." Klaare's voice was emphatic, authoritative.

"Anyway, will you try going to church with me? Just for the experience. I promise I won't try to convince you about my beliefs."

"Yes, I will go with you. It will be good to learn about Western superstitions."

"Good." Julie smiled.

Klaare looked at Dan.

"May I use your telephone to call my superiors? I must report."

"What do you mean? Where are you calling?"

"Estonia. I must call and report every few days."

Dan's mind raced. Calls to Eastern Europe from his home phone might not sit well with the State Department. Dan and Julie both had high-level security clearances when they left the service, and he needed his for his new career. Klaare's request put him on the spot. He wanted to be a good host, but here he had to draw the line. How could he say it?

"I'm sorry. I don't think we can do it."

"Why? I must report."

"We will have a phone installed for you, in your name. You will be able to call on it."

"I must report today."

"Is there somewhere at the university where you can make a call?" Julie asked.

"Yes, one of the professors said I could use his office phone."

"I'll drive you over to use it. We'll let Dan get back to work." Julie leaned over and gave Dan a peck on the cheek.

"Hey, unexpected dessert, thanks. Be careful."

Dan dashed about putting finishing touches to several little details in the basement. Overall, he was pleased with the way the apartment had turned out. He cleaned his paintbrushes and rolled up the drop cloth. The doorbell rang once and then again. He hurried up the stairs to the front door. He had scheduled the occupancy permit inspection, so it was probably the building inspector. He peeked out through the drapes and saw a new Cadillac parked at the curb with an elderly woman perched in the passenger seat. A tall slender elderly gentleman stood on the front porch, turned so he could see the car. Dan opened the door.

"Can I help you?"

As he turned to face Dan, he removed his hat, holding it in both hands.

"I live over in Castleton. You're the fellow who purchased this home from the Goldmeadows?"

"Yes I am."

"I heard you are in the process of remodeling it. This place has looked the same since I sold it to Mrs. Goldmeadow back in the seventies."

"You're Mr. McKenzie?"

He seemed to have not heard Dan's question.

"I grew up in this house. I shot skunks right out here in the front yard. You know, it's a funny thing about skunks: if you shoot one, they offer their own sort of revenge. It permeates all your senses and leaves a bad taste that can linger a long time. The best way to handle a skunk is to just give them a wide berth and let nature take them."

"You don't say?" Dan sized up his visitor with a wary look. *Why didn't he acknowledge my question?*

"The street was dirt back then. This entire town was full of skunks. Have you been seeing any? I'm sure their descendants are still about."

"No, I can't say I've noticed any. By the way, my name is Dan Winslow. You're Mr. McKenzie?"

"Pleased to meet you, Mr. Winslow. Yes, my name is John McKenzie. The woman in the car is my wife, Evelyn. She's too frail to get out."

"What can I help you with, Mr. McKenzie?"

"We were just out for a drive. I thought I would stop by to meet you. I was hoping you would let this sentimental old man have a look around the place. I can give you a little history of it if you care to hear."

"Sure."

McKenzie raised his arm in the direction of the driveway.

"You know those hedges along the driveway have been there since I was a kid. It was my job to keep them clipped. I hated them. It was before electric clippers."

"Come on in, Mr. McKenzie. Have a look around. As a matter of fact, you lead the way. It will be interesting to hear about the place."

The old man stepped into the living room. He surveyed Dan's handiwork and nodded with approval. He strolled from room to room without speaking until he paused at the kitchen door.

"I'm just a sentimental old fool. My father built this house. He built several houses in town. This is the one he built for my mother. Things became very difficult when he died."

McKenzie paused, visibly shaken. "Mother used to take in boarders. After she died, I sold the place. It would have broken her heart to know I did it. You understand why I want to make sure the right people live here—time came when I just wanted to give this town space, let nature take its course. Life is too short to be bitter. I've let God handle things. This house is my connection to my parents. You are doing a wonderful rehabilitation job here. My mother and father would be happy."

"John... can I call you John? And please call me Dan."

"Oh, by all means, call me John."

"Well, you said you sold the house to the Goldmeadows? Where did they come from?"

"Oh, my mother and Mr. Goldmeadow's mother were cousins. I knew I could trust the Goldmeadows."

"Trust them?"

"Yes, to sell it back to me or at least they would give me first option. I'm getting too old to be buying anything. They spoke with me before they sold to you. Since you are military retirees with no previous connection to this town, I felt I could trust you, Mr. Winslow."

"Why do you care?"

"Like I said, I'm sentimental. My father died in his prime. He had everything to live for. The town doctor ruled it an accident. A lot of the locals said it was suicide. Both of those notions are nonsense. My mother never made public her beliefs. How about if we just let it go—I would like to protect my family honor."

"Sure... well, I signed the agreement. You have my word I will give you first option."

"Trust me, Dan, should it come down to me purchasing this place from you, you will be properly compensated. When Goldmeadow called me to ask if it would be all right if he sold to you, I ran a complete check. Quite frankly, I found your military history to be rather intriguing. I could not have asked for a better person to relieve the Goldmeadows. You remind me a little bit of my father. My mother loved my father until her death. Say, if you'd like, I could mail you some old photos of the place."

"I would like it, John, but don't put yourself out."

"Sir, it will be my pleasure. I better get back out there with my wife. Tell Julie I said hello."

"I will." It was strange hearing Julie's name voiced by John McKenzie. He knew her name without ever being introduced or meeting her.

"Oh yes, and your sons, don't ever take them for granted. In the end, they are all we have. I hope you understand what I mean. These are fast-paced times and people get lost."

Dan took pause. McKenzie seemed to know a lot about the Winslow family. McKenzie's words made him feel out of sorts. "It was nice meeting you."

"It's a shame the way Goldmeadow let this place go. He was a book-smart kind of guy, not much going for him on the physical side, though. I don't believe in such nonsense, but he told me the place is haunted. I told him he was crazy, but he said the whole town knew it." John looked hard into Dan's eyes. "What do you think?"

"I have heard mention of it. It doesn't scare me or anything. We like the house."

"Good, it's what I was hoping to hear. Goldmeadow is a weird bird. If there was any haunting going on, it was probably him. Harry McDonath told me he became a hoarder. He left quite a mess for you to clean up. My apologies." John held out a check to Dan. "I hope this will cover your troubles. Harry and I feel real bad about the mess."

Dan took the check and glanced at it for an instant, then handed it back. John kept his hands to his sides.

"It's yours. Please take it. I'm sure it means more to you than me. You'll make Harry and me feel better if you accept it."

"It's too much, John. Fifteen hundred dollars is way more than what I spent hauling the stuff to the dump."

"Your time has value, not to mention the added stress. You take it. If for any reason you want to get word to me, just tell Harry McDonath. Take care, Dan, and thank you."

The two men locked hands in a firm grip. Dan couldn't say any more. The lump in his throat blocked the passage of speech even as the look in John's eye let him know all was well. John made his way down the sidewalk to the passenger door of his Cadillac as the window lowered. He spoke to his wife, but Dan couldn't make out the words. He looked back at the house as he made his way to the driver's side, slid in, started the car, and pulled away.

As Dan walked along the porch thinking about the shifting wind of the ceiling fan and the window that had slammed shut, he wondered if he would ever see John McKenzie again. If he believed in ghosts, things might make more sense. If he believed in ghosts and superstition, then the story he had just heard might offer an answer. He wondered where, how, and why John's father had died. John hadn't offered this bit of information, and Dan thought it impolite to pursue it. Now he was left to wonder, yet what did it matter? What had made the town doctor report it as an accident, and what had caused the locals to think it might have been a suicide?

Dan looked at his watch. The inspector was overdue. In fact, it was now past the inspector's quitting time. If he showed up tomorrow, Dan would be at work. He didn't want Julie to have to handle the inspection.

EIGHT

Julie's hand shook as she hit the speed dial to connect with Dan's cell. She looked at the kitchen wall clock, verifying the time. He should be on the interstate halfway home. The day shift ended a half-hour ago. She didn't want to talk to Dan. She *had* to talk to him. She couldn't contain herself any longer. Anger surged as she listened to the ring. She waited to hear his voice. Her vision blurred as tears welled in her eyes.

"Hey there, gorgeous."

"Dan," Julie began, pausing to take a deep breath, "the inspector was here."

"And he said my work is the greatest, right?"

"No, Dan, he failed the apartment. He won't give us an occupancy permit."

"What... how could it have failed? What did he say?"

"He said it was not up to standards—and when it is, you can call him back for him to do another inspection."

"But what needs done?"

"He was abrupt, even curt with me. He said it was up to us to know the codes and address them or hire a contractor who knows what he's doing."

After a long pause, Dan said, "This is exactly why I wanted to be there. Forget their permit. We have an exchange student living with us, not a tenant. They can't stop us from having a guest in our home. They're playing a game with us, Julie. Someone doesn't want us to rent out our apartment. I met every item in the code book and then some. Let's just move ahead—everything is going to be all right."

"I hope you're right."

"I'll be home soon. Love you."

Upon arriving home, Dan faked being in good spirits. He had to short-swing back to work in less than eight hours to work the midnight shift. He needed to nap after dinner. Julie would have to help Klaare move down to the basement. The big stuff had already been moved, adequate furnishings to make the apartment livable. Julie would make sure Klaare was comfortable.

Dan closed the bedroom door and turned on his white noise recorder. It soothed him. Ocean waves were his favorite; he selected ocean surf and sea birds, then lay back on a soft pillow. He stared at the paddle fan whirling over the bed.

"Don't change direction," he whispered.

He closed his eyes and drifted somewhere just this side of sleep. The ocean pulsed while the birds called as they always did. Dan envisioned a small beach between dramatic rock formations. It was along the coast of the Olympic Peninsula in the special place he and Julie had found while hiking under a dramatic darkened sky, a gentle breeze refreshing their faces. The gulls floated above sea foam. He could almost smell the sea salt, taste it on his lips.

A faint sound somewhere on the beach called out. A woman's voice heard beyond the relentless rolling of the surf. He strained to hear, but the words were muffled. They eluded him as he struggled to envision the woman on the beach. Awareness of the creaking house sounds brought him back to a murky reality. *This is just a recording.* A recording he had listened to a hundred times before. His eyes popped open, wide awake. He could still hear the faint voice. The words were not clear, but the tone was pleading, like a cry for help. He sat up, looking toward the noisemaker, his ears straining. Easing out of bed, he knelt to the white noise machine and put his ear directly against it. The words were more distinct now. He heaved himself to the door. "Julie!

Hurry! Come here, you have to hear this." He ran from the room. There was no response.

He took the steps two at a time, sprinting into the kitchen. It was quiet and empty. A bright green note lay on the counter. She had taken Klaare and the boys to the mall, to get some things for the apartment. He flipped it over to read: "We need to talk about Zane." He let out a groan. He had hoped to secure a witness to the voice on the machine, but it was not to be. He climbed back to the bedroom and tried to settle down. The waves and the birds were there, no voices. He lay questioning whether he had heard the voice or imagined it. The words he heard meant something. But what? He fell asleep with the question echoing in his mind.

Dan woke at ten in the evening, just in time to dress, then grab a travel mug of coffee and a hug from Julie. He did not mention the voice. He knew Julie would be the lone adult in the house and did not want to distress her with a story about mysterious voices. He saw no threat to her, save her own anxiety and fear, should he tell his tale.

"What's up with Zane?" he asked.

"I think he's falling in with a bad crowd."

"What happened?"

"He's just acting different, not like the same kid."

"Julie... more specific, please."

"He told me he doesn't believe in God. He said the Bible is just a bunch of fairy tales."

"Kids go through things like this."

"Maybe, but you need to help him come out on the right side of whatever he is going through."

"First chance I get."

"Oh, and can we take Klaare somewhere special on Saturday?"

My day off? "Sure."

He kissed her and slipped out the door. He spent the entire drive to work mulling over the words he had heard emanating from the noise machine. His job would leave no time to ponder the meaning behind the words. Later, on the long drive home, he could give it his full attention. Still, an answer eluded him, and he wanted an answer now. He coughed a dry cough. It felt like a piece of dust was caught far back in his throat. His coffee had cooled enough to drink a big gulp and quiet his cough.

###

Julie cleaned the kitchen after Dan left for work. The sound of Klaare's television in the basement let her know Klaare was still awake. She tapped on the door, heard dainty steps on the stairs; then the basement door eased open, revealing Klaare's friendly face.

"Oh dear, is my television too loud? I am sorry."

"No, I didn't knock to complain. I hoped you were awake. Dan left for work. It is so nice knowing there is another adult here in the house. I also wanted to see if you need anything."

Klaare opened the door wide, giving Julie a warm grin. "No, everything is fine down the stairs. I don't think I offer much protection should something bad happen."

"Oh, just having you here offers comfort. What are you watching? It sounds like an old show from long ago, but I can't make it out."

"My favorite American TV show—*I Love Lucy*—it is so funny." Her face lit up as she spoke, her smile filled with pearly white teeth.

"*I Love Lucy*—are you serious?"

"I'm sorry, this is not good?" Klaare's smile faded into worry.

"Oh, no, Klaare, I find it marvelous you can connect with our humor. It is wonderful. Of all the shows, I love knowing you are watching Lucy."

Klaare's smile returned.

"I don't want to keep you from your show. I just wanted to say good night and tell you how happy I am having you here. Also, Dan and I would like to take you somewhere on his off day. I wondered if you would like to go somewhere with us."

"What day is off?"

"This Saturday."

Klaare's face turned sad and her look distant. "Oh, the professors are planning to take me to a museum. I'm sorry. I should go with them, since I said I will."

"What time are they taking you?"

"They want to go early, when it opens."

"Hey, we're flexible. We'll take you wherever or whenever. You name it."

"You will?"

"Yes, we'd enjoy it."

"Have you ever heard of Mud Hollow Inn by the river?"

"I've heard of it, but we've never been there."

"I would like to go there to see some dancing, and they are having what you call Redneck Truck Rodeo or something. I will make sure we are not home late from the museum."

"Seriously, that is what you want to do?"

"I want to see America. I think it will be a bit of the real America. Am I mistaken?"

"No, you are not mistaken. If you can get home from the museum trip in time, then we will take you. Sounds like a lot of fun."

"Yes, I will look forward to it."

Julie said good night, and Klaare closed her door. Julie smiled to herself as she climbed the stairs to her second-floor bedroom. She unlocked the nightstand, her normal routine. The thoughts of taking her Ukrainian friend to a Redneck Truck Rodeo gave her warm feelings. Thoughts of watching mud trucks blowing through huge washes of brown slime while people shouted and cheered relieved her of lonely thoughts. She envisioned Klaare snapping photo after photo for the people back home. She could say she experienced Americana. Julie was asleep the minute her head hit the pillow. A cool breeze flowed through the window, bringing the night sounds with it.

###

The exhaust pipes rose alongside their cabs. Fire blew ten feet in the air as the engines screamed. Mudslinger tires launched chucks of debris toward the crowd. All the trucks were the same mud-brown color. The crowd ran from mound to mound to catch sight of the next mud-hole challenge. Klaare snapped photo after photo, not just of trucks but of the people in the crowd. She stood out in the crowd with her slacks and button-down. Dan offered to buy her a T-shirt, but she declined the offer. She insisted such garments are inappropriate for a young professional. Zane and Trent ran from one spot to another, angling for the best view and enjoying every minute.

Julie concentrated on the starting line as two new contestants moved into position. Flames shot above their exhaust stacks. She felt sonic vibrations in her body with every engine rev.

A deluge of ice water shocked her awake. She gasped for breath and bolted upright. The cold liquid ran down her neck into her nightclothes. The room was black, so black she couldn't tell if her eyes were open or shut. Drawing a deep shuddering breath, she sensed a distant light through the window. What happened? Was it all a dream? No, she was wet and cold. Her hand slipped behind her to grab her pillow. It, too, was soaked with cold liquid. Her eyes adjusted to the dim light. She could see no one, hear nothing.

She leaned toward the nightstand drawer, removing the pistol. Swinging her feet onto the floor, she crept across the room. She listened at the door but heard nothing, and she knew her door had not opened or she would have heard it. Her finger found the light switch. She held her breath and flicked it on. The light revealed nothing but her usual room... and the wet pillow. She wiped her hand across the wall behind the bed; it was dry. She stood on the bed, running her hand across the ceiling. It, too, was dry. There were no empty water glasses in the room. Had it rained outside? Had rain blown in through the window? She switched off the light and looked out at the night sky. A billion stars twinkled. The curtains were dry. She threw her wet pillow to the floor and climbed back into the bed.

Grabbing Dan's pillow to hug, she drew her legs up close to her body. Her back rested against the headboard. Her fist clenched the pistol. She remained positioned there for the remainder of the night. In and out of sleep in a sitting position, she waited for another water attack or worse. It never came.

###

Caressing her coffee cup, Julie stood at the living room window. The street was awash in bright sun. Cars carried their occupants to unknown destinations as they passed the house on Elm Street, none aware of the night's discomforting event, so surreal now. Had it all been a dream? The light of day made it seem so. An impossible event. She glanced around the living room; it looked so normal, so like every other day.

Zane and Trent had laughed during breakfast, excited about going to the truck mudder. They had shown no sign things were amiss. Julie chose not to share her experience with them. She even questioned her concerns about Zane. The boys seemed better than they had since school started. Now, though, she watched for Dan with great anticipation. Telling him would make it seem real again. She craved his response. His car appeared as he turned into Elm Street. Julie's heart raced.

She met him at his car door. He stumbled backward from the pressure of Julie's body thrust against him in an overpowering hug.

"Wow, I missed you too. Glad to be home." Dan felt winded; he coughed a dry cough. Julie's arms dropped to her sides. She backed away.

"What's up? Did I say something to offend you? I don't think I'm contagious."

"No, Dan, I'm upset about an event during the night. We need to talk."

"The kids?"

"No, but something strange happened." Julie filled him in with all the details, watching for his response. He never flinched. He used his best poker face and let her talk.

"Well, what do you think... overactive imagination? I'm telling you, it happened. My pillow is still wet this morning."

"I believe you. I've had a couple of strange events myself, but I don't think we have anything to fear."

"No? Well, I'm scared. The water... it was like ice, colder than anything you pull from the tap. It took my breath away."

Dan thought of the cold shock he received when he thrust his hand into Stony Creek. "Don't be afraid. I'm telling you, I have experienced things too. I've been told things; they make me curious. Maybe this house wants its secrets to be known. I think whatever this is, it is trying to communicate with us, not harm us."

"What if you're wrong? You're gone a lot of nights." They headed inside.

"Let's take it one step at a time. Maybe the father of old John McKenzie... the one who stopped by and then sent us pictures... I want to find out more about what happened to him. I want to go to the courthouse or the library to do some research. We're both too practical and tested to let this get to us."

"I don't know, Dan. I'm beginning to think moving here was a huge mistake."

"Come on, Julie, we've seen some pretty tense moments around the world. Don't let this old house scare you." He went to the desk and picked up the envelope of McKenzie's old photos that had arrived in the mail. He fumbled through them until he found the one of a smiling muscular man dressed in a white undershirt holding a small boy. He placed the photo on the kitchen counter.

Julie stared at the photo. "You know in the light of day... the bumps in the night don't seem real. Everything appears normal. It's when the light goes away... it's like the world changes."

"Nothing changes except our own thoughts. Our own thoughts are what we have to fear—it's better to control them than to let them control us. Look at this guy, Julie. He did not kill himself, and I doubt he had an accident. While you were at the mall, I heard a voice on the white noise machine. I was playing beach sounds. I thought I heard a woman saying over and over again, 'Help!'"

Dan looked at the photo again. "He looks pretty happy and competent. Do you think this guy died in the water? What water... at Stratton Beach? Fine. I would like to know more about our house's story and this guy." Dan looked around the room. His words were meant for someone other than Julie. He threw the picture back onto the desk.

"I'm sorry—I have a class, I've got to get going." She squeezed his hand. "I'm also going to take a DNA test as part of my genealogy research."

"I'm going to crash for a couple of hours. Then I'm going over to the county seat to start my snooping. I might drop by to see the old hillbilly, Lee McDaniels. He knows more than he lets on. Be careful, Julie."

"You, too."

Julie turned and was gone. Her parting left Dan's mind in turmoil. The house, Zane, McKenzie, and creepy Ed Knight. He trudged up the stairs and stared at the bed before he reached and felt Julie's wet pillow. He studied the paddle fan, then decided not to turn on the white noise machine. He sat in a chair staring out the bedroom window toward the backyard. Minutes passed before he tumbled onto their bed. He knew there was evil in the world. He was not naïve. The paddle fan whirled over his head. He watched, waited, and wondered if the cool stream of air would shift directions.

Evil was on Julie's mind as she drove to class. She was not naïve either. Her hope was based on Dan being right. Dan's belief in good spirits would help her, but she knew her fears would persist. She knew evil all too well. Her pain had not been at the hands of a ghost. This was a new evil she sensed, one more difficult to define and understand. In the light of day, it would be easy to be brave, but when darkness fell, she would be home alone, again. God is the light, but doubts creep about in the still of the night... in darkness.

NINE

A black Escalade proceeded up Elm Street. It hesitated in front of the Winslow home and again at the Knight home. The Escalade's tinted windows left nothing of the interior visible, even if Dan had been awake from his nap. Julie was still at the college. Like a stalking beast, the Escalade continued up Elm through two intersections without hesitating at the stop signs.

The college had always been the biggest employer in town. A third of the permanent population worked there. The local businesses depended on the cash influx brought by state budgets and student spending. It brought with it a structure, with third-generation townies managing the money flow. These structures encompassed family traditions, challenged by few. The way of things was well understood by all. Most people felt grateful to be employed. As the college's student population grew, no new on-campus housing was ever built. The college campus housing had room for half of the students. It meant the students were forced to seek off-campus housing. They fell to the mercy of slumlords.

Stony Grove had reached a tipping point where the homes rented to students exceeded the number of homes occupied by permanent residents. The situation had caused a deterioration of the wage tax base and challenged the public services departments. Town council posts were lifetime positions. No one could remember an election where a challenger ran against a council member. The mayor was third generation; his father had been mayor before him, and his grandfather was mayor before him. No one alive could remember a mayor by a different last name than

Whipple. It had all worked well for some, but the system was showing signs of sickness.

Foremost, the houses were showing their age. The landlords had failed to reinvest in their properties. The students lived in squalor. Basements were damp, electrical systems outdated, plumbing systems suffered chronic failures. Tree-lined streets looked peaceful on the surface, while roots ripped at rusted pipes under the street. Orange-stained plumbing fixtures in the homes were the norm. On a regular basis, the housing inspector issued occupancy permits for properties needing to be condemned. Yet he turned down permits for properties in good condition owned by the wrong person. The biggest threat to the system came from recent construction of an interstate three miles from town. The interstate allowed for quick transport into the city. New housing developments were springing up on the outskirts of town. The new residents brought change to the political demographics. The town fathers and their political futures were becoming more unstable.

The black Escalade slid into a reserved parking space in front of town hall. The driver's door swung open, dinging the door of the car parked beside it. The driver struggled to free his mass from the confines of the steering wheel. He emerged into the light of day, his skin pasty, black circles etched beneath his eyes that made him appear older than his forty-five years. Breathing with exertion, he struggled up the concrete steps leading to the doorway of the town hall. From there he pushed open the door, banging the wall, and headed straight for the mayor's office.

"Val! How are you this fine day?"

The mayor sprawled in an overstuffed, overpriced leather chair, behind a desk better suited to a New York law firm. He puffed on a cigar, blowing smoke like a steel mill into the air above his head.

"Cut the crap, Joe. Those thieves on Elm are still there."

Val leaned forward, both of his chubby hands gripping the edge of the desk.

"Yeah... we're working on it, Val. We turned down their occupancy permit for the basement apartment. I gave him some grief over his remodeling. He cleaned out the front yard before I could take legal action. There is only so much we can do."

The mayor snuffed out his cigar in the ashtray.

"Legal? What the . . ."

"Val, come on in. The hallway has ears."

Joe Whipple got up to close the door. It wouldn't open again for almost two hours. Their conversation consisted of a series of directives issued to the mayor by Val, who returned to the Elm Street encroachment on his territory.

"I own the rental house across Elm Street from the Winslows." He wiped his brow with a kerchief as he labored to breathe. "You tell the boys to leave those kids who live there alone. Any complaints about them—ignore as if they were being lodged at me. You got it? They're my kids, I own them."

"Yeah, Val, gotcha."

"No. I got... *cha*. Don't ever forget Valenta Wentreck owns you and this town." Val pulled the door shut behind him.

Val struggled to his Escalade. He stood by the driver's door catching his breath and looked about the parking lot with contempt, then stuffed himself behind the wheel and pulled away.

Val had made community offerings, such as a piece of land for a park. He named the park after his father. He never hurt himself financially except when he went to a casino or a pony track, gambling being something of a compulsion. Like his undisciplined consumption, it was a pastime he could not deny. He always said it was a good deal if the person across the table from him had tears in their eyes and by no means did he mean tears of joy. Yet at the blackjack table, many times Val had walked away broken. The gift of the land for the park came about because it was useless land with no development potential. This gift of land to the town gained Val many backroom political advantages and promises.

###

When Julie returned home from school, Dan was gone. She heard Klaare's television and giggles in the basement. Her tension faded. She had been hesitant before opening the front door. The sounds of giggling in the basement made her feel silly about her apprehension. She tossed her keys onto a tray on a small table by the door. Before they were done jingling, she heard footsteps on the basement stairs. A faint tapping on the basement door, then a voice whispered, "Ms. Winslow, you are home?"

"Yes, Klaare." Julie walked to the basement door and unlatched it. "It sounds like you are enjoying a good show."

"Oh yes, I'm watching *I Love Lucy* again. It is so funny."

"Good. Hearing you made me feel comfortable. It is so nice having you with us. Do you need something?

"Well, a man stopped by. I hope I didn't do a bad thing by answering my outside door. He asked me what I was doing in this house. He asked me if I lived in the basement. I told him I did." Klaare's face melted into a frown. Her eyes broke contact with Julie's.

"Who was he? What happened?"

"He said he was the building inspector. He said you do not have a permit to allow me to stay. Oh, Mrs. Winslow, I am so sorry. I can't believe I will have to move."

"You aren't moving. Dan will handle this when he gets back. Don't fret over this. You did the right thing. You have to tell the truth."

"I am sorry, Mrs. Winslow. In Estonia no one speaks up to the authorities. It is suicide."

"Well, this is America, not Estonia. Please call me Julie. Would you like some tea?" Julie signaled Klaare to come into the kitchen and closed the basement door.

"Oh yes, please. It would be nice to sit with you."

Julie filled a kettle with water, placing it on the stove. "Have you given any more thought to looking for a church with me?"

"Religion is superstition. It might not be approved for me to do such a thing."

"No one needs to know. It can be just between us girls. Personal choices are no business of the government."

"Oh no, I report everything I do, when I call Estonia. They want to have a complete report of my activities."

"Have you told them about how much you love Lucy?"

Klaare struggled but she could not keep from breaking into a grin. Her eyes twinkled.

"Aha! I didn't think so." They both chuckled.

"It's your life, Klaare. You don't owe it to anyone to report your every move."

"But they have paid my expenses. I do owe them."

"How were you picked? I'll bet you were chosen because you have done well in school."

"Yes, it is true."

"Coming here is your reward for years of hard work, Klaare."

There was silence as Julie placed cups, saucers, and tea caddies on the table.

"Ms. Julie, I have special tea downstairs from Estonia. Would you like to try some?" Klaare stood up.

"I would."

Klaare scurried down to her apartment to retrieve her treasured tea. Julie walked into the living room to secure the old Bible she had found in the trash in the front yard. She had never opened it, as she had her own favorite Bible. This old one would be good enough to loan to Klaare. When Klaare reentered the kitchen, Julie was seated at the table holding the Bible on her lap, hidden from view.

Klaare smiled, placing her bag of tea on the table. "I brought this from Estonia. It is very special tea. When we are done, I will read the tea leaves. It will tell us the future."

"Now, Klaare, I think *that* is superstition. You don't believe the tea leaves can tell you anything, do you?"

"No, Ms. Julie, religion is superstition. Reading the tea is not. You will see. A gypsy woman taught me how to read the tea leaves."

"I don't have a tea ball to put loose leaves in."

"Oh, we will just put the tea in our cups. It will sink to the bottom before we sip it. You will see."

Julie poured hot water into their cups, and Klaare pinched long tea leaves in. They sat letting the tea brew as they talked.

"How are Zane and Trent?"

"When he wants something, Zane is the boy I used to know, after he gets what he wants." Julie shrugged. "What worries me is he has made peace with the kids who were harassing him."

"It's not a good thing?"

"I don't think they are the type to be called friends. Zane doesn't know anyone else here, so I think he just wants to fit in. It is a dangerous situation to be involved in."

"Yes, I see. Who are these kids?"

"I've talked to the school counselor. He says they are bad news. The ringleader is the son of a professor, Dr. Bell."

"He is my political science teacher."

"You know him?"

"Oh, Ms. Julie, he is not someone you would like. The first day of class he said there is no God. He said the American Constitution restricts the government from helping people. He said Americans' rights come from the state, not God. He talks like my teachers back in Estonia."

"You're right, I wouldn't like him. Why not present the Constitution and have a discussion about it, rather than issue politically correct opinions."

"I didn't think much of it, other than I was surprised an American would say such things."

Julie held a poker face and tried not to overreact to hearing this revelation of the professor's atheism. In fact, she had suspected it of the two professors she knew, although they had never said so directly. Klaare rambled on about the similarities she had observed so far between America and Estonia. "Estonia is more modern than America. You have a lot of old buildings here."

Julie listened with a half grin. "Klaare, where did you grow up?"

"In Estonia."

"I mean, what was your neighborhood like?"

"Oh, I lived in a boarding school. My father is a general in the army. He did not want me to live on a military base. My boarding school is very near the university. It was an easy transition for me to start my college life."

"Well, have you traveled much around Estonia?"

"No, it is too dangerous. My father forbade me to travel except to come here."

Sheltered, Julie thought, *this girl has led a sheltered life*. Julie squeezed the Bible she held in her hands beneath the table. She was hesitant to present it. Klaare might take offense if it appeared she was pushing too much. Julie brought her hand from under the table to raise her teacup to her lips. The tea leaves had indeed settled to the bottom.

"I want you to have something while you are here. It's an old one, but they don't change. Please just look it over when you have time." Julie brought the Bible from under the table and placed it in front of Klaare.

"It looks very old. Wait, is it a Bible? I have never seen a Bible before. This is your book of superstitions? Thank you, it will be interesting. I will not be able to take it back home with me; it is forbidden."

"I understand, it is fine, I just thought if we go to church together, you should have a Bible to look at."

"Yes, it will help me understand what is going on. Yes?"

Julie was amazed. All her worrying had been for naught. Klaare was a paradox. She had no idea how to read this girl. After they sipped their tea, Klaare asked to read her tea leaves. She took Julie's cup with a smile, but when she looked into the cup, her face quickly changed. The alarm on Klaare's face startled Julie.

"Klaare, what is it? Tell me."

Klaare put down Julie's cup. She looked at Julie with a blank expression, then smiled.

"It says nothing; sometimes the tea leaves say nothing. It's all superstition."

"Klaare, I don't believe you. Tell me what you saw."

Klaare jumped up, clutching the Bible. "I will go read now. The tea leaves say nothing." Klaare bowed. "Thank you, Ms. Julie, this was very nice."

Julie sat alone with her imagination and doubts as Klaare disappeared down the stairway. The only sure thing she knew, Klaare was distraught.

And Julie would be alone after dark.

TEN

Dan pulled into the bait shop parking lot. Before the dust settled, he stood on the porch scratching Buck behind the ear. There was no sign of Lee, and it was getting late in the day. He broke into a coughing fit; it left him breathless.

"Hey, Buck, where's Lee? Is he somewhere about?" Buck panted through a doggie grin but offered no clue as to Lee's whereabouts.

Dan stepped inside the store. He could see the entire interior from just inside the door. Still no sign of Lee. He grabbed a bottle of water, twisted off the top, and took a long swig. It washed the dust from his throat, yet still he coughed. There weren't even whittling shavings on the floor of the porch. *The mare*, Dan thought, stepping to the end of the porch. He looked toward the shade of the giant oak where Lee's mare spent her days. No sign of her either. Dan had come seeking answers to questions aroused by his search at the library and courthouse. Now he had more questions and even fewer answers.

He sat down on the porch steps. Buck sat beside him, and they waited. Dan felt a tickle in his throat, coughing again. The parking lot dust was settled. *Strange,* he thought. Something had been irritating his throat, but he had never been allergic to dust. It didn't feel like a cold.

###

Ed Knight strolled into the fire department garage where a couple of volunteers were polishing one of the trucks. Ed had been a volunteer for years, but these days he just hung out with the boys at the station. They played cards in the evening, joked about old times, and waited for calls. Ed's back had gone bad, and the doctor told him firefighting was in his past. Still Ed didn't break the habit of loafing with the firemen. He oversaw fundraising and the monthly fish fry.

"Ed, how are you doing there, my brother?" Hank Davidson put his arm around Ed's shoulder, squeezing him. Hank stood a head taller than Ed. He was this year's fire chief.

"Good, Hank. Anybody up for a game?"

"No, I don't think so. We have a lot on our plate right now, but glad you stopped by."

"Why? What's up, Hank?"

"Val asked me to talk to you about some things. We need to go into my office for some privacy." Hank paused to look at Ed, who avoided direct eye contact even though Hank was his longtime friend. "Look, Ed, I want you to know this ain't from me. I'm just the messenger. Come in."

Ed's face went gray at the sound of Val's name. Ed followed Hank into the chief's office and closed the door behind him.

"Sit down, Ed. Make yourself comfortable." Hank dropped into his overstuffed chair flipping open a box of Cuban cigars. "Grab a few, one for now and some for later. Val dropped them off."

"No thanks, just tell me what this is all about."

"You know Val. He takes care of his people. He's going to take care of you." Hank didn't sound like he believed his own words.

"Take care of me? How's that, Hank?"

"He says the time has come for you to turn over your house, Ed."

"Turn over my house? What do you mean?"

Hank played with his cigar, then took a long puff before speaking. His words flowed in smoke. "Look, Ed, we've had some good times, all of us have. We're a brotherhood, right?"

Ed stared at Hank without responding. Hank knocked the ash from his cigar.

"You knew when you bought the house, Val let you outbid him. Remember, Ed, Val told you there would come a time when he would make it his. He told you that because you were one of the brothers. He could wait until the time was right. Well, the time is right, Ed. You're moving out."

"What if I say I don't want to?"

"Ed, you don't want to go there, do you? I mean, look, we all know each other better than our wives know us. We've all had our fun and covered for each other. Val's got the goods on you. And, well, there are photos. You don't want to have him unleash on you. He knows enough to ruin any one or all of us. He said he'll pay you market value."

"Why now?"

"Don't question him, Ed. Just take the money and move on. You know how costly a divorce is. Don't risk it. Your old lady would flip out if she knew some of the things we've done."

"Right, and the whole thing would snowball, Hank. There would be collateral damage."

"It's why I was chosen to be the one to talk to you. Hey, Ed, what's the big deal? It's just a house."

Ed sat staring at the floor. Val owned all of them. The house would be a small price to pay for silence, peace of mind.

"No big deal. Tell Val to start the paperwork. I'll tell Mary tonight. She won't be happy."

"She won't know it, but she'll be happier than she would be the other way. She'll get over it. You're doing the smart thing, Ed. Val wouldn't even give a second thought to destroying all of us."

###

Dan coughed again, a tight dry cough. Buck whimpered and put up a paw as if he knew something serious was in the making. Dan roughed the scruff of Buck's neck. The snort of a distant horse caught Dan's attention. He looked toward the old bridge in time to see Lee pop up over the creek bank. The sun sat low behind him, splashing shades of pink behind gray clouds. Lee's silhouette had a ghostly appearance.

It had all the trappings of an old Spaghetti Western. Lee sat tall in the saddle. The brim of his Stetson cast a shadow over his face. His body moved in sync with the horse. He was a natural. Lee looked as if he had been born on the horse. It was a scene out of the Gary Cooper era.

Dan stood up in anticipation of greeting Lee, but Lee's posture didn't indicate he saw Dan. Lee's head tilted downward as if watching the road in front of the mare. Dan thought Lee must have been aware of him because he continued past the point where he should have turned to go to the big oak out back. Lee didn't raise his head until he reached the porch steps where Dan stood.

"Howdy."

"Hi, Lee, evening ride? I was a little concerned when I got here and didn't see you."

"Concerned? What for? I left Buck here to watch over things whilst I checked my traps before closing up shop. Ain't nothin' bad happened, did it?"

"Well, no, not anything I'm aware of."

"What kin I do for you, Dan? You need some fishin' bait?"

"No, I just wanted to talk to you a little."

"We already talked, I'm thinkin'."

"We did. Since then I have had some new questions turn up."

"There ain't no percentage in me givin' out answers, Dan. 'Unless the questions are 'bout fishin' or maybe trappin'."

"Well, let's call this fishing."

"You know, a fella can get his self kilt askin' the wrong questions. There are dangerous people living in these parts."

Lee's right hand let go of the reins, reaching for a handle protruding from beneath his duster. He was quick, producing a relic single-shot black powder pistol. It all happened too fast for Dan to process, but Lee kicked the mare in the ribs and in a flash was at the edge of the parking lot, leaning off the side of the mare with shooting arm at full extent. There was a puff of smoke, a crack of thunder, then flames, as a burning ball ripped into the dry weeds. The weeds crackled to life, fanned by a breeze. Dan stood speechless, slack-jawed.

Lee dismounted with the ease of a man half his age. He removed his duster to beat out the burning grass. With the flames out, Lee tossed his duster over his shoulder, restored the pistol to his belt, and held the mare's reins as he walked back toward Dan.

"Dang vermin, they carry a virus, turns a horse's brain to mush."

"Vermin?"

"Possum. Ugliest critter alive, they get into the horse's feed and crap. The virus don't hurt the opossum, but it eats a horse's brain. Sad to watch, I tell ya."

"Did you get him? I didn't even see him."

"Git 'im? The lead ball took off his head, and the fire cooked him. I don't miss. I'll bury his charred remains later so's nothing gits sick feedin' on him. Just goes to show you some sayings are wrong. That bird got an early start on the night, but he didn't get the worm. They're night critters, you know."

"Yes, I know. It was amazing. How in the world did you see him in this dimming light?"

"It comes of knowin' good huntin' practices. Never expect to see what you're huntin' for. Just watch for movements where you shouldn't expect 'em. Keep in mind the size of your game. I didn't see the possum. I saw the weeds move. It had to be a small critter, a coon, a skunk, a cat, or possum. My head was processin' what it could be on my way to it. It was fifty-fifty to be somethin' I would kill. I don't never shoot cats or skunk."

Lee spit juice and inspected his pistol.

"Can we talk, Lee? Seriously, I need to talk to you."

"See the road over there?"

"Yes, I drove in on it."

"Yeah, well, did you know this road has tremendous historical significance?"

"No, I didn't know."

"I didn't think you would. Its historical significance is meaningful to us locals, and you ain't local, Dan. You're wantin' quick answers. You want a clear shot at your game. Well, just watch the weeds and be ready. If you live here a while, the answers might come to you, but then again, they may not, not even if you live to be a hundred. Now, I ain't knowed too many successful noisy hunters, and asking questions makes noise."

"Lee, I want answers to things having an impact on my family. I'm not wanting to know anybody else's business."

"Mr. Winslow, let me tell you how small towns work. There are people in these parts who are in their eighties and still hold grudges for grievances on the elementary school playground. Things move slow here, and ain't nobody going to appreciate you tryin' to hurry nothin' up."

"Lee, just answer me this. Do you know a fellow named John McKenzie?"

Lee spit tobacco juice into the parking lot dust. He tied the mare to one of the porch posts and took out a handkerchief to blow his nose.

Dan broke into an uncontrollable dry cough lasting several seconds. He took a swig of water.

"Sounds like you might be getting a bug."

"Maybe allergies."

Lee studied Dan for a moment.

"I know John... matter of fact, we were best friends when we were young'uns. We did a lot of crawfish huntin' together. It was all afore bein' smart mattered. As we got older, I guess ole John saw I wasn't the sharpest knife in the drawer. He's a real smart man, John is. Good guy, just ain't got no time for a fella like me no more. We were the three musketeers, McDonath, McKenzie, and me. Inseparable we were."

"He stopped to see me, wanted to look around the house. He said his father built it."

"Yep, right he did. John's father was a worker. Smart too, probably even smarter than John."

"John said he died in an accident."

"He called it an accident?"

"Well, no, he didn't exactly. What happened to him? Do you know anything about the incident?"

"Didn't think he'd call it no accident. I know it happened so long ago ain't nothin' 'bout it matters now. Can't change it no matter how much you talk 'bout it. I think we're done talkin', Dan."

Lee stepped up onto the porch, opened the door to the store, then stopped, turning once more toward Dan.

"Do yourself a favor, Dan. Sell the house and move away. It ain't healthy if you're goin' to be diggin' 'round these parts. Word is going to spread. We ain't talked a-tall, you hear me? Now, I gotta be gittin' closed up. I'll be riding home in the dark sure enough."

"Trust me, Lee. I won't even mention this meeting to my wife. Just so you know. A lot of things are public record and official reports. I just wanted to get your perspective. I know he was found in the Stony by three boys, one of whom was his son."

"There's the written record, and then there's the truth. Don't put too much stock in what you read. We did find Big Jim, though. I told you the Stony is dangerous. Mr. Winslow, you be careful. The road can be treacherous. Come on, Buck, git inside."

The door shut, leaving Dan standing alone in the parking lot. The sun setting, the light of day fading, Dan got in his car and headed down Lee's historical road. He liked Lee and knew he was no fool.

At the library, he'd read old newspaper articles about Stony Grove. He'd read Big Jim McKenzie's obituary, but it didn't say much. The time spent in the courthouse offered more insight. It became obvious, most of the land in the area was titled to three families. Two of the families owned large tracts of open land. The third name held title to half the homes in town and one large piece of undeveloped property. Dan studied the town's demographics and maps. Stony Grove had been founded on Revolutionary War land grants. The two families with the largest land holdings dated back to the time of the Revolution, the Stratton and Haines families. The map of the town indicated half the original layout of the town had been fulfilled. Streets ended in cul-de-sacs, and the original maps showed dotted lines and parcels sitting empty.

ELEVEN

Julie dumped her coffee into a travel mug, capped it, and grabbed her book bag. Everyone else had already left the house, so she checked the doors and took a quick look around the kitchen to see if all the appliances were off. She'd be late if she didn't hustle. Two minutes later she was heading up the driveway. Where the driveway crested onto the street, her car leveled out, giving Julie a panoramic view of the yard across the street. A young male, probably a college student, stood exposed, urinating on the grass. His hands rested on his hips. Julie threw the shifter into park. Her time as a supervisor in the military kicked into action.

Her words released in fury as she emerged from her car. "What do you think you're doing? You have no right to urinate in public in this neighborhood."

"Ah, come on, lady, don't act like you haven't ever seen one of these before."

"You're disgusting! What if a child was with me? Think of someone besides yourself."

"Ah, lady, get a life," he said, pulling up his zipper.

"Get a life?! Why, you . . ." All Julie could think of was that she had lived twice as long as this punk, been around the world, and served her country with honor. This slimeball was telling her to get a life. She wanted to scream. The student turned to walk back toward his house. It was Val Wentreck's house, a student rental.

"Hold on, bucko, what you just did was commit indecent exposure. There are laws against it. I'm calling the police. What's your name?"

"Kiss off, lady."

"What? What's your name?"

"Are you for real? I'm not telling you my name." He let out a chuckle.

"I'm sure the police can get the names of everyone who lives in that house."

He disappeared into the student rental and slammed the door.

Julie stood in the middle of the street somewhere between furious and flabbergasted. She couldn't move; she felt violated. *That mutant can't be a college student.*

Mary stepped out of her front door and walked toward Julie. "Julie, are you all right? Julie?" Mary looked concerned.

Julie didn't respond. Her ears were ringing, and her head was pounding. Gathering her thoughts, she concluded it had been a deliberate act. *I leave for school every morning, at the same time. What were the chances this guy knows my schedule? After all, he lives directly across the street from me. Yes, this was a planned act, but why?* Her thoughts both scared and infuriated her so much, she didn't even see Mary standing near her.

"Julie, are you all right?"

This time Julie turned toward Mary. "No, Mary. I'm a far distance from being all right."

"Well, I saw the entire thing. These college kids have nerve."

"I'm calling the police."

Mary's look turned disapproving. "Oh, Julie, let it go. They're just stupid kids. They'll graduate and move on. It's the way it is, the way it has always been, doesn't mean anything."

"Mary, what if a child sees something like this. Sorry, but it just isn't right. I'm reporting it."

"Julie, nothing will come of it. The police aren't going to do anything."

"It's indecent exposure, he broke the law. I think it was deliberate. I leave home at the same time every day. He wanted me to see him."

"That's a serious charge to put on a kid. This is a teacher's college. A charge of that nature could ruin the kid's life. He won't get a clearance with those charges. It's a moral offense."

"Mary, do you think someone like him should be a teacher? Would you want him to be your daughter's teacher? If nothing else, it proves he's too stupid to be teaching children."

"No, but I hate to make trouble. You're a pretty woman, Julie. Boys do stupid things to get the attention of pretty women."

Julie looked at Mary, dumbfounded by what she was hearing. It was just plain stupid. They walked into Julie's front yard. Julie decided to skip class. She was in no mood to sit in a room with a bunch of students of the caliber of the jerk she had just confronted and listen to a self-absorbed professor touting his progressive agenda.

"Julie, I also want to tell you, we're moving."

"You're moving? Why?"

"Ed told me last night, he's tired of the house. He says he wants out. He says he's going to spread the word down at the firehouse. He said a couple of the guys have told him if he ever wants to get rid of the house to let them know."

"You're serious, aren't you, Mary? I mean, this isn't something you and Ed are talking about; it's a done deal."

"Ed doesn't talk about doing things. He just tells me he's doing it. I have to go. I shouldn't have come over. Ed would be mad if he knew."

Julie didn't even bother to say good-bye to Mary. She watched Mary trot back to her house, then turned her attention back to the student rental across the street. She called in a report to the police, then sat down on her porch to wait for an officer to appear. The street looked peaceful now, not a soul on it. A light breeze ruffled a shrub near the walk. Other than the wind, all was still. Winter was in the air. As she looked toward Mary's house, a chill gripped her. She wondered what the new people would be like. She hoped Ed would sell the house to a young couple. It would be nice to have some young children on the street, once the college kids were made to act like future leaders, which they are supposedly learning to be.

A police cruiser drifted up the street, stopping in front of the Winslows' home. A lone officer stepped out, adjusting his holster and belt. It was Pete Peterson, she was sure. He looked around the area and then walked over to Julie on the front porch. Julie flashed back to the image of Peterson's knee in Zane's back, his pistol pointed at his head. Yes, it was the same officer who had responded to her call about the intruder, the intruder who had turned out to be her son. Julie flashed back to the day, the embarrassment of the moment and the joy Peterson took in it.

The town had two police officers, and she had already embarrassed herself in front of both. Suddenly, she lost confidence in her decision to place the call to the police. There was no sign of a smirk on the officer's face, but Julie sensed it. She knew he would be amused by her new complaint. Julie wanted to crawl into the house and draw the drapes shut. Mary's words buzzed in her head: *Nothing will come of it*. Why couldn't it have been Officer Monroe? Her chances would have been better with Monroe.

"Good morning, Mrs. Winslow. The dispatcher reported trouble on the street. What can I do for you?" Julie looked at his name tag. Yep, Pete Peterson. The officer's grin confirmed Julie's intuition.

She forced herself to stand her ground and respond. "The house across the street is a student rental. This morning one of the tenants exposed himself out on the front lawn. I would like him charged with indecent exposure."

"That's a serious accusation, Mrs. Winslow. Are sure you want to pursue it?"

"Yes, I want to pursue it!" Julie felt her control crumbling.

"Well, I didn't witness it, so I may need evidence. Did you take any pictures?" Officer Peterson smiled.

"No!" *Pictures—sure, I'm going to take pictures of...* Julie took a deep breath. She had made the call; now she needed to keep her head about her.

"Well, ma'am, don't be offended." Peterson turned Julie's anxiety on her. "Lots of people have security cameras these days. I'm suggesting you might have caught him on yours or maybe your neighbor has one."

"We don't have any security cameras."

"Well, did you get a good look at the perpetrator? Do you think you could recognize him if you saw him again?" The officer's smirk sickened Julie. He was enjoying himself at her expense once again, and it added to her disgust of him. She refrained from responding.

"Well then, were there any other witnesses?"

"Yes, my neighbor Mary saw the whole thing. She lives in the house across the driveway."

"Mrs. Winslow, why don't you go inside? I'll go talk to Mary and to the student across the street. Do you know the student's name?"

"No."

"After I talk to everyone, I'll come back to talk to you."

"Thank you." Julie disappeared into the house and stood at the window to watch as the officer knocked on the door of the student rental.

The door to the student rental opened, and Officer Peterson went inside. Julie moved to her kitchen to pour a cup of coffee. She heated it in the microwave, then stood at the living room window to watch for Officer Peterson to depart the house. She went to sip her coffee, but it was gone, and Peterson was still inside the house across the street. She set her empty cup on the windowsill. She swayed back and forth, her arms folded across her chest. A glance at her wristwatch marked the time. It had been twenty minutes since the officer went inside.

Then she saw Peterson emerge. He was laughing. He was *laughing*. Julie saw the offender step into the doorway. They shook hands, and the officer motioned with his hand as if blowing off a question from the offender. *Great*, Julie thought, *they look like buddies talking about football or something.* The officer and the offender continued to talk and laugh. Peterson's breath was visible in the crisp air. Julie walked out onto her porch and slammed herself down onto the porch swing. She was furious. She wanted to give Dan a call but controlled herself. She sat down on the porch swing to wait. Peterson walked away as the offender stepped back into the house.

Julie expected Peterson would head toward Mary's house, but instead he approached Julie. He strolled, looking up and down the street. There was no one else on the street, no vehicles or pedestrians. He began an exaggerated swagger, presumably meant to agitate her. She calmed herself with deep breaths and closed her eyes until she could hear the first porch step creak under his foot.

"Mrs. Winslow, I think I have resolved this matter."

"You do? How did you resolve it?"

"It seems there was just a misunderstanding. He claims he didn't intend to expose himself. He said he had an emergency call and leaned into the bushes. It seems your car startled him, and he turned to see what the noise was. Then he said you became hysterical. He tried to cover himself. Under the circumstance, I gave him a verbal warning. I think the matter is closed."

"It is an outright lie, and you know it."

"Excuse me, ma'am? I'm an officer of the law. A little respect, please."

"Are you going to talk to Mary? She will vouch for me. It didn't happen the way he said. Talk to her."

"No, it won't be necessary. I'll talk to Ed down at the fire hall tonight. Well, I have to write this up. You take care, Mrs. Winslow. Call us if you have any more trouble, but make sure the trouble is real. We don't tolerate nuisance calls. You know boys will be boys."

"Call you? Why would I call you?"

"It's your choice. If you do call, though, just make sure you have a legitimate complaint. Mrs. Winslow, while I'm here, I might as well warn you. That oldest boy of yours is under my scrutiny. I think he's leading some of the local boys astray. If you know what's best, you better crack down on him before it becomes my business... just saying."

Julie watched as Officer Pete Peterson got in his car and drove away. *What kind of town are we in? Why would someone do what this student did? Was it just a random act, or did he perpetrate it for a reason, and what if he becomes more aggressive?* She couldn't look at the house any longer; she didn't know who might be looking back and laughing. She wanted to talk with Dan. She stepped into the house, weary of the endless struggle in this town. She trudged upstairs to the bedroom, shut the door, and locked it. She fell on the bed and turned to prayer.

Julie rolled over and stared at the rotating paddle fan above the bed. Even in winter it helped to circulate warmth down from the high ceilings, as it was doing now. The fan continued to push air down on her. Her eyes closed, and she felt a gentle breeze on her face. *Thank you, Lord, for all my blessings. Please protect us from the evil I believe surrounds us.* She soon breathed more easily, drifting from prayer into sleep.

TWELVE

Something woke Julie, a noise, one which had become all too common. Dan's signature cough could be heard as he slipped out of his car in the driveway. Dan coughed so often now, he seemed to have almost become unaware of it. It worried her. She had never heard anyone cough quite like Dan did. She had been nagging him to see a doctor, but he always said he would when things slowed down. Julie sat on the edge of the bed listening as the cough grew closer. Dan was in the kitchen. Julie looked at the clock; she had slept most of the day. She gathered herself and headed downstairs to the kitchen.

"Were you napping? Sorry if I woke you."

"It's your cough, I can hear it as you drive up the street." She detected irritation in her own exaggeration. "But I'm so glad you're home."

"Glad to be home. Yeah, I just can't seem to shake this cough."

"I don't think you even realize it sometimes."

"I probably don't realize I'm doing it as much as I do."

"Dan, I can locate you in a crowd by following your cough. You need to see a doctor."

"I did stop at the doctor after work, as a matter of fact."

"What did he say?"

"Well, he says it could be some sort of allergy. He sent me over to the lab for an x-ray and some blood work. The x-ray didn't show anything, and the other results will take a couple of days."

"I'm glad you went. I've been telling you for weeks." Julie put her arms around him.

"I know, but other than the cough I've been feeling fine. It's only in the last couple days I've been feeling a little off." Dan held a glass under the faucet letting cold water overflow from it. He had been drinking a lot of water in the hopes of dislodging the dusty feeling in his throat. It never worked. Something felt like a feather in his throat, tickling his cough reflex nerve. He had tried cold water, ice water, hot water, coffee, tea, and beer, but nothing removed the tickle. Now, though, the cough seemed like the least of his worries. He felt rundown, more than he had ever felt before. His vision seemed to be changing, and the ache in his neck had spread into his head.

Julie rubbed his shoulders and back. *It must be getting worse if he went to see the doctor.*

He leaned over, placing his arms on the kitchen counter to stretch out his back muscles. Julie's hands worked magic, but he still felt bad. His head felt like it might explode. He turned to face Julie, holding her hands. He sensed her concerns, but there was more than just her worries about his cough. There was something else he sensed.

"Julie, how are you feeling?"

"I'm a little tired, too, Dan. I blew off classes today and slept most of the day. I think I'm depressed."

"Maybe you're getting what I've got."

"I don't think so, I don't have a cough." She pulled away from him, studying Dan's gaunt face, the dark circles under his eyes. She had never seen him look this way. His skin looked grayish. She wasn't a doctor, but she knew Dan. Whatever was going on with him, it wasn't an allergy. She decided he was not in a condition to be told of the incident with the college student and police. The way Dan looked now, Julie figured the punk across the street would have the upper hand. She refrained from confiding in him. There would be a better time.

"What's wrong, Julie?"

"It's just some neighborhood issues. Let's not bother with it now. You look terrible. I think you should lie down."

"No argument from me." He kissed her cheek as he walked past her on his way to bed.

No argument? Dan never took her advice without a counter remark. This worried her even more. She listened to him cough as he worked his way upstairs. She leaned against the kitchen wall, her emotions shredded by the day's events. There was a click, the sound of the outside basement door opening. Klaare. It was just what Julie needed to distract her thoughts.

"Klaare, is that you?"

"Yes, Ms. Julie. Sorry if I have made too much noise."

"Oh no, I am happy to hear you. Do you have any time to talk?"

Julie heard Klaare unlatch the dead bolt on the kitchen door leading to the basement.

"Yes, would you like to come down the stairs? I will make the tea this time."

"Sure, sounds wonderful." She followed Klaare down the basement steps to the apartment. "How were your classes today?"

"It was a long day. It is like I am still in Estonia. The professors seem to know a lot of theories, but I have my doubts about their practical experience. How were your classes?"

"I blew the day off. I got off to a bad start and went back to bed. Now I will be awake all night."

"Oh, too bad." Klaare filled her teakettle with fresh water and placed it on the stove.

Klaare's back was to Julie. Julie wanted to be cautious about what she said. She didn't want to confide in Klaare about the event with the student across the street before she told Dan, but she felt a need to unload. "You wouldn't happen to know any of the students living across the street, would you?"

"I know of them. They are not very mature, I think. Why?"

"At least one of them is worse than immature." She cast off her caution. Dan would understand her need to tell someone.

As Klaare turned back to Julie, she exclaimed, "Why, Julie, you look terrible. What happened? Something bad has happened?" Klaare touched Julie's arm.

"Well, when I went to leave this morning, one of them was urinating in their front yard. We had a confrontation, and I called the police."

"They are not nice guys. Two of them are in my international business class. They are always making smart remarks and disturbing the class. I see them with the other two around campus. Which one was it?"

"It was the tall blond one."

"He thinks he is so special. What did the police say?"

"They pretty much laughed it off. The way they handled it upset me." Julie dropped into a kitchen chair.

"Well, the one you're describing is Brian. He's the worst. It seems like he's the one who has the lease. I've heard him asking the others to give him their rent money. Maybe if you talked to the landlord you could get some action."

"I don't know . . ."

"What could it hurt?"

"Well, I have pretty much made up my mind to drop it. Do you know his last name?"

"Sure. Miller. His name is Brian Miller."

"Maybe I'll think about it." Julie could hear Dan's cough coming down through the furnace ducts.

"Your husband has a bad cough."

"Yes he does. He went to the doctor today, but it might be a couple of days to get test results."

The teakettle whistled and Klaare turned off the burner. Julie sat, thinking about how to deal with the student across the street. *I should call his mother, it might humiliate him, and as a mother of young men, I sure would want to know if one of my sons did something so inconsiderate.* Klaare poured hot water into a teapot and placed it on the table with cups. She went to her cupboard and retrieved the special tea whose leaves she had offered to read.

"Don't worry about what happened the last time. I would like to know more about how you learned to read them, though." Julie wanted to change the subject.

"I told you—an old gypsy woman taught me."

"But how did you come to know this old gypsy woman?"

"Oh, she ran a teahouse near our school. We would sneak over whenever we could. It was our great adventure during high school, harmless but forbidden. Breaking the rules made it more fun. She just wanted our company, so she gave us free tea. She told us wild stories about gypsy life. She had traveled all over Europe during the war and hid from soldiers."

"It sounds thrilling."

"It was, and I think her stories are what made me want to come to America. I want to be like a gypsy and wander the world."

"I got bitten by the same bug when I was a teenager."

"Excuse me, Ms. Julie, what bug?"

"It's just an expression. I mean, when I was young, I wanted to travel the world. It is why I joined the military."

"Oh, you must be brave."

"No, Klaare, I'm not brave... no more than you. Maybe I'm even less brave because I had the United States military backing me up, while you are going it alone." Julie stirred her tea.

"Ms. Julie, when I read your tea leaves, I saw evil. It wasn't clear what the evil was, but now I think maybe it was what happened today. If I can do anything to help, please let me know."

"You just saw evil in the leaves, nothing specific?"

Klaare held her cup near her face allowing the steam to mingle with her breathing. "Ms. Julie, the tea showed a widow. It upset me, though then I realized the widow may not be you. There is a widow, though. Someone lost a husband, and somehow it is connected either to you or maybe this house. It is something very close by."

"Oh, Klaare... I am so afraid. Dan's cough is getting worse. You can hear him now through the furnace vents. I hope . . ."

"No, no, I am sure the widow is not you. I'm sorry, I was not thinking."

"Talking things out helps. I have wondered about the tea leaves. I feel a lot better already. I've said some prayers. I think the Lord will help. There was a widow living in this house, years ago. It may be the widow the tea leaves speak of, but, Klaare, it is not something you should be involved with. It is something from the dark side. We need to let our fate be in the hands of God. We are not to try to see the future."

"It might be. You believe praying will help? I do not believe in it."

"You realize, by not believing, it doesn't work." Julie paused. "Oh, Klaare, why would anyone choose not to believe? Don't you believe in love? Did they teach you in Estonia there is no such thing as love?"

"Love—what does it have to do with superstition?"

"It has everything to do with God. God is Love—true and absolute love. Perfect love, a love we can only experience in his light. To survive, humans have a selfish nature. This prevents perfect love. Love and selfishness oppose each other."

"I've never heard it said in such a way."

"Want to have some fun? We can search the past instead of the future. I found some old letters when we were cleaning out the house. I haven't read any of them yet. We could read through them now." Julie gave Klaare a wide-eyed look as she stood up to retrieve the letters.

"Yes, it could be fun. I hope they are happy letters."

Julie wasn't gone long. The letters rested on the fireplace mantel in the living room. There were four of them, all addressed to Louise Haines, all in the same script. Julie studied the postmark dates so they could be read in chronological order—one for each year from 1917 through 1921. The envelopes were yellowed and brittle, but not to the point of crumbling. The letters may not have been read since they were first received, all those years ago.

The first letter was brief. Julie read it aloud.

My sweetest Louise,

I've missed you so much. Only have a few minutes to write. Hope this training is over soon and we can get on with ending the war. I'm sorry you fell in love with this guy from the wrong side of the tracks. I'll make you and your family proud, though. Keep me in your prayers, as I keep you in my every thought and prayer, every chance I get.

Yours always,
Jim

Klaare let one tear loose to roll over her cheek. Julie managed to maintain her composure. The letter was heartfelt, and she felt privileged reading it. It held the outpouring of a man's heart, a man born in another century, and yet the feeling was so contemporary. She pursed her lips as she placed the letter back in its envelope.

"Klaare, I think these letters belong to John McKenzie. I don't feel like reading anymore."

"I agree."

"Well, anyway... let's offer them to Mr. McKenzie, before we read any more."

"Yes."

"Do you see what I mean about love? To say you don't believe in God, well, you might as well just say you don't believe in love and what a sad world it is where love is lost. All good things come from love. When I pray, I feel God's love and grace. It calms me and gives me strength." Julie closed her eyes and sipped her tea. "The book I gave you is a love story. The Bible is the story of man's failings and God's love of man."

"I plan to read it. I have been too busy." Klaare sipped her tea.

"It is not an easy book to read and understand. You can read it several times and come away with different thoughts each time.

God doesn't want us to work at loving him. He just wants us to live by loving him. Just get in touch with all the things love does, and you will have found God. It changes the way you look at life, Klaare."

"No one has ever offered me such insight. It makes sense, I think. Funny how words can touch you even when they were spoken so long ago, like this letter. The Bible is the same?"

"Yes, it is the one thing I believe makes sense. When you are in touch with it, your spirit feels free. Free to look to God's love in every situation. Our spirit needs to be fed just as our body does. As we let go of the burdens of this world, our spiritual body feels freed. Truth is always relevant. It doesn't go out of style, and time does not change it." Julie turned toward the furnace vent, listening to Dan cough.

"I have been dismayed by what I've seen on television of the rituals of church. They seem so contrived—of men—and it seems preachers use God's words to gain control of people."

"Love, Klaare—use love as the litmus test. If something doesn't fit the definition of love, then it isn't from God. Run away as fast as you can because you are right, evil men use the Lord. I think I have found a pastor who is a teacher, he seems to be, and this is what a true minister should be." The church was the one Harry McDonath attended. "Klaare, will you come with me? Just come one time. Let's see if I know what I am talking about. Let's just call it an adventure. You know, the Bible warns us not to dabble in the dark side, such as Ouija boards, séances, or any means of talking with the dead. Tea leaves falls into this category. I think we need to talk with God and not look elsewhere for answers."

"Will you be going this Sunday?"

"Yes, and I think if you come along, you will be pleasantly surprised."

"There is something else I want to tell you." Klaare paused. "Some students I know say they are going to be moving into the house across your driveway."

"They told you this?"

“Yes, they said someone is buying it and turning it into a student rental.”

“I don’t think it’s possible. It’s not zoned for multiple occupancy.”

“I don’t know what is possible. All I know is, they were all excited about being my neighbor.”

Julie refrained from responding and sipped her tea. Likewise, Klaare remained silent and drank her tea.

Julie collected the letters in a neat pile, gave Klaare a hug, and returned upstairs. The possibility of students running wild in the Knights’ house and yard made her cringe. A panic overwhelmed her, but then she looked down at the letters in her hand. All things come to an end. *This too shall pass. I’ll just look to the Lord.*

THIRTEEN

Julie lay in bed, her head between two pillows secured by her locked arms. The bolsters had offered soundproofing from Dan's cough, but guilt echoed in her heart. Not seeing him off to work wasn't her style, but she couldn't face him. She knew she couldn't avoid nagging him to find a new doctor. It had been days since his tests. The reports offered no clue about his ailment, yet she could see his deterioration. The town doctor wrote it off as allergies or nerves from the pressures of the new job. He had given Dan a prescription for a cough suppressant, but it offered no relief. Dan and the boys had left half an hour ago. Today was a training day, which meant Dan started later and had time to drop the boys off at school. Julie didn't have class. She saw little reason to get up although she was wide awake. The scent on the pillows was Dan's, and even with his failing health the scent made her feel secure.

The ringing of the phone startled her. She snapped out of bed and snatched the phone from the nightstand. Her heart raced. Might it be the doctor or Dan or the school calling about the boys? She hesitated so as to calm herself before speaking.

"Hello?"

"Hello, may I speak to Mrs. Winslow, please?" It was a pleasant feminine voice.

"This is Mrs. Winslow."

"Oh... well, Mrs. Winslow, you don't know me. This is awkward for me, but I feel I must talk to you about my son. My name is Linda Miller. I'm the mother of Brian, Brian Miller . . ."

There was silence for a moment as Mrs. Miller listened for a reaction. "Mrs. Winslow... are you there?"

"Yes, yes, I'm here."

"Well, Mrs. Winslow, I received a call from a police officer the other day. He told me he was speaking off the record, but he wanted to make me aware of an incident involving Brian. If what he reported to me is true, I want you to know I am mortified, and my son owes you a sincere apology. Please, Mrs. Winslow, feel free to speak your mind. I can't imagine what you must be thinking of our family."

"You say a police officer called you... off the record? What was his name? Was it Peterson by chance?"

"No... no, his name was Monroe. I believe he said Jack Monroe."

Julie thought it strange that Mrs. Miller had been contacted by Jack Monroe. He hadn't been involved in the response to her complaint.

"You said Officer Monroe spoke to you off the record?"

"Yes, he said it wasn't an official call. He told me the situation had been glossed over and my son wouldn't have anything on his record, but he didn't think it was fair to the community to have this type of behavior condoned. I think he went out on a limb. You're a mother... I'm sure you would feel defensive if you received such a report, wouldn't you?"

"Well, yes, I guess I would." Julie thought of Zane's actions of late; she might be making the same kind of call in the near future. She felt compassion for Mrs. Miller.

"I feel badly now, though at first I didn't take kindly to hearing what Officer Monroe had to say. I became angry and defensive. I gave him an earful. Then, after he hung up, I settled down a little and reflected on it a bit. When Brian's father got home, we had a heart-to-heart, and he went through the roof. He was glad Officer Monroe let us know what our kid had done. In fact, my husband returned Officer Monroe's call to apologize for my son's bad behavior."

"Honestly, Mrs. Miller, I feel so bad about all this. It is a sad situation for everyone involved. I don't intend to press the issue."

"It *is* sad, and I just want you to know it will never happen again. My husband is a proud man, proud of our family name. He waited a day to calm down before he spoke to Brian. I'm so glad because he wanted to kill him."

"I don't know what gets into these kids—it scared me because I was afraid there may be more going on than just this incident. Without knowing the family or his history, I was afraid he might be a creep of some kind. Can you understand?"

"I do... yes, looking at it from your perspective, I can understand the concern. It's his landlord who should frighten you."

"His landlord, what do mean?"

"My son said his landlord told him they could have a free month's rent if he did things to gross you out. Do you have some kind of issue with his landlord?"

Julie held the phone away from her ear. Speechless, she tried to grasp what she'd just heard. Landlord... she wasn't even sure who the landlord was. Julie flashed through her memories of recent days trying to envision anything strange or any incident that would have sent anyone on a vengeful course. What would instigate someone to do such a thing? In the distance, someone called her name.

"Mrs. Winslow, Mrs. Winslow, are you there?"

"Yes... I'm here. Who is the landlord? I don't even know who owns the house."

"His name is Val Wentreck."

"I don't know him. Why would he target us? Did Officer Monroe give you any insight into this Val Wentreck?"

"Sorry, he never mentioned anything along those lines. He reported the facts of the incident. It was almost like he was reading it off a police report. He did stress to me it could cost him his job, but he was willing to risk it. This thought was what made me a believer, since the man had nothing to gain from calling to notify me. It was an ugly truth, one I didn't want to believe. Well,

Mrs. Winslow, again I'm sorry about what happened. I hope you figure out why their landlord would put them up to such a thing."

"Thank you, Mrs. Miller, and God bless you." The phone went silent before Julie completed her blessing.

Julie dropped back onto the bed. *No resolution*, she thought. Now there were bigger unknowns, more questions. The situation had grown from creepy to creepier. She couldn't handle it alone anymore. As sick as Dan was, she needed him. She needed him to know. She needed all her senses on alert. She wanted to shower but not get undressed. She could imagine the sound of the shower masking sounds from other parts of the house. Quickly she disrobed and donned her street clothes. She would only shower when someone was home.

It turned into a day of neurotic cleaning and organizing punctuated by quick glimpses out the windows, an instantaneous survey of the street or backyard. Her movements were frantic. Half the time she wanted to run but to where? The rest of the time, she thought she should nail the doors shut. Then she thought about Officer Monroe; he offered a little hope. There had to be some other decent people in town. They couldn't all be as creepy as Officer Peterson, Mary, the Miller kid, and this Val Wentreck.

When she heard stones crunching in the driveway, she threw down her dust rag and ran to the kitchen window. Before she even looked out, she heard the cough. The sound was almost comforting to her now; she decided she loved the sound, for it meant Dan was close by. As she peered out the window, she saw Dan wrestling with a couple of bags of groceries. She had just shopped. They didn't need groceries. She ran to the door to open it for Dan.

"Julie... I missed you this morning. Aren't you feeling well?"

"Oh, Dan, I'm so glad you're home." Julie grabbed the bags of groceries, setting them on the counter. She threw her arms around him, burying her head into his chest.

"Wow, this is my kind of greeting."

"We have a lot to talk about."

"Well, can I tell you about my day, or do you want to tell me about your day first?"

Julie paused. She needed time to become unfrazzled. Letting Dan talk would give her the opportunity. She hoped he had uplifting news, though.

"You go first, Dan. What's in these bags? I just shopped."

"I know, I know, but I work with a guy. I guess you would call him a health nut. I've been double-checking some of the things he's been telling me, and I think he might be onto something. Anyway, I figure, what do I have to lose? He claims a person can fight any disease if the immune system is built up by eating the right stuff. I bought all these things to fight whatever this is I have."

"Oh, Dan, I think you just need to find another doctor." Julie regretted saying it before she uttered the word *doctor*. This would be her last nag. With her thumb and forefinger, she squeezed her lips tight and gave Dan her sorry look. "I'm sorry, go ahead."

Dan started pulling out one item after another. He held them up with a gleam in his eye and explanations on his lips.

"Mushrooms, good for the immune system, and did you ever hear of sulfa drugs? Mushrooms are loaded with chemicals whose properties build the immune system. Sulfonamide is the basis of several groups of drugs. I'm going to be eating a lot of mushrooms. I'm hoping you'll support me on this, Julie. I'm serious about using nutrition to heal myself."

"What else, Dan?"

"Vinegar." Dan held up a bottle. "Apple cider vinegar with the mother to be specific, a couple of tablespoons a day—and garlic—lots of garlic. I want garlic in everything I eat. You're going to want to eat it, too, so you won't smell it on me."

"Wonderful, Dan, but what about other people? You will still offend other people."

"Julie, I'm talking about beating whatever is attacking me. I'm not going to worry about offending anyone."

Julie brightened. *Offend people*, she thought, *sounds like just what I want to do, Dan. Let's go for it.*

"I've got a whole bag of onions. I'm going to eat an onion a day. Blueberries, lots of blueberries—I'm going to eat them, juice them, and mix them into yogurt. I want to be committed to this. This isn't something you can do halfway or occasionally. I want this to become our lifestyle. Julie, I'm a sick man. I know it. I feel it, and I am responsible for it. I've quit believing in the pill pushers. Oregano kills fungus infections, so I bought oregano oil supplements."

"I'm with you. Do you think eating like this I can drop a couple of pounds?"

"Eating this stuff may not help you lose a pound, but not eating what we're used to eating probably will. I'm done eating flour and sugar. We need to get away from those things, they're poison. We need to cut way back on meat too. As a matter of fact, I may try to go off meat altogether."

"It's a little radical... I don't know."

"Start reading, Julie, go online. I'm telling you, you'll start to understand. The immune system starts in your gut. You must keep your gut healthy if you want to be healthy. Meat loads down the gut, not to mention all the crap they feed the animals to get them fat fast."

"How long do you think this is going to take?"

"How long? A lifetime. I hope this is our future. I'm hoping you will help me by adopting this as our lifestyle from now on."

"Okay, but how long to get you well?"

"I can't say, but I know this is going to work. I'm going to beat this and be stronger for it."

"Dan, I think I'm going to double down on prayers."

Dan gave Julie a long, loving look, then started to stash away his home remedies. Julie thought about what she wanted to say but kept it to herself for the time being. She would pray for strength to bear their troubles. She wished there was something they could eat or drink to make their issues in this town all better. When Dan put the last item away, he turned to Julie with a hopeful smile, wanting her blessing.

"And so, how was your day?" Dan's smile faded. Julie looked sicker than he felt.

"Dan, Klaare tells me the Knights are selling to one of the student rental landlords."

"What?! It'll ruin our house value. We can't share a driveway with a bunch of students."

Dan headed for the door. He couldn't believe the Knights would do such a thing, after all the work he had done to fix up the house. His heart raced. He wanted to hear it from Ed, not a rumor from Klaare.

"Dan, what are you going to do?"

"Talk to Ed. It's all I ask, just talk to Ed."

Dan stood at the Knights' front door. Ed answered the door without an offer for Dan to come in or even a hello. Dan saved the niceties himself. "Did you sell your house to a student slumlord?"

"I'm under no obligation to tell you one way or the other."

"I'll pay you five thousand over the asking price."

"That's not going to happen. The deal is done. You could think about selling. Things are changing, the town is changing."

Dan walked away from the Knights' front door without saying another word. He felt sick, physically and emotionally sick. He had a feeling of loss and defeat.

When Dan came through the front door, Julie took his hand and led him to the living room couch. It was time to lay it all on the line for Dan. He didn't think things could be any worse, but Julie knew things were much worse. The boys were due home in half an hour. She told Dan every detail of the events of the last week. Perfect timing, as the boys burst through the front door before Dan could vent his built-up rage.

Dan wanted to confront the punk across the street, punch Officer Peterson, and get in Val's face. All this would have to wait. Sick or not, Dan made up his mind the town and the disease were not going to beat him. Once his mind was made up, there was no turning back. Zane excused himself and headed for his room. Dan knew better than to address Zane's issues at this moment. Zane would get the full brunt of his anger, and it wouldn't be fair.

Trent plopped down beside Dan, to share his thoughts on his latest favorite author. "Dad, I've been reading the James Herriot series. Do you know those books?"

Dan smiled. To focus on *All Things Bright and Beautiful, All Creatures Great and Small*,

is exactly what the doctor ordered, or should have.

FOURTEEN

Days passed, and the winter weather ran mild, yet it felt brutal to Dan. Much to Julie's delight, he concentrated on his new diet—his battle plan, as he called it. They spoke in private about their speculations on why this Val Wentreck might be targeting them. No other incidents had occurred, but the entire idea seemed surreal. Dan seemed more interested in regaining his health than focusing on Val, and he saw stress as a detriment. He remained watchful but refrained from obsessing. Julie went to her classes, conducted research into their family histories, and life began to take on routine. Even Zane seemed a little better.

Dan was on the evening shift. Julie read a homework assignment as the boys sat at the dining room table working on math when the phone rang. Julie reached for the phone, looked at the number, but she didn't recognize it. She hesitated. No one she knew would call this late in the evening.

"Hello?"

"Hello, is this Mrs. Winslow?" It was a man's voice, an older man.

"Why yes, it is."

"Hi, Mrs. Winslow, this is Bob Flynn, your husband's supervisor. Dan is fine, but he had a little trouble this evening at work. His vision went a little fuzzy on him. We've transported him to the emergency room at the Memorial Hospital to get it checked out. It seems he was seeing flashes of color, and lights had halos around them. He had a little trouble focusing."

"Dan's at the hospital now?" When the boys heard Julie speak, they ran to her side.

"Yes, I'm sure everything will be all right, but I don't know if he should be driving. Is it possible for you to pick him up?"

"I'll find a way, yes. I'll head in right now. We'll make arrangements to get his car later."

"Great, I'll relay the message to the man who drove him to the hospital. Be careful driving. You know how slowly they move in emergency rooms. They just left here a few minutes ago."

"Thank you." Julie slipped her phone into her purse.

"Boys, I have to go get your father."

"What's going on?"

"Listen, I don't know much except he was seeing lights and halos, but your dad's a tough guy. He'll be all right. Now, you two take care of yourselves and be good. I don't know when I'll be home. Finish your homework and pack a lunch. Remember, Klaare is downstairs."

Julie grabbed her purse and headed out to her car. It was windy, and the smell of rain was in the air. The streetlight and trees caused strange shadows to dance on the garage doors. She was parked in the driveway even though Dan had cleaned out the garage months earlier. The garage doors needed to be replaced so it was easier to just park outside.

She jumped as a dark wraith passed near her head. It happened again. Her heart raced. She looked toward the streetlight at the end of the driveway. Bats. Three bats circled the light in jerky patterns.

When she arrived at the emergency room, she was directed to Dan's room. The employee who had brought him had just left. Dan stared off into the distance with a concerned look. It scared Julie because he didn't acknowledge her at first, but she had entered from a direction that was not in his line of sight. In a matter of seconds, he turned toward her and smiled.

"Dan... what's up? How's your vision?"

"It's fine, good as new. It lasted about a half hour or forty-five minutes. No big deal."

"No big deal? What did the doctor say?"

"They took some pictures of my head. The doctor hasn't come in yet. You'll hear what he has to say at the same time I do. I'm glad you're here." Dan held out his hand for Julie to take.

"Your boss said you were seeing color flashes and halos around the lights."

"Yeah, it must be like what people see on acid trips. It was freaky. Scared me."

"I'll bet."

Julie was just about to sit down when the doctor pulled back the curtain divider and stepped into the room. He was older; a large man with massive hands, he looked more suited for manual labor. His eyes gleamed with intelligence.

"I'm Doctor Raymond Betters. I like to be called Ray. You're Dan, and this lovely lady is... ?"

"Yes, I'm Dan, and this is my wife, Julie."

"Pleased to meet you both. I looked at your pictures, Dan. I hope you don't mind, but I must tell you, I've never seen a skull constructed like yours." A grin spread over Ray's face. "It's thick, Dan—very thick. You are a true bonehead."

Julie couldn't believe what she had just heard and couldn't contain her laugh.

"Does it have something to do with my eyesight going fuzzy?"

"Nothing at all, it's just a side observation. Evolution has taken care of it in most modern skulls by developing enlarged sinus cavities. You have almost no sinuses. Your head must weigh a ton." The doctor shook his head. "I'm sorry, I'm into studying bone structure. My amusement is at your expense, but I had to share it with you."

Dan grinned. He liked the doctor's humor, and he glanced at Julie who struggled to contain herself.

"I've been telling him for years, Doctor. Thanks for your confirmation." Dan had to admit he liked this guy's candor and bedside manner. It demonstrated Ray had the ability to speak the truth, and yet his words lightened the mood... until Dan coughed.

“Strange cough, have you had it long?” Ray’s face showed concern.

“Yeah, for a while. I’ve been seeing my family doctor about it. He thinks it is allergies.”

“A chronic cough might be serious.”

“Sure. He just prescribed cough medicine. I had tests run, but the results didn’t show anything. What about my eyes, though?”

“Let’s have a look.” The doctor shined a light into Dan’s eyes and had him move them left to right, then up and down. He held two index fingers in Dan’s periphery and asked him to tell him when they disappeared. Dan watched them until they were almost even with his ears, then told Ray he could no longer see them. Next, Dan followed Ray’s finger as he brought it to the tip of Dan’s nose, and then Ray sighed.

“Do you get headaches? I mean severe headaches. Sit up and let me listen to your chest and back.”

“When I was a kid I did. My parents took me to a doctor about them once. As I’ve gotten older, they have become less frequent,” Dan answered as he positioned himself for the stethoscope.

“Did they call them migraines? Did they make you sick and last a couple of days?” Ray placed the cold stethoscope through the side slit of the hospital gown onto Dan’s back, causing a shudder. “Breathe normally.”

“Yes, they did. They were migraines, why?” Dan punctuated with another cough, then cleared his throat.

“Take a deep breath and hold it... Okay, exhale.”

“How’s it sound?”

Ray didn’t respond to Dan’s question but instead continued to listen to Dan’s breathing and his heart.

“Well, with your sinuses the way they are, I would say you are prone to sinus headaches, but if you’ve had migraines, I suspect there’s a possibility what you had tonight was an optic migraine. It’s like a headache, except it’s in your optic nerve. Does that make any sense to you?”

“I guess so.”

Ray moved the stethoscope around to Dan's chest and listened. "Take a couple of deep breaths and hold them, then exhale."

Dan broke into a cough with each deep breath.

"Look, Dan, I want you to see a specialist about your eyes, a neurologist. This may never occur again, and then again it might start happening on a recurring basis. I think it's best to get it checked out. As far as the pictures go, I saw nothing to indicate a growth of any kind, nothing to impact your vision. I don't see your vision situation as anything threatening. It may be more on the order of an annoyance. I think you need to follow up with the specialist about the cough. Your lungs sound clear, but I think you should be a little concerned about it." The doctor handed Dan a note with a recommended neurologist's name on it. Ray shook Dan's hand and offered his best wishes to both Dan and Julie.

The ride home was quiet for the most part. Dan stared out the window at passing streetlights, watching for halos and flashes of color, but they didn't appear. He called work to let them know he wouldn't be missing any days, but they told him to stay off until he had a release from the neurologist. Julie smiled when she heard this; it meant the old bonehead would have to follow up. She wouldn't have to nag him. Dan coughed and cleared his throat every few seconds. Julie refrained from commenting, which contributed to the silence. In a way, it was a silent nag Dan must have sensed.

"Am I annoying you, Julie? I mean with this constant cough."

"Yes, Dan, you are. It's not so much the cough. It's just one more thing in our recent life making no sense, and it can't be resolved easily. I don't think your mushrooms are helping."

Dan rolled his head to the side without responding.

"You're a bonehead, Dan."

"Not funny."

"Is too—and now it has been certified." They both broke into a laugh until Dan's laugh turned into a cough.

"I hate to miss work. I haven't been there long enough. If I take off too much, they might decide they don't need me."

“Let’s think happy thoughts. Christmas break starts in a few days.”

“Oh, I guess I better get the decorations out.”

The next morning Dan took advantage of not going to work by sleeping late. Julie got up with the boys and made breakfast. She wanted to let Dan sleep in, so she headed to the university library to research.

The tapping noise started around nine. Just a light tap at first, it caused Dan to stir, but with each pause, the sound got louder until he opened his eyes. He had to gather his thoughts. He couldn’t make sense of the sound. He sat up and pulled the curtains back on the bedroom window. In the driveway, he saw steel fence posts.

Dan got out of bed to get a better view. A man was driving the last post into the ground in the parking area ten feet from his garage doors. The line of posts, ten in all, ran from the street down the middle of the driveway to the parking area outside the garage. Dan unlatched the window giving it a hard tug. It didn’t move. It was painted shut. He tapped on the window, but the man driving the post gave no indication he heard Dan’s signal. Dan hopped around the room as he slipped on his trousers. The excitement caused him to break into a cough as he headed down the steps two at a time.

His bare feet touched once on the floor between the bottom of the stairs and the front door. He stopped at the edge of the grass where it met the gravel. His hands rested on his hips as he stared down the line of posts toward the man installing them. When the man turned to walk toward Dan, he appeared unfazed by Dan’s presence. He carried a sledge hammer in one hand and a roll of plastic caution tape in the other, the type of tape used to mark crime scenes.

“What are you doing? This is my driveway.” Dan ended in a cough.

“You think? Well, I’m buying this house off the Knights. So I own half this driveway, and I don’t want anyone using my half.”

"What?! You're crazy! You won't be able to get to your garage."

"I don't need to. This is going to be a student rental, and I want them to park in the street."

"What do you mean *them*? This is zoned for single family. You can't put a bunch of students in it. I will be a violation of the zoning code. Without the use of my driveway, you're hurting the value and use of my property. You're crazy." Dan stiffened as the tension escalated.

"Are you threatening me? I think you are. If you threaten me, I'll own you."

"I'm not threatening you. Look, I'm not feeling well, and I would like to reason with you."

"I'm moving five students in as soon as Ed Knight gets his stuff out."

"What's your name?"

"Black, Fred Black. I've lived in this town all my life, and I know people, so don't tell me what I can and can't do. Ed and I go way back. We're volunteers at the fire department. He told me about you. He said you might make trouble, so I'm getting a jump on things. You aren't using this driveway anymore."

Dan grabbed the nearest stake and ripped it out. Then he walked back toward his house without another word spoken. He felt lousy, weak and shaky. The light of day hurt his eyes. Conflict was the last thing he needed. He resolved to find an attorney within the hour and let him sort out the legal rights to the driveway. For now he would park in the street.

Fred Black had gotten in his pickup truck and left by the time Dan returned with the keys to his car, which was under the carport behind the garage. As Dan walked up the driveway, he pulled out each post and tossed it into Ed Knight's old yard so the driveway would be cleared for his exit. He parked in front of the house. He just wanted to go back to bed. Instead, after placing a call for an appointment with the first lawyer he spotted in the phone book, he cranked up Christmas music loud enough for the entire street to hear. *Revenge*! *Being happy is the best way to get revenge on a scrooge.* Dan decorated the shrubs in front of the house, strung lights around the porch, and put up their artificial tree in the living room, all the while coughing from the irritating chill in the air.

FIFTEEN

Early the next morning Dan paused in the lobby of the Children's Hospital to admire the Christmas tree. Hundreds of presents were stacked at its base, donated gifts from well-wishers. *Children gravely ill... I've had a wonderful life. The children in this hospital have already faced things I cannot imagine. Why do adults try to make other people's lives so miserable?* It was a thought; it was a prayer. Dan made a silent promise to bring a gift to place under the tree.

Dr. Cohen is considered one of the best in the world at immunology, and happens to have his office at Children's Hospital. He and his receptionist were the only two in the office. There was no wait. Dr. Cohen took Dan into his examining room for what he called "a thorough look-see and listen-to." The exam wasn't anything any other doctor hadn't done. So far Dan was unimpressed. He had expected someone more like Dr. Betters, who had sent him to Children's Hospital to meet with Dr. Cohen, who appeared reserved and meek. But then the doctor started asking questions, pointed questions about Dan's lifestyle, and soon his brilliance began to show. The questions probed into details Dan hadn't considered. The interview lasted almost half an hour with Dr. Cohen taking concise notes. Every time Dan coughed, the doctor paused with a studious look. Dr. Cohen scribbled a note and handed it to Dan.

"Well, Dan, I think I have a pretty good idea of your lifestyle. I want you to take this to the lab on the first floor. These are expensive blood tests, but I believe they will confirm my suspicions. We'll discuss the finding on your next visit. Do you have any questions?"

"Well, I'd like to know what you suspect."

"Let's wait. I don't like to share my guessing. I want facts. When I know, I will be straight with you. You will know everything I know. Now, I want you back here as soon as the results come in. It will probably take several weeks. See the receptionist and schedule for late next month. If there is a change in the time frame, we will call you."

"What about the holidays?"

"Disease doesn't take holidays. Someone is here twenty-four-seven."

As Dan passed through the lobby, a child in a wheelchair stared at the Christmas tree. Another boy held his mother's hand as they entered from the street. Even with a knit cap on, it was obvious he had no hair—no eyebrows or eyelashes. *Cancer treatments*. Dan's throat knotted, and his eyes welled. Whatever was wrong, he hoped he had the courage he witnessed on the children's faces in the lobby. The urge was there, but Dan contained his cough until he reached the street.

He sensed this doctor had the tools to determine what his illness entailed and it wouldn't be good news. The next week would be agony. He needed a diversion. *Hillbilly Lee*, he thought. He headed straight for the bait shop. He flipped on the radio to the local news station: "A suspicious fire has leveled Castleton's largest house. Emergency crews are searching for the elderly homeowners. If anyone knows the whereabouts of John and Evelyn McKenzie, please call the Castleton police."

It took an hour to get to the bait shop, an hour lost in his own thoughts, struggling with the unknown, always flashing back to a vision of sick children. It was a comfort to see the old mare tied to the oak tree behind the bait shop. Dan parked under the oak to have his car in the shade, but most of all, he just wanted to greet Lee's stupid old horse.

Dan ran his hand down the mare's neck, talking to her about nothing. His voice was soothing, his touch gentle. He struggled to clear his throat, avoiding a loud cough the harshness of which might spook the mare. She let out soft whinnies as if conferring with Dan's whispers.

"You're a therapy horse, aren't you, girl? Yeah you are."

"Well, Mr. Winslow." The voice startled Dan. He thought he was alone with the old mare, but Lee had crept up on him, real close.

"Ah, Lee, you startled me."

"Sorry. It's the Comanche in me."

Dan studied Lee. *Comanche? Don't even question it,* Dan thought. With someone like Lee, the possibilities knew no bounds.

"How about we go sit on the porch, Lee?"

"Sure. I'll fetch us some water, and we can talk fishin' or huntin'."

Lee and Dan walked to the porch. As Dan sat in one of the rockers, old Buck's nuzzle worked its way under his hand. Lee handed Dan a bottle of water, welcome on such an unseasonably warm, dry day.

"What've you been up to, Mr. Winslow? You and the missus ready for Christmas?"

"Come on, Lee, call me Dan. I put up our decorations, my wife buys the presents."

Lee nodded with a smirk.

"Me and mine don't decorate."

It wasn't a surprise for Dan to hear. "Did you hear anything about the big fire over in Castleton?"

"Can't say I have. I don't listen to the news much. Before I took up this hillbilly lifestyle, I used to listen to the radio in my car, but the old mare ain't so equipped. No use knowin' what you can't do nothin' about anyhoo, so why know it?"

"Well, the fire was at the McKenzie house."

"You don't say. I hear he had a big house. How's John and his wife?"

"It seems they're missing. The house was a complete loss. They're searching the rubble for bodies. It's a suspicious fire because it went fast and furious, like an accelerant was used."

Lee dropped into the other rocker. His face was void of color. Dan watched his eyes wander off to some distant place.

"What is it, Lee? What are you thinking?"

Lee didn't answer; his lips began to quiver like he was about to talk, but he didn't. Instead, he took a swig of water. Dan let it go. He gave old Buck a pat and sipped some water. When he saw Lee's eye well with a tear, he looked away out of respect. Lee wiped his eye with the back of his hand, letting out a sigh. Dan held in a cough.

"My wife's doing poorly... the doc says it won't be long."

"Sorry, Lee, you never mentioned her being ill."

"Private thing I 'spect, until a point, and then it might be best to let others know. She's been suffering long, and I suppose it will be a blessing for her when the time comes, but I ain't ready. McKenzie and his wife were good people; I'm sure they weren't ready to go either. I suppose people my age are coming due. When we were young'uns, the three of us done the blood-brother thing, cut ourselves and mingled our blood—me, McKenzie, and McDonath. We considered ourselves of the same clan when we ran the woods. I guess I was the one never quite growed out of it. I always held out hope old John would drive up someday and forgive me... it'll never be now."

"Forgive you?"

"Don't never you mind."

"Blood brothers, I've heard it, stories from back in the day." Dan coughed until he took a sip of water.

"Still soundin' bad, Dan... they got any suspects?"

"I haven't heard. Probably some druggie. I doubt they had any enemies. It sounds like they were real nice folks."

"Real nice folks. Evil has its way. Evil got no regard for nice folk. I know for a fact, evil has been working its way on the McKenzie family as long as I can remember."

"What do you mean?"

"Still questionin' things, don't matter much now. I might as well spill my guts."

"Sorry an event like this . . ." Dan stopped talking, deciding to listen.

"It all started with his father, and it ain't never stopped. Stony Grove is full of churches, but evil feasts on the citizens just the same. The three of us found John's father in the first calm water after the rapids up on the Stony. It was a day to never forgit, seeing his dad bobbin' facedown like he was. John said he knew he was murdered. Now this. Enough said."

"Help," Dan mumbled to himself as he thought. *The voice on the white noise machine, it's what she was saying.*

"What did you say?" Lee gave Dan a hard look.

"Don't mind me. I have a lot on my mind." Again Dan launched into an uncontrollable cough.

Lee stood and stepped off the porch, then walked to the middle of the parking lot where he picked up a stone and tossed it at the mailbox at the edge of the road. He hit it square away, then kicked hard at the dust around his feet. Dan watched without saying a word. When Buck let out a whimper, Dan comforted him by scratching behind his ear. Dan coughed so hard, it startled the mare across the parking lot.

Lee returned to the porch.

"Sounds bad, my friend. You better go see someone."

Friend. It was strange, but it struck a note with Dan. He knew Lee wasn't the type to throw out words of endearment freely. Dan appreciated his new friend's concern.

"I just came from a doctor's appointment. I'll hear within a week what's causing this... maybe."

"Life sure slips by quick. One day you're catching crawdads, and the next thing you know, you're a dried-up, useless old man. No matter to me, I guess, I been useless all my life, but John, he *did* things, made things happen. If you hear who might have done it, would you stop and let me know?"

"Sure thing, Lee, will do."

Lee unsheathed his whittling knife and commenced to make shavings. Dan sat with him for a spell, but they didn't speak. There was no discomfort in it. Eventually, Dan gave Buck a brisk head rub, stood, and walked to his car. He could have sat there all day if it weren't for his annoying cough, which Lee didn't need to hear. Dan gave the old mare one last pat before he got in his car and drove away.

Dan pulled up in front of his house. Iron stakes dotted the middle of the driveway again, bearing flags of yellow caution tape fluttering in the breeze. Dark clouds gathered out beyond, over the Gorge. The weather was taking a change; a cold front was moving in. Dan felt a chill. The sight of the flagged stakes triggered a sigh, initiating a cough. True to form, an announcement of his arrival for Julie.

The front door opened with a gleeful greeting. Julie was anxious to hear about the doctor visit and to tell him her news.

Dan returned her greeting as best he could. She gave full consideration of his failing health with her concerned look and focus on him. He put his arm around her as much for balance as for affection, and they stumbled onto the living room couch. Julie let Dan rest before she said a word. Dan closed his eyes and laid back his head.

"How'd it go with the doctor?"

"Just another doctor's visit and lab work. I have an appointment in a week. By then the lab results should be in. Nothing else to report. How about your day?"

"Well, I have some news. Two of our neighbors approached me about the stakes in our driveway. They're not locals. They're transplants like us. They say they are disgusted with the slumlord mentality of the town and want to form an action committee to put pressure on town council to enforce the zoning laws. They want to put a stop to cramming half a dozen students into single-family homes.

"They brought up a good point about the wage tax. These students don't work, and they have replaced tax-paying home owners. Stony Grove is deep in debt, Dan. There is a council meeting tonight. It's the last one of the year. They are going to attend it, and I think I'm going too." He let out a groan. "Dan, you don't have to go. I know you aren't feeling up for it."

"Let me lie down for a while. If I feel better, I'll go. I want to go, you know I do."

Dan took a nap after dinner, and when he woke up, he felt well enough to go to the council meeting. At the town hall entrance, Julie introduced Dan to several people, including the two neighbors she had spoken to earlier in the day. Tensions high, the neighbors were suspicious of each other. Even if they all appeared to be displaying sincere outrage, the people gathered on the Borough Building steps didn't know each other well or who was related to whom. People speaking in loud voices caught the attention of town council members of long-standing community lineage walking up the steps. The scene had the appearance of a community in the process of an awakening.

Half the faces in the audience were new to the council members. An air of contempt filled the chambers. Val Wentreck sat in the front of the chambers facing the gathering, while the town council members were seated to his left about ten feet away. One of Julie's new acquaintances pointed out to Dan who was who as the two of them peered into the council chambers from the front entrance. Val occupied a reserved seat at the public meeting even though he held no official public office. To Val's right sat Fred Black, described by one of Dan's new acquaintances as Val's personal secretary and henchman. The wheels turned in Dan's head. It didn't take a brain surgeon to figure out the who was responsible for prompting the sale of Ed Knight's house, but why? The crowd of town newcomers refrained from entering the chambers until a few minutes to starting time, as they continued to exchange experiences and dealings each had with the local townies. Several invited Julie to their churches.

When asked by a neighbor about the state of his driveway, Dan could only offer the obvious. There were stakes driven down the middle. The new owner of Ed Knight's house didn't want Dan trespassing on his side of the driveway. In addition, Dan mentioned the plans to convert Knight's house into a student rental. Dan assured everyone he had sought legal counsel and had an appointment next week, the results of which he would be willing to share. The neighbors were outraged.

They had already dealt with enough empty beer cans in their yards. Then there were the Sunday mornings spent hosing vomit from the sidewalks. The big question on all their minds was the impact on property values and the tax base. They all showed sympathy and concern for Dan and Julie's situation, but they also had their own concerns. The slumlords were driving down property values and then buying cheap. The story was the same all over town. The new residents in the outlying areas hoped the business district would someday morph into more of a village setting.

Julie stood in the center of a group of women relating her experience with the student living across the street. Julie caught herself as she studied faces and assessed her listeners. Cautious at first, she decided to tell the entire story. *The truth is the truth, and it needs to be aired.* The ladies were aghast at what had transpired with the student, and when Julie mentioned Officer Peterson, several others took the opportunity to interrupt her with their own tales.

Some ladies shared their experiences involving Officer Peterson. Some refrained from speaking yet displayed knowing looks. Julie wondered if the worst of Pete Peterson might be too much to share in a public forum for these reserved ladies. The outrage toward Officer Peterson took the conversation off on a tangent as half the women tried to talk at once. Julie interrupted them to get back on track. She shared about the phone call from the student's mother and the landlord's offer of a free month's rent. Julie told it all, all except the call from Officer Jack Monroe. There was no need to put a Good Samaritan at risk.

Dan felt a surge of energy as he listened to the support gathering in the crowd outside the council chamber. *We have numbers, which gives us strength; the council will listen.* This would be his first experience with local politics and his naiveté showed. A woman with a tablet walked among the group taking names, phone numbers, and email addresses. The energy needed to be organized and harnessed to be effective. It would take work, but in the end it would be worth it. The woman with the tablet approached Dan for data and then asked for a commitment to hold a meeting at his house next week. The meeting would present the perfect opportunity to share news from his discussion with the attorney concerning the paper alley.

A group leader needed to be chosen, one who could speak for them. Dan agreed to host the meeting although he feared being pressured into a leadership role. His health just wouldn't support a demanding post. He had attracted a lot of inquisitive looks as he went into his coughing spasms, which hit at regular intervals throughout the evening.

A Stony Grove squad car pulled into a reserved spot in front of the Borough Building. The police offices were just down the hall from the council chamber. Officer Peterson stepped from the squad car, adjusting his uniform. As he approached, a strange silence gripped the gathering on the steps. He swaggered until he reached the group surrounding Julie, a sinister grin enveloping his face.

Julie sensed an unease and apprehension within her group. One minute they possessed the spirit of wild horses; now they cowered like sheep. It made her wonder if they could tough it out in the ensuing battles that were sure to take place. Like a sixth sense, they were all aware of an undefined threat; all felt it and withdrew inward.

"Evening, ladies. Beautiful night, isn't it?" The tone in Peterson's voice reinforced everyone's beliefs. The man was no good, and not a single person responded to him. He stopped dead in his tracks to let out a snicker.

"Did I say something wrong?" He paused for effect. "It is a beautiful night, is it not? Or maybe . . ." No one responded. "Oh, maybe... you're not ladies." Peterson selected certain ones in the group with whom to lock eyes.

"Your day will come, Pete!" a quivering feminine voice called out as Officer Peterson began to climb the steps past Julie's group, his back already to them.

Peterson turned to look at a slightly built woman of about thirty standing next to Julie. He stared at her in a menacing way, but then as he spoke, his eyes shifted to Julie.

"Sandy, you can't threaten an officer of the law." His voice had a sickeningly sweet tone to it. He smirked as he stared at Julie. "My day already came, Sandy, remember?"

Julie didn't speak, not out of fear but rather out of her unwillingness to give him ammunition or insight into her thoughts.

Peterson bounded up the steps toward the Borough Building doors where Dan stood blocking his way. Peterson stopped, waiting for Dan to step aside. Dan didn't move as he stared at Peterson. Peterson's demeanor seemed to crumble even with the protection of his uniform. Even with Dan's poor health, Peterson apparently sensed a threat before him.

The whole crowd stopped breathing until Dan stepped aside just enough for Peterson to squeeze by. Everyone knew it would not be a moment soon forgotten by either man cr the crowd. Peterson headed toward his office, giving the briefest salutations to a couple of embedded townies. The mood for the meeting had been set, and neither side wanted to take prisoners.

A man next to Dan leaned close and whispered, "He lives in one of Val Wentreck's rentals, rent free. Wentreck claims he is doing the community a service by helping to support local law enforcement... he owns Peterson."

Dan remained stoic, no emotion on display.

SIXTEEN

The council meeting was due to start in five minutes. The crowd on the steps began to flood the chamber room. Conversations did not ebb; the room hummed like a beehive. Some people took to their seats, while others remained standing. There appeared to be no order to the gathering; then the gavel smacked the table as the president of the council called the meeting to order. Those standing plopped into their chairs, the buzz subsided, and the president spoke.

"I hereby call this meeting to order. First order of business will be roll call, but we'll start the meeting with the pledge of allegiance."

During the pledge Val remained seated, although he did put his hand over his heart. After the pledge, the president proceeded to call out each council member's name, each committee chair's name, and the names of other officers present. He then asked for the previous month's minutes to be approved. The gavel tapped the table. Each officer and committee chair took a turn standing and reading reports, which would be entered into the records. It all seemed so proper and well structured. The reports of special committees followed. Forty-five minutes passed.

"Is there any unfinished business to address?" As he finished speaking, the president struck the table with his gavel again. "Very well, I call for new business."

Ten people had raised their hands to be recognized for unfinished business without being recognized. A man in coveralls who had his hand raised spoke out.

“I want to discuss unfinished business. We have asked council–”

“Sir, you have not been recognized. You have no right to speak; you are out of order. I have closed the discussion of unfinished business; please be seated or I will have you removed.”

“Wait a minute. I have a right to speak—”

“Sir, you are out of order.” The president pounded his gavel on the table. “Remove this man from the chamber.” The president looked over at Val who was nodding his head in approval. Officer Peterson, who had stood at the back of the council chamber guarding the door since the meeting began, walked over and grabbed the man’s arm. The man shouted obscenities as Peterson escorted him to the parking lot. The others who had raised their hands to discuss unfinished business remained silent.

“I would like to remind everyone—I run this meeting, and we adhere to a certain structure to maintain order. Anyone who does not comply shall be removed from this chamber. I am limiting tonight’s meeting to one hour. Is there any new business?” By now a total of fifty-five minutes had passed. Twenty people raised their hands.

“Yes. The man in the blue shirt, please state your name and your business.”

“Yes, my name is Paul Morgan. My wife and I moved into town four years ago. I would like to know why the zoning laws are not equitably enforced. It seems some people are allowed to sidestep the rules.”

“Sir, I do not see an agenda sheet on this subject. Did you fill one out and submit it two days before the meeting?”

“I didn’t know I needed to.”

“It is in the procedures. You can obtain an agenda sheet Monday through Friday between nine and five from the secretary. Out of courtesy, sir, I will address your concern anyway.” The president looked toward Jason Reilly, zoning inspector. “Can you answer the man, Jason?”

"Well, yes, sir, I can. We enforce the codes to the letter as spelled out in our procedures. There may be times discrepancies take on an appearance, but I assure you, sir, it is because you may be unfamiliar with the range of flexibility allowed under the law to the inspection officer."

"Sounds reasonable, Jason. Thank you for addressing Mr. Morgan's concerns."

"Wait a minute, I have specific examples I can cite. Like—"

The president slammed down his gavel. "Sorry, but I need to adjourn this meeting. We are out of time. Get an agenda sheet for the next meeting."

Grumbling rose in the crowded chamber. No one could believe their grievances were not going to be heard.

"Order, order. We have a special closed meeting scheduled this evening in my office. You are all dismissed, this meeting is closed."

The president proceeded to his office behind where he sat, and the council members followed. Dan stood dumbfounded, his eyes wandering the front of the chamber until he met Val Wentreck's eyes. Val's stare was cold and menacing. During the meeting Dan had noticed every time he gazed toward Wentreck, Wentreck's eyes were locked on him. Wentreck now broke the stare and proceeded into the president's office. Fred Black tagged along behind. *A special closed meeting? Wentreck and Black are not government officials of any sort, just private citizens like the rest of us. What right do Val and Fred have to attend this meeting?* His blood boiled.

Dan held Julie's hand as they departed the Borough Building, neither one of them in a mood to join any of the small groups of citizens gathered in the parking lot. Several people either gave a wave of their hand or a "good night," and Dan politely nodded. He realized little could be done until election time. All they could do now was create a never-ending annoyance. He couldn't wait for his appointment with the attorney on Monday, but now all he wanted was to go to bed.

As they arrived home, the house was dark except for the Christmas lights. The boys were already asleep and hadn't thought to leave a light on for their parents. Dan and Julie sat at the dining room table and whispered so as not to wake anyone.

"Dan?"

"Yes."

"I want to run away. I just want to walk away from all this. There is evil here."

"Julie—"

"No, those men, Val and Fred," Julie whispered, "I think they are capable of doing anything they choose without feeling the slightest remorse. The fire in Castleton is suspicious. For whatever reason, Mr. McKenzie wanted to control who owns this house. It is also obvious those men have a problem with us living here. I don't think they care what happens to us. They don't hate us. They just want what we have."

"I'm not one to run away from problems, Julie. Maybe if they took a different approach about the whole thing, I might have just considered taking an offer or letting Mr. McKenzie buy it back, but they drew a line in the sand and now McKenzie is gone. I don't want to run away now. I want to take a stand against this evil."

"You are also sick... and I don't want to be a widow."

"Julie, as sick as I am, I think I am stronger than those two. They are going to find out what I'm made of. I'll know more after I talk to the attorney. We can make arrangements for you and the boys to live somewhere else until this is settled."

"I'm not living anywhere without you. I am afraid for the boys, though. I am afraid this house might catch fire. This whole thing is crazy."

Dan finally let out a cough.

"Dan, I'm sorry."

"I'm fine, I was holding my cough in way too long. We better get to bed and try to sleep." He gave her a peck on the cheek, and they climbed the stairs to bed.

"Dan, I'm going to pray before I go to sleep, and on Sunday I'm going to church. Klaare said she would go with me. She's a sweetheart. I think you should pray with me, Dan."

"I will, Julie, I will."

Their prayers were silent prayers. Without discussing it, they both prayed for strength and for blessings and good health for the other. They sought forgiveness for their flaws and lack of faith. They fell asleep before they finished, resting in the silence of the night as the hours passed.

A scream broke the peace. Dan recognized Julie's voice. His heart jumped. He grabbed the lamp from the nightstand. Julie sat with her hands on her face gasping for breath. Dan took a quick look around the room. Everything appeared normal except Julie's hair. Julie's back was to him; he couldn't see her face, but her hair was slick and shiny.

"Dan! Ice water, I've been doused with ice water again!"

"That's crazy... it's impossible."

Julie twisted around to look at Dan. Water dripped from her nose and chin. Dan looked at her pillow. It was soaked except for the outline of her head. Dan put his hand on the wet pillow. It felt cold, cold like ice water. He looked at the ceiling for water marks. There were none. He knew there was no overhead piping above the room. He stood, feeling the walls for moisture. They were dry. He checked the window, and it was latched closed. He walked to the door to check if it was locked. It was. He heard footsteps approaching. "Mom, Dad—we thought we heard a scream."

Dan opened the door to see Trent and Zane leaning on the door frame. "We're fine, guys, just a strange splash of water woke us up."

Julie dried herself with Dan's T-shirt.

Zane scanned the room. "Weird, where could the water have come from?"

Dan used his authoritative voice. "I have no idea but it is cold, like ice. You guys can head back to bed. Maybe in the morning we'll be able to figure it out." They didn't seem convinced but turned to go as he closed the door.

Julie covered her face with her hands as she sat down on the edge of the bed. Dan placed the lamp back on the nightstand and sat beside her. He put his arm around her. Neither one could think of what to say. Julie grabbed her cold wet pillow and tossed it across the room. Then they both started to laugh, slowly at first, but soon they fell into a full-blown belly laughter, complete with snorts. Dan wrestled Julie back onto the bed and under the sheets, making ghostly reverberations. What else could they do? The place was haunted, there was no longer any doubt, yet they decided to make a joke of it. They covered their heads with blankets like little kids. It was all too much.

"Our house is haunted, Dan," Julie whispered. "It makes everything else seem so trivial, doesn't it?"

"Yes, it does! Look at it this way: if you ever had any doubts about an afterlife, this kind of reinforces your belief in one."

"I wonder if this ghost is trying to tell us something. I wonder if it's Big Jim."

"Well, I would say he told you to wake up—and didn't they find Jim in the icy waters of the Stony?"

"He doesn't scare you, Dan?"

"No, it gives me hope. Are you afraid?"

"Just a little apprehensive, I suppose, not knowing what is going to happen next. I don't think he's out to harm us."

"I don't think we should tell anybody about it. Don't mention it in front of Klaare."

"Maybe I'll make some obscure references and see if she has had any of her own experiences with our friendly ghost. I am going to pray more, for sure."

"If we ever want to sell this place, it would be best if we didn't advertise our experiences here, any of them. As far as prioritizing our troubles, I put my health as number one, this stupid town as number two, and this ghost at maybe third or fourth." He paused a few seconds. "Julie, I think Big Jim was murdered. When I was at the library reading news articles, I found one that said the town doctor was found in the Stony. He was found in the same spot as Big Jim, three years later. Whatever or whoever is haunting our house may be trying to lead us with clues. Do you think you can get back to sleep?"

"Yes, I'm going to pray myself to sleep. Good night, I love you."

"Good night for the second time tonight. Love you."

"Oh, Dan, let me end this on a happy note. Tim called today. He said to tell you he is stopping by on Sunday."

"Sweet. It'll be good to see him."

Julie lied: she knew she could not go back to sleep. She lay in Dan's arms, mulling the research she had been doing. She made a decision to follow up with Pastor Kirk's offer of researching through the old church records. Within a few minutes Dan was snoring. It made her feel secure for a while, until he coughed. He didn't wake. She whispered a prayer for him. *What would I do without you? How could I go on?* She pulled the covers from over her head. Enough light drifted in through the window to illuminate the room. Even with everything going on, it felt like their room was a haven in a world gone mad. A room where nothing could hurt her, not even a ghost. She breathed easily, counting her blessings, and then soon fell asleep.

SEVENTEEN

On the Sunday before Christmas. Julie woke early, showered, and rushed to the kitchen to start coffee. She heard Klaare in the basement and called an invitation for breakfast through the door. Klaare accepted and said she would be up after she showered and dressed. Julie whipped eggs, placed tempeh in the skillet, and cut veggies to fill an omelet. This would be the fourth Sunday she would take Klaare to church; she seemed to enjoy it.

Faith Community Church, a nondenominational church on the edge of town, was Harry McDonath's church. It's why she had chosen it. The pastor presented himself like a teacher. Other ones she had visited were too ritualistic. All she wanted from a church was a study of Scripture, with an emphasis on serving in love, without much in the way of rituals or pomp. She poured herself a cup of coffee while waiting for everyone to get moving.

Klaare came into the kitchen first, looking lovely. Her hair was always groomed, but this morning it looked exceptional. She wore a form-fitting pale blue dress, elegantly simple, yet on Klaare it appeared striking. Julie put down her coffee for a hug when she approached.

"Honestly, Julie, I don't know what to think about church, but I am looking at it as an adventure. Is it wrong? I feel like the Bible you gave me tells a remarkable story. I hope when we go into church, we will be walking right into the story in some way."

"Oh, Klaare, what a beautiful way to think of it. I like this church more each time we visit. It is most unfortunate that some pastors lack imagination, and some are self-absorbed. They are just human, with the entire range of worldly elements we all possess. This one seems to have a special gift. You must keep in mind, in the end God is love; He is not religion or church. God wants to live in our hearts. I hope you come to believe it. This pastor is supposed to be a teacher, so just think of church as another class."

"You make it so exciting. I like the way you think about it. So many people seem to get bogged down in rituals and such. This is what scares me away from religion."

"Don't believe in religion, God wants us to believe in Him. The pastor reads from Scripture and reminds us Jesus just wants us to accept Him as our savior, admit we are sinners, and ask forgiveness for our sins and weaknesses. It's simple, a focus shift. Men tend to overcomplicate things. They do our Lord a disservice. Now, would you like some coffee or tea?"

"Coffee will be fine, with a little cream, please."

"Let's not read the coffee grounds." They both laughed.

Julie poured Klaare a cup of coffee. Dan coughed as he descended the stairs. Klaare studied the concern on Julie's face.

"When will he hear from the doctor?" Klaare whispered.

"Not until the end of the week, the day after Christmas."

Dan walked into the kitchen standing tall with a cheerful grin.

"Good morning, ladies. You both look stunning, and breakfast smells delicious."

"Morning, Dan. You look lively this morning." She handed him a cup of black coffee.

"It's a decision... I chose to feel good and have a good day. My little brother will be here soon, and I plan to make it a great day. Klaare, your dress is nice. Are you looking forward to going to church?"

"I am, very much. I told Julie I feel like we are going on an adventure."

"Ha, it's the exact word I used to describe buying this house, an adventure. Hopefully the pastor is the sort to support your expectations. Some can be rather boring."

"Dan!" Julie slapped Dan's shoulder.

Klaare smiled. "Will you come with us, Dan?"

"No... the boys and I are going to wait until Julie sorts through the churches. When she settles on one she wants to attend regularly, we'll all go with her. I'm not much of a churchgoer, but I am a believer, always have been. I'm just not into religious pomp."

"He's a heathen, Klaare, plain and simple. I've been trying to reform him for years, but I like his wild side. I don't want to break his spirit, just tame it a bit. Dan, this is the church. I've decided. So you better get prepared."

"You do not believe in church, but you believe in God?"

"Oh, I believe in God. Like I said, it's religion I have a problem with. It's a war—good versus evil. I consider myself a warrior. Our enemy shows up in the most unlikely places, even in churches."

"This gets more exciting all the time. I have read these things in the Bible you gave me, many battles."

"Don't let me influence you. You make up your own mind. It's what Jesus wants us to do, choose. God is love. Jesus offers forgiveness if we accept him, accept his way of loving. We simply believe He is God, He is Love, trust in Him and put Him in charge of our lives. We are, of our own free will, to accept or deny, though to deny is to accept chaos. No one can force another person to accept the Word of God. Each person must make his own choice. If someone is using force, he does not speak for God. Love doesn't work that way."

The noise of the boys jostling each other as they stampeded down the stairs brought a silence to the conversation in the kitchen. They pushed each other through the kitchen doorway, bursting in with laughter. They caught sight of Klaare, and the clatter stopped. Both had a not-so-secret crush on Klaare. They stood straight and speechless, eyes wide. Dan grinned as he recognized the symptoms of puppy love. They hadn't known Klaare would be having breakfast with them. He wondered if they would even be able to eat.

"Good morning, boys, we have a guest for breakfast. She's going to church with me."

"Morning, Mom," they said in unison.

"Hi guys." Klaare's smile was genuine.

"Good morning, Klaare," Zane said, grinning from ear to ear.

"Good morning." Trent almost made eye contact before he retreated to the dining room table.

"Mom, is there anything I can help you with?" Zane offered.

Dan walked into the dining room with a chuckle. Zane asking to help was more than he could take.

There came a knock at the front door.

"That'll be Tim," Dan announced.

"What... I wasn't expecting him until this evening."

"I invited him for breakfast." Dan winked at her as he headed for the door.

He opened the door. "Tim, my brother, I've missed you."

Dan threw his arms around his brother in a bear hug.

"Come on in. You are just in time to feast."

"Great. I could smell it from clear out by the street."

The brothers walked into the dining room. Dan positioned himself to catch Tim's reaction to seeing Klaare. Zane and Trent caught Klaare's expression upon seeing Tim. They were outmatched. Tim had good looks and well-groomed maturity.

Breakfast was served and consumed, and the boys jumped to clean up, if only in a last-ditch effort to impress Klaare. Julie and Klaare headed for church.

With the women gone, a wrestling match broke out in the living room, but it was all in good sport, and Dan had Zane laughing within minutes. Tim sat sipping coffee. Zane laughed so hard, he had to break from the match, barely making it to the bathroom. It took all Dan's strength to tussle with the boys, something he had long taken for granted. When things settled, Dan began to cough, while both boys watched with worry. Tim put down his coffee.

Dan's coughing had ruined the moment. Zane and Trent asked if they could walk to the soccer fields to kick a ball around.

Dan thought it was a good idea. He wanted to talk to Tim in private.

"So, how's Houston?"

"Houston is over."

"Totally? You had a lot of capital invested, didn't you?"

"Everything... financially and emotionally."

"What happened?"

"I got bought out. Bridget's dad made me an offer. Bridget said I should take it. I got the message. You know, my brother, I joke a lot about women, but I never cheated on Bridget, and I never lied to her. It's hard to maintain a relationship when you are on the road eight months a year."

"Too bad. What are your plans?"

"I have a million-step plan... coming here is step one. I have no idea what step two is. I'm lost, my brother, I'm lost."

"You're welcome here as long as you want."

"I'm not one to impose. I'll check in at the hotel."

"Ah, come on, we have room for you."

"Are you kidding... this place is haunted."

The brothers laughed.

"We each need our own space. I appreciate your offer, but what I need is to be near family, not in the family. It'll work out better. I may be here for an extended time. I'm not short on change. It'll be quite a while before I have to do anything for work."

"What did you think of Klaare?"

"She's a looker, no doubt, but I think I've taken the cure. I've traveled enough, loved enough, and been hurt enough to last me a while. Bridget and I had planned to get married next June. Three weeks ago, we were on the beach, soaking up the sun. Then, two days ago, she dropped the bomb on me. No explanation, I don't know if she got tired of me or met someone else or if her dad's business interests had something to do with it. My brain is numb. After three years, you would think I deserve an answer... I took her old man's offer."

"How'd you do?"

"It was generous for where we currently sit, but I know the potential five years out is worth a thousand times what I got. I just wish I knew why all of a sudden I was no longer welcome."

EIGHTEEN

It looked more like a bright white chapel than a church. It sat just off an old farm road outside of town. Nestled in a grove of ancient hemlock, a small creek trickled down a ravine between the parking lot and Faith Community Church. A footbridge spanned the ravine. A white gazebo perched on the edge opposite the parking lot offered a tranquil place for reflection. It was the perfect setting for a love story. The parking lot was three quarters full, yet it was a half an hour before the service would begin. People gathered at the entrance under a large roof covering a drop-off area.

Julie and Klaare sat in their car watching as more cars pulled into the lot. As people walked past Julie's car, they smiled and waved. Even on this fourth visit Julie was assessing and building up courage to face a crowd of strangers. Klaare just followed Julie's lead. After a few moments, Julie opened her door, offering a nervous sigh. Klaare followed suit. Unexpectedly, Julie heard her name called out. She turned, looking to see who might be calling to her. It was Harry McDonath.

"Julie, how are you? It is so good to see you."

"Hello there, I thought this was your church—this is our fourth visit, but I haven't seen you here. I'm so sorry about your friend Mr. McKenzie."

"Yes, John and his wife . . ." Harry could say no more. He took a deep breath and changed the subject.

"It's a fine church. I missed the last few Sundays, went to church over in Castleton. Our Pastor Kirk here is a military man like you and your husband. Where is your husband?"

"He didn't come today. He's sending me to do a little recon work... Oh, I'm sorry, let me introduce you to Klaare. Harry, this is Klaare. She's from Estonia, a graduate exchange student at the college. She's staying with us."

"Nice to meet you, Klaare. How do you like our little village?"

"I love living with the Winslows, but the village is not very pleasant."

"Julie, I've heard rumors about the goings-on. Are they true?"

"I don't know what you've heard, but we have been having some trouble. It has not been the dream I thought it would be."

"I'm so sorry, and now my old friend John McKenzie and his wife... oh dear. The world can be so ugly." He looked away toward the woods behind the church.

"Have you heard anything about the McKenzies? I mean other than what's been in the papers about the fire being suspicious. Who would do such a thing to such a nice gentleman?"

"He's a good man and a gentleman. He used his wealth and influences to help a lot of people. He's a good friend." Harry stopped speaking again, he looked at his watch. "We'd better head over to the church."

"Do you think it was some drug addict robbing them?"

Julie, Klaare, and Harry crossed the footbridge and walked past the gazebo. They were almost to the front door of the church when Harry stopped. Everyone had entered the church except the three of them.

Harry looked at Julie and then Klaare. "I know I can trust you. All my years as a real estate agent have taught me how to read people." He took a deep breath. "I don't want to divulge much at the moment, but because I was your agent when you bought the house, I'll give you my opinion."

Julie waited for him to continue. Whatever he said, she would let it go at face value and not question it further. Harry looked serious and took another deep breath.

"No."

Julie wanted to ask more, but his one word spoke mountains. They walked on into the church. Just inside the front door a greeter smiled, shook their hands, and handed them a bulletin. It was a sincere smile and handshake.

Julie's mind wandered. She just couldn't concentrate on meeting new people. The foyer had groups of people chatting and hanging up their coats. The congregation looked to be made up of simple folk, farmers and lumberman types. Many offered Julie and Klaare warm greetings as Harry introduced them, but none of their names stuck in Julie's mind. She felt guilty about it, but the word *no* just kept echoing in her head. *Who, then, set the fire at the McKenzies'? Who do you suspect, Harry?* Julie looked at him and knew that he sensed her question without her speaking it.

Organ music drifted into the foyer announcing the call to be seated. Klaare held Julie's arm as they waited their turn to enter. The church was full. The only open seats were near the front. Julie and Klaare felt self-conscious as they walked down the aisle, the last two to find an open spot. In the past they had arrived early, securing seats in the rear of the church. Julie clutched her Bible against her chest. Klaare, wide-eyed, looked about, admiring the stained-glass windows, the large wooden cross behind the altar, the artful tapestries, and wooden planking high up on the cathedral ceiling. The church appeared much larger inside than it looked from the outside. Julie bowed her head, closing her eyes in prayer. Klaare watched her but did not follow her lead.

Julie glanced toward the back of the church where Harry sat with friends. They all had their heads bowed for prayer, but as if he sensed her, Harry opened his eyes, catching Julie's gaze. He tightened his lips and gave her a knowing nod, then closed his eyes again. Julie looked around the church, wondering who knew what. These were simple folk, but they weren't stupid. They weren't town people, but from the surrounding countryside. She thought they probably owed no loyalties to the town, but who was related to whom? She wanted to let go of her suspicious thoughts and just make simple friendships. She made a mental note to speak with the pastor to schedule times to research the church's voluminous history. The choir director took his position, then raised his arms.

The choir broke into song with beautiful voices, robust and joyful. The hymn was "For the Beauty of the Earth" by John Rutter, and it wasn't just heard, it was felt. She touched Klaare's hand. It was a moment to be shared.

When the choir ended the hymn, the congregation bowed their heads in prayer. All but Klaare—who continued to look around for a minute before she closed her eyes and bowed her head. Only she knew if she prayed or even knew what was going on, but she went through the motions just the same.

Pastor Kirk, a tall, lean man of about sixty, took his place at the podium. His white short- cropped hair framed a handsome face. Square of jaw, with broad shoulders and straight posture speaking about his nature as a marine, he had the look of someone people would follow into battle. His words flowed loud and clear so even the elderly far back in the pews caught every word. Confidence and enthusiasm made his words musical. He read Psalm 145:1–6, a psalm of praise by David. Following the reading, he greeted the congregation and welcomed all new visitors, his gaze landing on every unfamiliar face, for he knew every one of his flock. Klaare smiled when he looked at her. He made all the visitors feel special.

The choir sang another hymn, "Revive Us Again," followed by the Invocation. When Pastor Kirk asked if there were any praises, hands went up. One by one people offered praise to the Lord for answered prayers. Thanks were given for Uncle Charlie's gout easing up, Ms. Alice's healing broken hip, the easing of Brother Tom's financial troubles, and on and on. When the congregation finished, the pastor turned to the choir and announced the next hymn, "The Comforter Has Come." Klaare seemed swept away, and Julie couldn't have been happier.

Pastor Kirk asked for prayer requests, and just like with the praises, raised hands were called on one by one. When he asked if anyone else had a prayer request, Klaare's hand went up. Julie was shocked. *What on earth would Klaare request a prayer for?* The pastor smiled and pointed at Klaare.

"Yes, what is your request? You're new to us, but you are welcome and we will pray for you."

Without hesitation Klaare spoke. "I would like everyone to pray for Julie's husband, Dan Winslow. He is a very sick man. He has a severe cough, and it does not come from a cold. He seems to be getting worse."

Julie couldn't believe Klaare had the courage to speak like this in a group of strangers. Her eyes teared up. Julie had given thought to making a request but held back. *Oh Klaare,* she thought, *you are a beautiful person, inside and out.* Julie squeezed Klaare's hand as a tear rolled down her cheek. The pastor sensed the emotion of the moment, and as he petitioned the Lord on behalf of all the prayers requested, he fervently asked for healing for Dan Winslow. In a moment, Julie knew she had been right to choose this church and hoped Klaare had found God.

Julie's decision was again confirmed as the pastor gave his sermon. His intent for the next several weeks was to review elements of the foreshadowing of Christ in the Old Testament starting in Genesis. He read passages of Scripture followed by insightful analysis leading up to the birth of Christ and current-day relevance. His words flowed quickly, concisely, and without personal judgment on the ways of man. He offered the Word of God and the Way of God in such a humble way, Julie could detect not an ounce of ego in his voice. The pastor's looks were not meek or humble, but when he spoke, humility filled the church. He finished by stressing the true meaning of Christmas. He invited all to attend Christmas Eve candlelight service. This was a man of God. When the service was over, the pastor stood at the door of the church taking each person's hand and thanking them for coming to hear the Word. Julie and Klaare knew they were not in a group of strangers.

Harry McDonath walked with Julie and Klaare across the little bridge to the parking lot. “I’m so sorry to hear Dan’s not well.”

“We would appreciate your payers.”

“Well, did you enjoy our little chapel in the woods?”

“Yes, it feels like home.”

“Klaare?”

“I did enjoy the service... I hope I didn’t speak out—”

“You did fine, Klaare. Don’t think any more about it.”

“You know, Julie . . .” Harry paused, seemingly gathering his thoughts. “This town has a history—a lot of what is going on now started a long time ago. We’re clannish and insular. People around here don’t forget or move on. It’s kind of hard for you to understand people’s interactions and doings.”

“Honestly, I am having a tough time adjusting. This area is so beautiful, it is hard to imagine why people act the way they do, how they can be so ugly.”

“It’s all in the Bible,” Klaare murmured.

“What is, Klaare?” Harry raised an eyebrow.

“Oh, I gave Klaare a Bible and told her to start reading it before we came to church.” Julie gave Klaare a motherly look.

Harry offered Klaare a pleased smile. “Well, Klaare, I agree, I think every type of interaction known to man is in the Bible. It is mankind’s service manual. It’s the message Pastor is trying to get across.”

“No—” Klaare words were cut off by Harry, but being a little hard of hearing, he hadn’t noticed Klaare’s attempt to interject.

“I’m quitting real estate.”

“I hope it doesn’t have anything to do with us.”

“No, this old man has just seen enough, and I’m tired. It’s not the same anymore with all these newfangled gadgets and computer search engines. I have no interest in learning them. People can bother you any time of the day or night. They want you to respond yesterday, or they dump you. It's time. It was a good run, but times have changed."

"You'll love being retired. it'll be good for you to just relax. Oh, I almost forgot. When we were going through all the trash the Goldmeadows left behind, I found four old letters. They were from Jim McKenzie to Louise. I intended to turn them over to you to give to John McKenzie, but now, well . . ."

"Oh, how nice, Julie. I am in touch with John's children. I can see to it they get them."

"Thank you. I can bring them next Sunday or drop them off at the real estate office." They all stopped at Julie's car. "Well, I hope you enjoy retirement."

"I've worked twenty years longer than most folks. I'll tell you a secret if you promise not to tell anyone."

"Trust me. I have no one to tell. Klaare, you promise too." Klaare gave a positive nod.

"I have a friend at the state capitol. The university is going to have a huge student housing expansion. They don't want word getting out just yet because of an investigation into bribery and kickbacks. Julie, you take care of yourself. If I can be of any help, let me know. Maybe in a few days we can talk a little more. Let's see how things unfold. I'm not one to push an issue. Let it come about naturally, I always say. A few skunks might expire without the benefit of releasing their revenge."

"Sure, you take care. It's our little secret. Come on, Klaare. We'll see you next Sunday then."

Julie and Klaare got into the car and soon pulled out of the church parking lot. Julie's thoughts were on the secret Harry had just shared with her.

Klaare clasped her Bible with both hands.

"Mr. McDonath seems like a nice man. It is a shame he lost an arm. It must be very painful to be shot."

"What... what did you say, Klaare? Did you say shot?"

"Yes."

"Who told you he was shot? Dan and I wondered how he lost his arm. Are you sure?"

"It says so in the Bible."

"What... in the Bible, it says Mr. McDonath was shot? Klaare . . ."

"I tried to tell both of you, it is all in the Bible."

"The Bible I gave you?"

"Yes, there is a lot written in it. I will show you when we get home."

NINETEEN

Dan arrived at the attorney's office first thing Monday morning. He entered a copper-lined elevator, pushing the button for the third floor. The elevator moved swiftly; then the doors opened with a ding. The law building had a sterile feel, more sanitary than a hospital and quieter than a library. In the broad empty hallways, Dan could hear his own footsteps on the white marble floor. He struggled to contain a cough he knew would echo through these cavernous corridors, eventually disturbing the entire building. Dan entered a door marked "Mathew Proctor Attorney at Law" and found himself in an office reception area furnished with overstuffed leather chairs. *High dollar—maybe I should cancel,* Dan thought. He wanted to run, but before he could, a serious-looking receptionist greeted him.

The receptionist took Dan's name, checked her appointment book, then asked him to have a seat. He sank in between two fat leather arms studded with shiny copper. He wondered if he would ever be able to stand back up. Being the first appointment of the day, he optimistically anticipated being attended to promptly, but as time passed, his naïve hopes faded. The world, at least this high-dollar world, did not run on his schedule. The leather made him sweat; he knew his pants would be sticking to him when he got up, so he shifted about. No one else entered the office during Dan's forty-five-minute wait.

The door next to the receptionist flew open. Out stepped a giant of a man who looked like he could play hoops in the NBA. He extended his hand on an arm that seemed to reach halfway across the waiting room. Dan's hand was by no means small, but it was engulfed by Proctor's. He struggled to get out of the chair. Standing, he tried to discreetly use his free hand to pull at the seat of his pants. The entire setup proved intimidating.

"Mr. Winslow, so nice to meet you. I'm Mathew Proctor. Please, please come into my office."

Dan followed him, still trying to get over feeling awestruck.

Plaques of honors, degrees, and certificates covered the walls, leaving no room for a family photo or personal item. The mahogany desk wouldn't have fit in Dan's living room, and the chair behind it looked like a throne.

"Have a seat, Mr. Winslow. I like to get right to the meat of the issue. By the way, I'm sorry I kept you waiting, but I have a court appearance this afternoon, and I've been reviewing briefs—I lost track of time. Now, what brings you in and why do you think you need an attorney? You won't be charged for this visit if I determine your matters can be resolved without me. I'm a fair man and I'm expensive. Now, go ahead—state your case, sir."

Dan sat down in the client chair. Once again he sank low, as if to suggest his position was subordinate. He summarized the situation in Stony Grove, his driveway dispute, the student rental zoning violations, the town council's corrupt meeting. He went off on tangents and offered his understanding of the law. His emotion had the best of him, and his speech became a rant.

He was clearly displaying anger, something he had promised himself he would not do. He felt horribly ill and at the mercy of evil. He had dealt with so many shady characters and impossible situations since arriving in this town. Mr. Proctor took notes when Dan first began to talk but soon sat back in his chair and listened as Dan vented. Mr. Proctor, hearing enough, stopped him.

"Mr. Winslow, excuse me. There is no need to continue."

"I'm sorry, Mr. Proctor, I'm not myself. I promised myself I would not do what I just did."

"It's quite all right, but I have to tell you. I cannot represent you in these matters."

Dan's hands gripped the arms of his chair to try to regain some sense of control.

"Quite frankly, Mr. Winslow, to represent you would place me in a situation of conflict of interest. You see, I already represent some individuals in your community. I can offer you some free advice, however. I suggest you play dumb, don't talk about these things even if you know what you are talking about." He leaned forward, toward Dan. "I suggest you seek legal counsel from outside this county. I'm an honest man, Mr. Winslow, but I earn my living from my understanding of the law and representing clients in legal matters, sometimes running along a fuzzy line. It is the conundrum of my profession. I have been known to walk away from clients for those reasons. My nature tells me you are a client who deserves my services, but my wallet tells me you can't afford me. I will offer you some free advice and insights without being specific or violating my fiduciary relationships with my clients." Mr. Proctor studied Dan's face, waiting for him to speak.

"I never expected this. What can you tell me?"

"The key to all your troubles is your driveway."

"My driveway, what do you mean?" Dan thought about the Bible writings Julie had shared with him yesterday afternoon. Writings he would not share with Mr. Proctor. Especially now that Proctor had divulged his loyalties were elsewhere. Thank God he hadn't spoken of them during his rant.

"It's not—not a driveway. It's what is known as a paper alley. It extends the entire length of your property and your neighbor's. It was laid out during the initial survey and plot planning of Stony Grove. It is a valuable easement to those whose land is situated behind your property. You see without an easement, the property is landlocked and of no value."

"I'm not sure I understand. I mean, I understand about the property owners being landlocked, but how does this paper alley thing work? Why isn't it just an alley?"

"Because in the beginning when the town was slow to grow, other properties were developed first. If an alley is not used within twenty years of its recording, it becomes inactive. To open it up requires the permission of every property owner bordering it. If the property owners used the land designated for the alley by installing fencing, growing trees, bushes, or a building on it, then it further complicates matters. It's about all I can divulge to you without violating fiduciary relationships. Please accept my apologies and understand, my other clients involve long-term relationships. I hope you understand, and the best of luck to you."

"Thank you, Mr. Proctor, I respect where you are coming from. I guess I'm going to have to reassess my situation."

"Mr. Winslow, you hold a valuable piece of real estate. You might want to consider parting with it, for just compensation. Why trouble yourself when you can just take the money and move on?"

"I'll think on it."

Dan took Mr. Proctor's advice about playing it dumb and quiet. He had no intention of giving even the slightest consideration to selling to the likes of Val Wentreck or Fred Black. What better place to start following good advice than right here with the man who offered it, a man who had to be considered suspect, as an associate of the enemy. "Thank you for your time, Mr. Proctor, I'll show myself out."

Walking down the hallway of the law building, Dan finally let loose with his cough. It echoed widely, as did his footsteps, but the reverence he held upon entering no longer ruled. Contempt was in his heart.

He had enough fuel in the car to make it back to Stony Grove. There he slipped into the service station on the edge of town. At the pumps, he got out and began to fill his tank. Dan heard it before he saw it, a brand new one ton dually with stacks rattled up to the other side of the pumps. Dan never looked up from filling his tank. Behind him he heard the pickup's door slam, someone fiddled with the fuel hose, and then the sound of fuel. A sudden cough surged in Dan which he couldn't stop. He let go the handle of his nozzle, placed his hand on the side of his vehicle to catch his balance. The coughing continued, and Dan began seeing white spots before his eyes. Light-headed, he gathered all his strength to keep from passing out, then heard a voice from behind him.

"Sounds bad, really bad, like you're gonna die."

Dan knew the voice but couldn't place it. As his cough subsided, he turned, and Fred Black smiled.

"I'm all right."

"You don't sound like it. You know, I got nothin' against you. Just so you know, I'm gonna own that house of yours before it's all over. What do you want for it?"

"It's not for sale."

"Everything is for sale. Even you have a price."

"You can't buy me or my house."

"A price doesn't have to be money. Sometimes a price is something in trade, like peace of mind. You got a might pretty little wife."

Rage surged before the words were half spoken, but all Dan could do was choke and cough. He couldn't catch his breath long enough to speak. He felt weak.

"Maybe I'll just wait to work it all out with Widow Winslow. She might even take a special liking to me after you're gone. She won't be the first widow ole Fred has scooped." Fred racked the fuel hose on the pump and hopped into the pickup. The ground at Dan's feet rumbled as Fred revved the engine of the dually.

Dan couldn't catch his breath due to anxiety and fatigue. He felt as if Fred Black had held a chunk of kryptonite and dangled it in front of his face. Helplessly, he watched his antagonist drive away.

Dan stopped fueling before his tank was full and slumped into the car. He sat until another fuel customer pulled up behind him. He looked toward the gas station building, where four boys stood outside the door. They lit cigarettes, blew smoke. They were the guys Zane had come to call his friends. Bad news.

It was all Dan could do to drive the rest of the way home. *Fred will never get our house.* The gauntlet had been tossed down. Dan would dig in with everything he had. He knew Julie would be with him. Also weighing on him was Zane; he had to rein him in. Mathew Proctor likely represented Fred and Val; what were the odds he would pick the attorney of the enemy.

###

Julie let herself into the side entrance of the church, near Pastor Kirk's office. She stopped to say hello, even though she hated to bother him while he was working. "Julie, welcome. Make yourself at home. The library is in the basement, just down those stairs."

"Thanks for letting me research here. I hope to find details about my ancestors. They've been here since the revolution."

"Happy someone is making use of all the information and trivia written down over the past two hundred years."

###

Walking into the kitchen where Julie was preparing lunch, Dan kissed her neck. He made a growling noise. Happy—he just wanted to be in touch with happy. Even though his appetite had waned lately, the aroma of garlic was tantalizing. Julie sautéed mushrooms, onions, and garlic to mix into angel hair pasta and olive oil. She had a loaf of garlic bread heating in the oven. He didn't feel like eating, but he would. For his health, he knew he had to. Julie wilted handfuls of spinach by mixing it with the hot pasta.

"Hey, Dan, you startled me. How'd it go?"

"I guess I should have coughed more before I came into the room."

"Not funny, Dan. Your color . . ."

"What about my color?"

She hesitated. "You look grayish, how do you feel?"

"Well, grayish, I guess. I just ran into Fred Black. He said he was going to buy this house off Widow Winslow. He said you might even get to like him after I'm dead. It's how I feel, dead."

"Not funny, Dan. Don't say such things. Did you really see Fred Black?"

"Yes, and he really said it. I wanted to hurt him, but I'm too weak. All I did was cough."

Julie put her arms around Dan and rubbed his back. She rested her head against his shoulder.

"More importantly, I saw Zane's new friends. They were hanging out at the gas station, smoking. The professor's kid looks like a real loser."

"What can we do?"

"I'll think on it, push the pause button."

"I researched all morning. Didn't find too much yet. Oh, and the doctor called... the immunologist. He wants you to call him right away. He gave me his personal cell number. It's on the paper, on the counter. He said your test results are back, at least some of them."

"I'll call him after we eat."

"Call him now, Dan. Lunch won't be ready for twenty more minutes."

Dan picked up the paper and went into the living room. He sat on the couch, closed his eyes, and whispered a little prayer. He wanted to know, but he didn't want to know. He dialed the number.

"Hello."

"Hello, this is Dan Winslow. My wife said you called."

"Oh, yes, Dan, we need to talk. I would like you to come into my office first thing in the morning. Can you be here at eight?"

"Sure, I can be there. My wife said you have my results back."

"Yes, yes, yes... I put a rush on some of them, the ones I had suspicions about. The others aren't quite so critical. We can go over everything in the morning."

"Can you tell me what you know?"

"In the morning, Dan. This evening I'm going to do some research on your prognosis. Oh, by the way, would you happen to be a spelunker by chance?"

"You mean someone who crawls around in caves? No, not at all, why?"

"Do me a favor, Dan, and do a lot thinking tonight. Try to remember if you might have done any crawling around in confined spaces in the last six months."

"Okay, I'll think about it. See you in the morning." Dan sat back. *Strange—confined spaces, spelunking, what does any of this have to do with this cough? The garage! I cleaned out the garage... it was like a dark, old cave, but it was long before this cough started . . .*

He dozed off mid-thought.

Julie came in to check on him. She didn't wake him. She just watched him breathe. He sensed her. His eyes opened, looking tired. Julie sat next to him putting her hand on his thigh.

"Lunch is ready," Julie whispered. "What did the doctor say?"

"He'll tell me first thing in the morning. He's researching my prognosis this evening. He asked me if I was a spelunker—strange, huh?"

"A spelunker, what . . ."

"I don't know. The only thing I can think of coming close to spelunking is when I cleaned out the old garage. Remember how packed it was?"

"Come on, let's eat." Julie's hand pushed down on Dan's leg as she stood, so he grabbed it and pulled her into his chest for a hug.

"Remember yesterday when Klaare showed me the Bible I had given her? I can't stop thinking about it."

"You mentioned it yesterday. You're talking about Mr. McDonath being shot while he was coon hunting with Lee."

"The Bible just lists events, it doesn't give much detail. The first is the burning of the resort down in the Gorge, followed by Jim McKenzie's death, the accidental shooting of Harry McDonath, and then the doctor's body being found. Why would Louise McKenzie list those four events in her Bible? Is there some connection between them? Maybe I'll find out more from the church records."

"I don't know. Is there anything else in the Bible?"

"There are, but I can't make much sense of them. They're not in Louise's hand. They match the letters written by Jim McKenzie; he lists some Psalms, like Psalms 12, 55, and 59. Maybe you can make some sense of them."

"I'll have a look, but not right now—I'm too exhausted to think. I have to get up to go see Dr. Cohen. I already know what these guys want. They want to open the alley."

"Open the alley?"

"Yes, our driveway is what is known of as a paper alley. It is the single access to plots of land in the field and woods behind our house. Wentreck owns the land, purchased by his grandfather way back in the roaring twenties. I saw it when I was looking for information at the courthouse. Then I wasn't even aware of Val. Now it all makes sense. Maybe the battle over this alley involved Val's grandfather and Big Jim McKenzie."

Julie helped him to sit up. "I know about the paper alley, Mr. McDonath told me. It didn't seem to matter much at the time." They supported each other down the stairs. "You know, in the letter I read, Louise's maiden name was Haines."

"Interesting. The Haines family owned the land between us and the Gorge. According to the records, they sold it to Wentreck. Where are the boys and Tim?"

"Tim took them and Klaare into the city to shop for Christmas."

"Nice, just me and you?"

"And maybe for tomorrow night as well. Zane says there is a Christmas party tomorrow night at the professor's house."

"What? I thought they weren't believers."

"It's what I've been told. I guess they celebrate the holiday, though."

"They should, they get a nice break for it. Zane isn't going."

"He'll be upset."

"So?"

TWENTY

Dan arrived at Dr. Cohen's office twenty minutes early. It was now twenty after eight, and he was still sitting in the waiting room. The long drive and now this wait had given him too much time to think. Apprehension gripped him. He held in his cough as if doing so might change the doctor's findings. He tried to tell himself he wasn't sick—the whole thing was just his imagination or maybe the stress from the situation about the house. Dr. Cohen was going to tell him he just needed to rest. Spelunking? No, there was more to all this than just stress.

The nurse stepped into the waiting room. Dan tried to read her face. She had a concerned look about her as she announced his name, then asked him to follow her. Dan felt a burning in his nose, his breathing inadequate. Light-headed, he entered the examining room where the doctor sat waiting for him. He hadn't heard a word, and yet he already sensed what he was about to hear wouldn't be good. When he sat, it was as if his head had not lowered with his body, as if he were looking down at himself and the doctor.

"Good morning, Dan." The doctor's voice didn't hide a thing. This wasn't a good morning at all.

Dan nodded in response.

"Dan, I believe in being blunt... you are a sick man." The doctor pursed his lips and gathered his thoughts. "I don't understand how you are functioning. In all my years, I have never seen anyone as sick as you are without having them flat out on their back in a hospital. You are a naturally strong person. I think it has given you an advantage."

"What do I have, Doc?"

"You have two issues, both of which are dire. One is hypogammaglobulinemia, very serious, Dan. It's a serious weakening of the immune system, and I have never seen an immune system as devastated as yours, except maybe in an AIDS patient. I tested you for HIV; the results were negative. Your other problem is histoplasmosis." Dr. Cohen looked at Dan, waiting for questions.

"What does all this mean... and why did you ask about spelunking? I don't go into caves. Is it possible this is related to my military service?"

"Well, histoplasmosis is caused by a fungus in bat and bird droppings. Let's deal with this first. Climbing in caves in the Ohio River Valley is a major source, but it could also be from being in an old barn or shed. With a good healthy immune system, a person will normally suffer effects like those of a cold. However, with a compromised immune system this type of infection is deadly. Have you thought of any place you have been where there might have been bat guano?"

"I was thinking about it last night. Closest thing would be when I cleaned out an old garage; it had a lot of debris from bats and birds—but I did it months ago."

"Say three to six months ago?"

"Yeah, about right."

"How long have you been coughing and feeling sick?"

"About two months or so."

"So, would you say you started to get sick maybe three or four weeks after you cleaned out the garage?"

"Yes, that's right."

"The perfect incubation period. Dan, with your hypogammaglobulinemia I have to be honest with you . . ."

"Go ahead."

Dr. Cohen adjusted his glasses and rubbed his eyes. "Nothing is certain. Your case has me baffled. There is a possibility you have, in fact, a rare and powerful immune system. Even though it is beaten down so much, you still have been able to maintain relative health. The fact you can drive here and walk into my office says there is something going on we don't quite understand. Based on all the tests, you are dying. Based on the tests, I would say you might have five years. It's what the data tells me. Looking at you tells me there's something more to it than the data." He paused, giving Dan time to let it all sink in. "I'm going to give you an inhaler to help you breathe and ease your cough."

"What caused this hypo gamma mess?"

"Hypogammaglobulinemia."

"Isn't there anything you can do to get rid of this? Five years?" Dan felt faint; this was surreal. No, this wasn't what he expected. He expected bad news but not this.

"I'm sorry, Dan, but it's what the test results show. As far as what caused it, your immune deficiency could have been something you were born with. Then again, it could have been caused by your body being saturated with fungus or molds. As far as your military service, I would like you to think about it. Were you ever overexposed to radiation or involved with chemical weapons? You know the military—they may not have even told you. Make a list of where you've been stationed. The treatments I can do might not be wise at this point." Dr. Cohen spoke in a compassionate tone.

"You're not going to treat me? Well, I'm going to do my own research on this. I will look into my military duty stations. Offhand I can't think of any hazards, but you never know, like you said."

"Good idea. I like my patients to be involved. We need to be a team, Dan. I can't cure you. I can help you cure yourself. I'm going to do more research. Listen, with your permission and understanding I would like to start trending your condition. I want you to come in every week for blood tests. I would like to know your lifestyle. Keep a journal for me. I'm going to recommend a diet for you, with lots of natural, organic fruits and vegetables, along with oregano to battle fungus and infection. I'll print it out for you. You can get it from my receptionist. Keep track of everything you are eating and drinking. The treatments we can offer have extreme side effects. My plan is to hold off on those unless your condition deteriorates. It's your call, though."

"I'm eating lots of stuff for my immune system already, like onions, garlic, and mushrooms. I started researching it for myself a while back. I eat blueberries every day. Did you ever hear of noni juice? Well, I'm drinking it."

"Be careful, some of the claims made, like those made by noni juice producers, aren't documented. Noni won't hurt you, I just don't know if it will help. But as well as you are doing, I don't think we should panic. I'm afraid the treatments I can offer would be devastating. They could interfere with your natural recovery. If you start to fail, we can always hospitalize you. Do you agree? If not, I can have you admitted and we can start treatment today."

"No, I agree. Let's see how I do. I can't be hospitalized right now. I have a lot on my plate. I'm not even sure I have a job anymore."

"Dan, there should be one thing on your plate right now, your health. I'm sorry to be the one telling you this. Your situation is almost one hundred percent fatal. It's just a matter of time. I'll do all I can for you, but I would like to see how you do on your own. I'll give you something to mask the symptoms and make you more comfortable. Albuterol is an inhalant, it will help you breathe easier. You went to a neurologist about your vision, didn't you?"

"Yes, he said he thought it was an optic migraine."

"I would like to contact him. Could you leave his name out at the desk when you leave?"

"Yes, of course. Do you think my eye problem is related to this?"

"Yes, I'm afraid vision issues are a symptom. It may have been an optic migraine, maybe not. Let's just cover all the bases."

Dr. Cohen showed Dan how to use the inhaler. Then he went into greater depth about the effects on the body of the two ailments and warning signs to watch for. Five years kept ringing in Dan's head. In five years, how old would the boys be and how much quality of living would he have over those years? Dan tried to listen to the doctor, but he kept drifting off.

"Can you give me any other insights as to how you are managing your health other than diet?"

"Julie . . ." Dan stopped talking.

"Who is Julie?"

"Julie's my wife, she prays for me. She seems to always get what she prays for."

"Right... well, you tell her to keep praying; it just might be what's keeping you going. I've been a doctor for thirty years, and believe me, I have seen miracles. I've seen people pray, I mean really pray, and things have occurred I can't explain. Rest is important also; get lots of sleep. Avoid stress. Don't worry about your job." Dr. Cohen chewed on his pen.

On his way toward Stony Grove Dan mulled over everything Dr. Cohen had said. He also flashed back to his days in the military, searching for a possible answer. Nothing came to him. About three miles before Stony Grove, knowing Julie would not be out of class yet, Dan turned down the road leading to the bait store and Lee McDaniels. He was in no mood to be blown off by Lee. He wanted answers, answers to everything. He felt cursed and haunted. He wanted to know by whom. He felt a cough coming on and took a snort of the inhaler.

Lee sat on the front porch whittling and rocking. Dan slowed so as not to stir up any dust in the parking lot.

"Hi, Lee. How are things going? How's the missus?"

"Hi, Dan, everything is good. Missus was having an up day when I left her."

Dan stepped onto the porch, scratching Buck behind his ear, then dropped into the rocking chair next to Lee.

"Did you hear anything from them doctors you been seein'?"

Dan thought long and hard about how best to respond in order to get Lee to talk about things. Dan hadn't confided in anyone yet, so he wondered if it was proper to tell Lee before his own family. Julie and Dan had both witnessed several deaths over the course of their military careers. The prospects he now faced were more personal, but still his battle experiences had left him jaded about his own mortality. Julie wouldn't see it the same way. He didn't know the best way to break the news to her.

"I've just come from a specialist, an immunologist." Dan pondered another minute and decided just to let things rip. "I'm a dead man, Lee. The doctor thinks I have five years at most. He said I'm the sickest man he's ever seen not in a hospital."

"Do tell. You ain't contagious, are you?" Lee stopped whittling but continued to look at his piece of wood.

"No, I'm not contagious. I have a lung infection, an all-over infection—but my body isn't up to fighting it. I'm not sure what to tell my family. You're the first one I've told."

"Too bad, seems everything is dying lately." Lee looked sincerely grieved.

"Lee, I want you to know, Val Wentreck and Fred Black are making my last days miserable. Do these guys mean anything to you? I know you don't like talking, but can you give me any insights into either of them or both?"

Lee drew back his knife and tossed it in the direction of the porch post in front of him; it hit hard, sticking solidly into the oak.

"They ain't no friends of mine. They are the worst of the worst. I warned you, you didn't make any friends when you bought the house. I told you to sell and run. Now you want me to spill my guts and make myself a target?"

"I hate to tell you this, but you're an old man. You don't have much time left either. We're both in the same boat. You said your wife is dying. What are you afraid of, Lee?"

Lee didn't respond for quite some time, and Dan refrained from saying anything more. When Lee spoke, he stared at the floor.

"I guess I've been a coward all my life. I guess it's why I play the hillbilly. It's what you're getting at, isn't it? You're trying to tell me for once in my life to show some courage."

"Lee, I don't know if I'm saying all of that, but I guess what I am saying is causing you to think it. So, yes—I guess I am."

Lee stood up, struggling to pull his knife out of the oak post.

"Your driveway is a paper alley. It is the only access to property owned by Val Wentreck."

"I know. An attorney explained that to me. When we moved into the house, we found an old Bible and some letters. They belonged to the McKenzies, Big Jim and Louise."

"Don't say?"

"Yes, in the Bible there are handwritten notes about when Big Jim was found in the creek." Dan spoke in vague terms, wanting to let on like the notes contained more than they did. He wanted to prime the pump to get Lee's words flowing.

"I guess you know all you need to know then."

"The Bible also talks about Harry McDonath getting shot. It also mentions the old doctor having an accident in the Stony."

"Do tell."

Dan could tell by Lee's body language he had hit a nerve.

Lee stood up. "My wife doesn't have much longer. She always wanted me to take her away from here. She wanted me to show some ambition. Shake things up a mite. I guess I failed her. I failed myself."

"It's what I'm telling you, Lee. This is your chance. It won't change the past, but you can change the future."

"I'm going to fetch myself a bottle of water, would you like one?"

"Sure, that would be good."

Lee put his hand on Dan's shoulder as he walked toward the door to the store.

"It's going to be a long story, and it happened so long ago. Long ago, but the impact still lingers. Some things just never seem to go away. I guess—truth be known—I am a coward. Maybe it's the real reason John McKenzie turned his back on me. It didn't have nothing to do with my smarts. I've been hiding behind a lie so long I forgot what the truth was. Give me a minute, Dan."

When Lee returned, they sat for a while listening to the cicadas' song.

"You know, when I was in Latin America, the mariachi song 'La Cigarra' romanticized that those creatures sing until they die," Dan said.

"You been a lot of places, haven't you?"

"I've been all over the world."

"I've never been anywhere. I've lived my whole life in this valley. I never even went anywhere on vacation." Lee spit a swallow of water at a fly on the porch post. He hit it.

"Well, Lee, everyone is entitled to their choices."

"Yep, I just never went anywhere. Now I kinda wish I had, but it's too late. Well, let me make my first confession."

Dan and Lee rocked in sync, a gentle, easy motion.

Dan broke the silence. "I'm listening."

TWENTY-ONE

"We were just kids doing what kids in them days did. It was two years after we had found Jim McKenzie's body in the Stony. John had pretty much quit going with Harry and me on our night coon hunts, so he wasn't with us this night. After his daddy died, he stuck close to home. He studied a lot, but his focus was his mother. John was a good kid; Harry and me had turned a little wild. We weren't awful bad, just went off on our own a lot.

"Well, the night didn't have no moon. The woods were real dark. We didn't have no lights or nothing. We didn't even have a coon dog, but we took some powerful smellin' chicken fat with us to smear on the rocks along the Stony. We were too poor to be wasting food for bait. Harry smeared the rocks downstream of us, and we climbed on some boulders to watch for coons." Lee stared off as if he were envisioning the night. "Those woods were dark. You couldn't see much out beyond the rocks, in the hemlocks. The light color of the rocks below us would allow for us to see coon silhouettes, though. Harry and me sat smoking cigarettes. We talked in whispers about girls. We weren't real serious about getting a coon. It was more about being out by ourselves in the dark. Them were the best years of my life.

"There were a lot of strange things went on down in them woods. Most of it took place farther down than where we sat. Down toward where the old resort was. You know the fire is one of the biggest mysteries around these parts. You want to solve a mystery, that's the one. Like I said, it belonged to the Strattons, still does, matter of fact. Val Wentreck's grandfather, Dimitri, made moonshine in a little cave above the creek. It was prohibition, you know, so Dimitri was making good money. The Stratton and Haines boys ran the Gorge, though. They hated each other with a passion. It was kinda like the Hatfield and McCoy feud you hear talk about. Old Dimitri played them one against the other and got all of them drunk. If you ask me, it was them Haines boys what set the fire at the resort."

Lee shifted in his chair, glancing at Dan. "At the time, the parcel of land Val owns—the one he needs the paper alley for—was Haines property. They owned a lot of these hills around here. The family was an old loggin' family. They had a start with a six-hundred-acre Revolutionary War land grant. Same as the Strattons, both original settlers. Folks say their hatred goes all the way back to the two veterans who first laid claim to the grants. Well, it weren't too long after the fire the Haines family up and sold Dimitri the land. They sold it real cheap; kinda makes you wonder if there weren't more to the reason for sellin' than they were just tired of ownin' it. I always thought ole Dimitri had the goods on the Haines family. It was just afore us boys found poor Jim McKenzie . . ." Lee paused as if he had just put a couple of thoughts together he hadn't ever put together before. He just sat and stared, and Dan let him go. He figured Lee needed to dust off old thoughts.

"The resort was more speakeasy than anything else. Lots of gangsters from Louisville and Lexington came for booze, gambling, and women. Like I told you before, I was too young to understand it. When it burned, I was just learnin' to stretch my legs and wander, I recollect. Heard plenty of talk about it around the dinner table, though. Mother said the valley was flowin' in sin. My old man seemed a little more tolerant of it. I wonder if he didn't partake in it a little himself . . ." Lee swatted at the gnats hovering near his face. "To be truthful I knowed he did. I also knowed it was why we were the poorest family in these parts. If'n I'm going to be honest with you, I might just as well be honest with myself. I can't be too hard on the old man when I ain't measured up much better. We both suffered from the same curse."

"Lee, this is all pretty incredible. What a history."

"Don't mean much 'cept to kin. Evil has its way. You don't have to be directly involved with it to be used by it. I consider myself passively evil. I have struggled with it most of my life. I'm guilty, tried, and convicted by my peers, my punishment self-imposed. I'm a passive liar to boot."

"I don't understand—maybe you're being too hard on yourself."

"I ain't being as hard on me as what God has planned for me."

"Ask forgiveness. I don't know what you did, but if you admit to it and ask forgiveness, all will be forgiven. You don't need to confess to me, do it in private... just you and God."

"Truth be known, talkin' like this is making me feel better." Lee looked around. "Maybe God's listenin'."

"He is."

"Well, I got things on my mind I ain't never spoken, things what need to be in the light. I'm an old man. You said it right, if I don't show a little courage now, it ain't never going to happen. I know this—evil has its way. Evil don't mind if you're an innocent witness to its doings, it'll leave you alone and maybe even reward you for your silence, but if you lash out and work against it, it will surely strike at you. If I had spoken back then, I might have been a hero. Speakin' now, I'm using the voice of a coward. All the same, evil won't be takin' kindly to me for what I say."

"Do the right thing... do what's best for you." Dan took a long drink of water to suppress his cough reflex.

The wind swirled a dust cone across the parking lot, while Lee apparently mulled over his thoughts and searched for courage.

"The song says, we are all just dust in the wind. When you reach my age, you begin to realize it. Well, Dan—here goes . . .

"Like I said, we were waitin' for coons to get a whiff of chicken fat, smokin' and jokin'. We was all of fourteen, just pups. There was a crack in the hemlocks. Being in the military, maybe you've experienced the zip of lead cutting through air. When you hear it, you know it's close."

"Yes, I know the sound. It's a sickening sound, the sound of terror."

"Yep, and you don't know what to do. Harry and I just froze for a split second, and then the second crack sounded. I saw the flash on that one. Next thing I know'd, Harry tumbled off the boulder onto chicken-fat-smeared rocks below us. He never flinched after he landed. I rolled myself around the back side of the boulder as I listened to crack after crack from the hemlocks. I heard lead cutting the air and pinging off the rocks around me. I wanted to holler to tell them we wasn't aggressive, but I knew it wouldn't gain me nothin', so I just lay there for the longest time listenin'. I didn't have my rifle because I dropped it in the initial commotion. It fell to the ground next to Harry. I felt like a coon caught in the chicken coop. I ain't ashamed to tell ya, I wet my pants."

Lee stood up to pace the porch. "Pretty soon the shootin' stopped, but the dark silence terrorized me even more. I know'd someone was out there. It was the next shot, the one what never came, that scared me the most. Someone wanted us dead. I couldn't bring myself to even look over the rock to see if anyone was approachin'. All I could picture was a piece of lead shattering my skull. I wasn't comfortable, so I tried to shift my body around. That's when I realized my leg had jammed in a crevasse. I was a trapped coon just waitin' to be finished off. I folded my arms over my head. It seemed like hours, but I guess it was just minutes when I heard voices.

"There was an argument going on between at least four men. It was drunk talk, tough talk, and they sounded mean. Mean enough to kill each other, so I knew it was hopeless to try to reason with them. I could make out one of them was using a touch of reason, while the others switched between curse words and laughter. The one of reason seemed to be of authority, though, because when he spoke the others went silent. The best I could make out was three of them had got themselves drunken mean and wanted to kill somethin'. The somethin' they came across to kill just happened to be Harry and me. Not because we were a threat or the fact they had any particular reason to do it, it was just the thrill of bein' mean. There are those what takes pleasure in beating a woman or a child. It don't have to be reasonable at all. I seen people kick dogs as sweet as old Buck here.

"My money was on the voice of reason I could hear in the dark. He tried to convince them there weren't no need to pursue no more killin'. His thought was to call it a huntin' accident. One shot fired by mistake killed another coon hunter. Everybody would feel bad and life would go on." Lee stopped his pacing. "The others, drunk beyond reason, wanted to eliminate witnesses and bury the bodies so as to never be found. The voices were getting clearer and closer. My life depended on a decision bein' made afore their arrival at my trap. Their killin' plan sounded too reasonable for me. I thought I was going to throw up, and my head pounded with the sound of my heart. I curled in a fetal position with my eyes closed. I didn't want to see what was coming. I was afraid if I saw their faces, they'd figure killin' me was the only option. I never prayed." Lee looked hard at Dan. "Ya hear me? I never prayed. I think that is what saved me. I think evil witnessed a blackness in my heart, my potential. Looking back, I know I had few options. Prayin' should have been one. I wouldn't be talkin' to you now, but except somethin' spared me to live this wretched life I have lived. It weren't God who saved me, and I didn't ask him either."

He heaved a regretful sigh. "The voices stopped down at the bottom of the boulder where Harry lay—and I didn't know if he was alive or dead. I could barely hear them. After a time, the one with reason announce Harry wasn't dead. He was out cold from the fall. In none too good a shape, but breathin'. If they killed us and buried us, they would spend the rest of their lives worryin' 'bout the bodies being found. One bullet could go down as an accident, the man of reason said. One of the drunks countered with there's another one on the loose, there had been two of them sitting on the rocks." Lee slumped down in his rocker again. "The man of reason argued a boy's word against four grown men wouldn't hold water. He said, 'We're Strattons. Ain't nobody going to give us any trouble in these parts. We don't kill kids, our own or nobody else's.' Strattons! I thought, must be the old man and his boys. One of the drunken ones got real rowdy 'bout this time. He said he didn't mind killin' the offspring of vermin. Said he'd kill his own if they didn't mind him. Let's just hold their heads in the Stony like Dimitri did... He was in midsentence when I heard flesh on flesh, and he went silent. He must have been knocked out cold because the man of reason told the other two drunks to drag their brother home. I heard them draggin' him—sounded like it was quite a struggle for them. Afterwards, there was just silence. The peepers even started back up with their chirping. I heard the hoot of an owl off in the hemlocks. I know'd I was going to live, and I hadn't prayed for it.

"I felt it was safe to move, so I stirred a bit. The night air smelled good when I lifted my head out of being buried under my arms. I looked straight up toward the sliver of sky the rocky creek bed provided in the dark forest canopy—a place were no trees growed. Black clouds raced across the void. From the corner of my eye I caught a red glow, the end of a cigarette. My eyes widened as I adjusted for a better look. It was the silhouette of a man. I couldn't make out the features in his face, but I knew it was old man Stratton. He had been a sittin' and studyin' on me for a spell without me knowin'. It gave me a bad case of the shivers, I'll tell ya.

"He told me he was glad I hadn't run off too far because he wanted to have a talk with me. He asked me if I had been shot. I told him I had not, but I was stuck in the rocks. He asked me if I had heard them talking, which I acknowledged. He said he was glad I had, but he wanted to stress some of the finer points with me. First, he wanted me to answer his questions. 'Answer them the right way, boy,' he said. He asked if I knew who he was. I said no. He asked me if I know'd how many of them there were. I said no. He asked me how many shots I heard fired. I said one. He asked me how Harry got hurt. Just a stray shot from another hunter, I said. He told me I was a good boy as he stood up. He told me his sons were good boys too when they ain't liquored up. He said he had come down to find his boys and reached them just as the shooting had started. The sound of gunfire guided him.

"That was when he stepped forward and climbed down the boulder to get real close to me. He pulled out his bowie knife—holding it a millimeter from my throat. It's when my bowels let loose. I thought we had an understanding, but then nothin' ain't never a sure thing when dealing with mentally unstable individuals, such as them Strattons. He looked right into my eyes and talked real slow and quiet-like, 'Don't ya ever let me hear you let out a whisper of this night's truthful events, or I'll kill your momma, daddy, and your dog. Killin' you will take days. You will beg me to finish you off. Now, if you keep quiet, I'll see to it my family takes care of ya... got it, boy?' It's what he told me, honest injun. It's when I made a pact with the devil hisself." Lee scuffed the heel of one boot along the floor.

"Lee, I can't imagine it. I've been in some tight spots, but at that age to suffer like that, I can't imagine it."

"Well, he just left me there with my leg all stuck and such. His partin' words were, 'I'm gonna leave ya the way I found ya. I don't know if the other boy's going to live, but he won't remember nothing but what ya tell him. The town will be out lookin'. I might even be on the search. It'll give strength to your story if they find ya just like ya are. I'll be watching and listening, boy. Don't think I won't be quick dispatching those folks of yours and snatching ya should I hear the wrong thing.' Then he put away his knife and walked off into the dark."

"So cold, he didn't help you at all?"

"He wanted me to know how cold he could be. His kids weren't all crazy for no reason. They were his kids, for sure. They were in their early twenties when all this happened. Eventually, them boys learned to tame their crazies just like the old man. They went on to be real successful at business, showin' a touch of their crazy side when it was needed.

"Well, I lay wedged in them rocks until around noon. Harry never did stir. Some men from the fire department searched for us at our moms' requests. They carried Harry out on a stretcher, but I was good enough to walk out. Harry was unconscious for two more days. The lead had shattered both of the bones in his forearm. The new doctor in town had no choice back then but to amputate. I ain't never went straight about it with Harry. John called me on it, he wasn't a believer in the stray bullet theory, but he never made no trouble about it. Only called me out on it in private. Afterwards he seemed to have no use for me, and I have always had trouble looking Harry in the eye. I try to act friendly when I see him on occasion, but to this day I feel naked in his company. I'm best off livin' down here below the Gorge with my woman. Never had no kids, amen." He glanced upward. "Spent my time drunk most days. Sometimes I think I've spent my whole life wedged in a rock just awaitin' to be rescued. The Strattons took care of me all right, kept me right close to them."

"Lee, I can't tell you how sorry I feel about all this. Like you said, you were just a kid."

Two tears rolled down Lee's cheeks and were gone. When Dan looked at him again, the color was also gone from his face. It was as if his lifeblood had been in those tears. Dan scratched Buck behind his ear. No one spoke for a long time as they sat and rocked, both thinking about the story of Harry McDonath losing his arm. Dan wanted to ask Lee more questions, but he knew Lee was spent.

Dan looked at his watch. Julie's class would be letting out. There were no good-byes; Dan just stood and rested his hand on Lee's shoulder, then walked away. Halfway to his car he stopped to look back at Lee, who had stood and was leaning against a porch post.

Dan gave Lee a nod. As he got in his car, he offered Lee a slight wave, which Lee returned. On the drive to town, Dan thought about hauntings, spirits, and evil. Sure, people speak of haunted houses and haunted places, but Dan remembered what his brother had said about being haunted by the women he loved; it was spoken in jest but . . .

TWENTY-TWO

Julie and Dan arrived home at the same time. They parked in the street in front of the house. Dan put his arm around Julie as they walked onto the front porch. It wasn't lost on Julie: Dan hadn't coughed or cleared his throat. They sat on the porch swing holding hands.

"What did the doctor say?"

"He said a lot of stuff."

"Can we be a little more specific? I noticed you're not coughing."

Dan had learned in battle not to think so much about what might happen and concentrate on what *is* happening. Speculation could also be a distraction. It needed to be considered, but without emotion.

"No, I used an inhaler he gave me. It lasts a couple of hours. It's nice to have a little relief from my symptoms. He says he's not going to treat my condition right away. I have a couple of serious problems."

Julie stared into Dan's eyes. "What kind of problems?"

"Well, I have a compromised immune system, he used a fancy word. Basically, it means my immune system is down, down real low. He said he wants to monitor me, take blood tests over time to see which direction it's heading. If it goes lower, he'll begin treatment. If it perks up, he'll just keep monitoring me."

"What causes it?"

"He can't pin it down just yet. It's not contagious. He said it could be faulty from birth or some environmental issue I've encountered, like a chemical or nuclear exposure. He wants me to think back over my life and list any potential hazards, you know like in the military. I'm not thinking well today; maybe you can do a little thinking for me."

"What other issue do you have?"

"Fungus, I'm infected with a fungus found in bird and bat guano. I think it's from when I cleaned out the garage."

"Oh great. I am so sorry. Buying this house has been a nightmare. It's my fault, all of this. I am so sorry." Julie stood up to pace the porch. As she came back near the swing, Dan stood to pull her into a hug.

"Blame is not what we need. I could blame a whole chain of things bringing us to this point. It is not your fault, Julie. What I need from you is just love, kindness, and caring—but guilt will ruin it. I don't want guilt motivating you; I want love."

"Oh, Dan, I'm still sorry. So how is he going to treat this fungal infection?"

"He's not, he says my immune system needs to battle it. But oregano oil helps kill fungus."

"But your immune system isn't healthy."

"No, it's not, it contributes to the problem. If my immunity doesn't recover, then I don't."

"You don't—"

"I'm going to build my immunity, Julie."

"Dan, if something happens to you . . ."

"One day at time. I'm here right now... don't speculate. The good news in all this is, according to the numbers I should already be flat out in a hospital, dying. But I'm not and Dr. Cohen says he doesn't understand it. He said the truth is what it is. And it impacts us; we don't impact it. We don't have to know the truth for it to be so. He says something unknown is keeping me going. I told him about your prayers and my diet. He thought both were excellent. He wants me to keep a log of what I eat."

"I'll double down on the prayers—no, triple down."

"Thanks. I love you, and your prayers."

"Love you. Don't you dare leave me."

Dan collapsed back onto the porch swing. He wanted to get better for Julie. He couldn't bear to see her blaming herself for his illness. There was an uneasy tension in the air. Julie pulled a bundle of Christmas cards out of the letter box mounted by the front door. She handed them to Dan and massaged his shoulders as he opened them. Aunts, cousins, friends—then one from his employer. He dropped his hands to his lap after just a quick read.

"I've been terminated for excessive leave." *Evil never takes a break.*

"Oh... what about health insurance?"

"We can go on Cobra, but we'll have to pay for it."

Then the front door opened. It was Zane.

"Where do you think you're going?"

"I'm going to the Christmas party."

"I told you, you can't go."

"I won't let you label me a nerd, Dad. Everybody is going."

"You're not."

Zane took a couple of steps, but Dan grabbed him by the arm.

"Son, don't make this ugly."

"I'm old enough to make my own choices. You and Mom want me to stay a baby. I don't believe in the same things you do."

Dan held back. He remembered the feelings he had as a teen, the rebellion.

"These people aren't the type to be real friends. I don't believe you, Zane. In the long haul, you'll admit to yourself what your mother and I believe is right. You are just trying to break the strings. You go to your party, but keep your head straight. Be honest with yourself. I think you'll conclude these are not your type of people."

Dan looked at Julie. He wanted some sort of acknowledgment or approval of how he handled the situation. Her lips tight, she nodded. Dan let go of Zane's arm. Zane stepped from the porch without another word. He walked to the street, then started to run. He ran until he was out of sight.

Julie sighed. "Our boys are growing up."

Dan stared down the road. "We can't just tell them the ways of the world; we're going to have to let them feel the pain."

"It scares me."

"Me too."

Dan sat back down on the swing beside Julie.

"I hear we might have a white Christmas." As Julie rubbed Dan's back, he leaned forward.

"Nice."

"Some of the neighbors want to have a meeting this evening. Do you feel up to it?"

"Sure. It's not what I would like to do, but we need to develop a plan. There is nothing to be gained by putting it off. What the heck, let's call it a Christmas party."

"My thoughts exactly. I'll make a call. We have a call chain set up. I'll just be a minute. Are you staying out here? It's so nice out, I would like you to."

"I'll grab the old Bible. We can go over the Psalms listed in the notes; let's try to make some sense out of them."

Dan leaned back in the swing, keeping an eye on the street. The swing faced the Fred Black house. He watched as Fred carried painting supplies from his pickup truck to the house. Fred glanced at him, but it was quick. *Maggot*, Dan thought as he watched a black Escalade stop behind Fred's truck. Fred leaned close to the open driver's window. As Fred stood at the window, he made quick glances at the driveway and Dan's house, nodding in acknowledgment with whatever the driver was telling him. Fred watched the Escalade ease away, his hands on his hips. By the time Julie came back to the porch with the Bible, Fred had withdrawn into his house.

Julie carried an energetic smile and the Bible as she stepped back onto the porch. The yard brightened as a gap in the clouds allowed the sun to fill the space. She placed the Bible on the swing, then resumed rubbing Dan's back and shoulders. He had no complaints.

"Look at Psalm 12."

He paged to Psalm 12. He read it to himself. Then he read it aloud and said, "The troubles we face are nothing new. Man has not learned a thing in two thousand years."

"Is it perfect or what? I'm going to start the meeting with it tonight."

"This chapter was marked as important back in the nineteen twenties. This town hasn't changed much over the years. I guess people are people, in all times. Everyone lies to his neighbor, and lips often speak with deception. We need God on our side. This place is overrun with evil." Julie was paraphrasing the words aloud.

"We need all the help we can get. This is a battle, and I'm afraid there will be casualties and collateral damage."

"Now you're talking like the military man I fell in love with."

"Just remember, I'm already wounded. I'm beginning to believe my issues have been orchestrated by some power other than God. Why else do my numbers say I'm dying and yet my spirit says no? What's the missing factor?"

"Dan, look at Psalm 59:6. It talks about snarling like dogs, returning in the evening to prowl the town. This might be in reference to whoever used to hang out down in the Gorge. What went on down there?"

"I stopped to see Lee after seeing the doctor. He told me some things about the Strattons, Harry, and the old town doctor. Let me tell you . . ."

###

Representatives of twelve neighborhood households gathered in the evening, two dozen in all. Chairs were moved from the kitchen and dining room into the living room, forming a large circle. Christmas music played in the background. Julie opened the meeting with a psalm. There were no objections. She read

Psalm 12, and everyone just looked at each other, stunned. After a moment of silent gazing, Julie made an announcement. "Coffee and hot water for tea are on the kitchen counter, along with plenty of cups. Help yourselves whenever you'd like."

"Hi, everyone, for those of you we haven't met, I'm Dan Winslow and this is my wife, Julie. I know we all *feel* like we might know each other, but I don't think we should take it for granted. So if you don't mind, could we all take a turn and introduce ourselves? Just tell us your name and what street you live on."

Each member of the gathering took their turn to introduce themselves. The meeting continued with the selection of someone to take minutes. The first order of business was to define the group's purpose, and it was agreed their main initiative would be to work toward transparency in the local government and maintaining the values of their properties. Under rules of engagement, it was considered wise to refrain from undocumented accusations or character attacks at council meetings and to ask well thought-out questions, support each other's needs, and help research historical references. They planned to prepare evidence for council, such as photos of extensive litter and neglect in rental property yards. When a homeowner felt the need for emotional support during confrontations with students, others in the group would respond to calls for help.

There was little disagreement as to the needs and objectives as stated. The meeting lasted well over an hour and the next meeting was scheduled for the first Tuesday evening of the next month, after the holidays. Julie finished the meeting by reading Psalm 55:23. Half the group departed at the end of the meeting; half stayed to socialize and drink coffee. Julie walked around with a tray, offering raw chocolate energy bites.

"Dan, your house is beautiful. I can't believe you've accomplished all of this rehabilitation."

"Thanks... I believe you said your name was Frank?" Dan extended his hand.

"Right, Frank Riley. We moved here about three years ago. We love our house, but the students are brutal. Every day I'm picking up beer cans. It ticks me off—the lack of respect these clowns have for other people's property. I work construction—it's demanding work I do to pay for my place—and some little jerk tosses an empty beer bottle onto my grass as if it's a trash can. No respect—these kids should be living on campus."

"I heard a rumor," a woman interjected, speaking from behind Dan.

"Lynn, right?"

"Yes, there is a rumor about an investigation going on. I work at the university. Talk has it, heads are going to roll as high up as the university president. It seems certain people have come under the influence of these slumlords. It's been going on for years. Seems they influence them to refuse building funds for new dormitories. The crap is going to hit the proverbial fan. If it turns out to be true, this little group may not even be necessary."

"Great news. You should have said something during the meeting." Frank took a sip of coffee.

"I shouldn't even have said it now, but I'm real excited about it, and what the heck, it's time for a change, not just in this town but at the university. Everybody who works there isn't crooked, but there are some key positions in need of a shake-up. I'm glad it's planned."

Dan smiled. "I wonder what caused the idea for a shake-up. I would like to think it came about as an honorable step toward correcting a problem, but knowing how politicians are, it might just be a regime change. Big contractors might have paid off the right people to get them to kick out capital for building new dorms. The local media will play it out, exposing corruption."

Everyone within earshot smirked.

One by one the stragglers departed, and as the door closed on the last one, Dan flipped off his shoes and flopped onto the couch with a sigh. Julie sat at the end of the couch, picked up his feet, and started massaging them.

"Let's clean up in the morning."

"No argument from me."

Dan closed his eyes as Julie's touch worked magic. His breathing eased. He could feel himself drifting off. He yawned, picked up his inhaler, took a quick hit. It would be hours before he would cough. He just wanted to sleep, right here on the couch. The front door latch clicked; then the door burst open. Zane ran across the living room and bounced upstairs, unaware his parents were sitting on the couch. They heard the attic door close.

"He's home early. It didn't look like he was coming from a good time."

"Should we go talk to him?"

"No, we'll see him in the morning. I'm not feeling well enough. I need to chill out."

Dan closed his eyes as Julie continued to rub his feet. He drifted off into sleep. Julie's thoughts switched from Zane to the house and then to the town; when her mind settled, she mulled over the Psalms. They offered her peace, reassuring her that their experience was not unique in the eyes of the Lord. She relaxed.

Suddenly there was a knock on the front door.

Dan opened his eyes. "Who could that be?"

"I'll get it."

"No, Julie, its late—let me get it."

Dan staggered to the door and drew back the curtain covering the ornate window of the door. It was Officer Jack Monroe, back to the door, scanning the property before him. He was in uniform, though Dan could see his personal car parked at the curb. *He must be off duty*, Dan thought. Jack didn't notice Dan peeking through the window.

Dan opened the door.

"Officer Monroe, good evening, it's awful late. What can I do for you?"

Monroe turned to face Dan.

"May I step in, Mr. Winslow?"

"Certainly, call me Dan." Dan held out his hand. Jack Monroe gave a firm handshake.

"This isn't an official visit."

"It seems like you do a lot of unofficial work. I wanted to thank you for helping us with the tenant across the street."

Jack Monroe just nodded and pursed his lips.

"I just came to warn you. I hear a lot of ugly talk around the Borough Building about you. It might be wise to watch your step. Organizing the neighbors is making some people feel uneasy."

"I'm not organizing anybody. I'm just another one of the neighbors. These people are organizing themselves."

"I didn't come to argue the point, just to tell you, *you* are the focus. You are the one singled out as the troublemaker. True or not, you have the target on your back. I just wanted to tell you to watch your step... and your back. This isn't a threat from me, I'm on your side."

"I appreciate your concern, Jack, thanks."

"Well, you didn't hear it from me. This visit never happened. I've got a family to support, but I just can't sit back while... well, we all know what this town is like... is your son home?"

"You mean Zane?"

"Yes... I don't want to alarm you, but the campus police raided a party. They called the state police for backup. I went off duty just as it came across the radio."

"Zane came home about twenty minutes ago."

"Good, he seems like a nice kid, but I've seen him with some of the town's worst. Just want you to know. Initial reports are it was a drug bust. I think public nudity brought attention to the event. These kids... well, I'm glad your son wasn't involved."

"Thanks, Jack, thanks for keeping us informed."

Jack walked out to his car.

"Dan, what do you think?"

"I think Jack is a good man."

"I mean about you being a target?"

"It doesn't scare me for myself, but it does scare me for you and the boys."

"Do you think Zane was at the party?"

"Yes, I do. I also think he left before it got raided. I think he made a wise choice in leaving."

"We'll talk to him in the morning. Let's get some sleep."

TWENTY-THREE

Dan descended the stairs to the smell of coffee and toast. Tim sat at the counter talking to Julie. The boys were still in bed. "What brings my favorite, and only, brother here this fine morning?"

"Hey, brother. Julie called me and said you needed some help."

Dan gave Julie a quick questioning look. She just raised her eyebrows and rolled her eyes.

"Anytime is good, Tim. Umm, yeah, I was hoping you could help us with Zane. He needs to hear things about life, but not from us. We just wanted to talk with you about it while the boys are still asleep. Later or maybe on Christmas you can do us the favor."

Dan looked at Julie with a "was that right?" kind of look. She responded with a wink.

"Sure thing, what's it about?"

"Partying and hanging with a bad crowd. He has to learn in his own way, but hearing it from you might carry enough weight, he may avoid some of the pain we went through."

"No problem, I'm looking forward to Christmas. You could have just asked me this on the phone."

"We haven't seen enough of you since you went to the hotel. I wanted to make you a good breakfast in exchange for your help."

"Thanks, Julie, and I'm sorry about not stopping by more."

Julie heard Klaare stirring in the basement. She walked over and tapped on the basement door.

"Klaare, would you like to come up for breakfast?"

"Sure, give me a minute."

Julie winked at Dan.

"Hey, I better get out of your hair," Tim said. "I'm driving to Louisville this morning. I better get an early start."

"I just came downstairs. You stick around and visit with me a minute. You know I'm not a well man."

Tim accepted another cup of coffee. The two brothers drifted into the dining room. As they sat down, Klaare opened the basement door. Dan watched Tim's eyes glance toward the kitchen.

"She's a good kid, Tim," Dan whispered.

Tim shook his head. He took a sip of coffee. In the kitchen Julie and Klaare spoke in whispers. Julie came into the dining room first carrying plates and silverware. Klaare followed behind with dishes of scrambled eggs, fruit, and toast. As she entered the room and her eyes caught Tim's, they both looked away. Klaare's inexperience made her shy. Tim's excuse was in his wounds.

This is going to take work, Julie thought.

"What are you going to Louisville for?" Julie asked as she fetched a carafe of coffee.

"I have to stop at an attorney's office to sign some final papers. It's going to take longer to drive there and back than the appointment itself will take. I wanted to do a digital signing, but there are a couple of items I need to clarify."

"If you would like company, Klaare is on Christmas break. I'll bet she would love to ride along. It sure would beat sitting in our basement."

"Oh, Ms. Julie, I wouldn't want to impose . . ."

"It won't be exciting. It'll be a long, boring ride."

"It doesn't have to be. It's Christmas season, the city is decorated, and there are some nice places to eat. Go look at Christmas displays."

Dan gave Julie a tap on her leg with his shoeless foot. There was a nervous silence as everybody filled their plates and began to eat. Tim looked at Klaare, catching her eyes looking at him.

"Would you like to go with me?" Tim asked.

"If you don't mind, yes, but I don't want you to feel you have to entertain me."

Julie kicked Dan under the table, a little harder than he had tapped her. The talk lightened up after the initial tension subsided. Tim managed to tell a couple of travel anecdotes. Having Tim around provided comfort for both Dan and Julie. Klaare and Tim helped clean up the dishes before they headed for Louisville.

Dan sighed. "You are too much."

"What?"

"You know what, women just can't stand to see a man unattached."

"It's just not natural."

Trent bounced into the kitchen. He hugged his mom, gave her a kiss on the cheek, and said good morning to his dad.

"Have you seen any signs of your brother?"

"No, Dad, he's still in bed, covers over his head. We're all better off with him hiding out."

"Trent! Not nice."

"*He's* not nice. I hope I don't end up like him in a couple of years."

"I'm going up to see him."

"Are you sure you want to?"

Dan went upstairs, tapped on Zane's door, then went on in.

"Are you awake, son?"

A growl came from under the covers. The pillow was positioned over his head.

"How was the party last night?"

No noise this time. No movement under the covers. Dan reached down, removing the pillow covering Zane's head. When Zane rolled his head around, his eyes looked yellow and sick. His skin was pale.

"Ah, Dad . . ."

"Do you have anything to confess?"

"No... it was stupid. I left early."

"Did you do any drugs?"

"No... I don't use drugs. The other guys were smoking weed, and when I said I didn't want to, they made fun of me. Then they brought out some white dust. The girls were acting wild. I could tell it was going to get ugly fast."

"Is this the whole truth?"

"Yep... you were right. They aren't friends. They were going to use those girls. Before the girls showed up, they joked about them. I'm thinking before I showed up, they joked about me."

"It's tough finding out about these kinds of things. Don't take it too hard. We all go through it. Uncle Tim and I took our turn. Listen, you aren't going to find many people who care about you the way your parents do. Someday you may find a girl who does, and if you do, consider yourself lucky."

Zane rolled back over, covering his head with his pillow again.

"I'll leave you alone... oh, and the party got busted." Dan left the room.

When he reentered the kitchen, Julie stood at the stove making an omelet for Trent. Dan gave her a hug and whispered in her ear.

"I think Zane is going to be all right, and we're going to have a beautiful Christmas. Love you."

Julie smiled. "Will you help me wrap gifts?"

"You bet."

Dan poured a cup of coffee and went to sit with Trent. As Julie brought Trent his breakfast, Zane walked into the kitchen. He received a pleasant smile and a whispered good morning. No confrontation. He poured some orange juice and sat with the others.

"Can I fix you anything?"

"No hurry. Mom, I'm sorry for the way I've been acting."

Julie went to him and hugged him. She kissed him on the forehead.

"I love you." She was too choked up to say any more.

"Me too."

"I'll scramble you some eggs."

“Nice... and some toast?”
“You bet. You sound like your father.”
Zane gave his dad an approving glance.

TWENTY-FOUR

Christmas Eve day it snowed with huge, exaggerated flakes. Trent and Zane were running around the front yard throwing snowballs at each other as Uncle Tim pulled up. Tim couldn't get out of his car fast enough. He joined in the battle, grabbing Zane, wrestling him to the ground, and rubbing a handful of snow in his face. Trent stuffed a handful of cold snow down the back of Tim's neck.

The temperature was a mild thirty. Mild enough so the activity made them all sweat. Dan and Julie walked onto the porch to watch the circus. Christmas music followed them out the open door.

"Come on, Dan, give me a hand. Your boys are getting the best of me."

"Sorry, brother, I'm the walking wounded. I can't risk it. Maybe Julie will help."

Julie ran into the yard, scooping up snow to make a snowball, but it broke apart soon after leaving her glove. She didn't pack them tightly enough. Zane hit her square in the back with a big glob, and Tim grabbed him again to shove snow down the front of his shirt. The play kept time with the Christmas music until Klaare came around the side of the house and joined the fray.

For a minute everyone stopped, until Klaare tossed her ready-made snowball at Tim, hitting him squarely on the forehead. The aim was good, but the snowball was soft. They all laughed as the snow melted and ran down Tim's face, like a whipped cream pie.

The game was over; Klaare had won. Julie and the boys retreated to the porch swing to sit with Dan. Klaare wiped Tim's face.

"Anybody for some hot spiced cider?"

It was unanimous. Julie went in the house to fetch it. Dan soon followed to give her a hand. They sipped their cider as Bing Crosby sang "White Christmas." The boys decided to go into the house. The adults left for a walk on the deserted streets of town. With college on winter break most of the houses were dark and empty. It was as if these four were the last people on Earth. Dan and Julie lagged far behind, giving Tim and Klaare space. They walked for about forty-five minutes before heading for home. A black Escalade slowed as it passed them. Val Wentreck.

"What a miserable . . ."

"Dan, think happy thoughts. Don't let seeing him ruin our Christmas."

"Sorry, Julie, you're right. Still, he turns my stomach."

"I get it—but let it go. Feel sorry for him instead."

The Escalade disappeared, and Dan's blood pressure returned to normal. He put his arm around Julie and coughed.

When they opened the front door, the smell of Julie's cooking, the warmth of the house, and the sound of Christmas music snagged every sense. It was like walking into a dream. The boys were sitting on the floor near the tree as they had done every year since they could crawl.

"Geesh, this is a scene out of *It's a Wonderful Life*," Tim joked.

"Oh, Julie, it smells so wonderful, can I help you in the kitchen?"

"Sure, Klaare, I would love it."

Dan brought more hot cider for the guys. They played Scrabble, making up silly words and laughing. The Christmas mood touched them all. Julie gave the boys their gifts as the hour approached midnight. It was their tradition to open the gifts on Christmas Eve so they could sleep later in the morning. The boys took their time opening one gift at a time. Most of the gifts were practical, such as school clothes. Dan gave Julie a necklace. Julie gave Dan a fishing rod and tackle. Klaare and Tim gave each other looks.

Tim headed back to his hotel as soon as the gift opening was complete. Klaare went to the basement, and the Winslow family retired to the second floor. The house became quiet. The huge snowflakes continued to fall outside.

###

Christmas Day was perfect. Everyone, including Klaare, went on a road trip to Grandma's gathering. It was an open house affair, welcoming about forty relatives over the course of the day. Everyone was charmed by Klaare.

In the days following and leading up to New Year's Eve, Tim became a regular visitor. He either hung out with Dan or was downstairs with Klaare. Early in the afternoon on New Year's Eve, Tim and Dan sat in the dining room enjoying a cup of coffee.

"I'm wondering what you're going to do about your job, brother."

"Yeah, Happy New Year, huh?"

"Not to worry. I got your back. I can pay off your mortgage or whatever it takes."

"I appreciate the offer. I don't want your help, but it's nice to know it's there. I don't know at this point what I'm going to do or be able to do."

"Well, just say the word."

"Thanks."

The two men sat in comfortable silence.

New Year's Eve came and went without much fanfare. The New Year slid in peacefully. The six of them played board games and listened to music, waiting for the ball drop on a muted TV. About half past midnight, Tim heard his cell phone chirp, a text. As Tim read the message, the color left his face. He turned off his phone, and everyone sensed his disturbance. He heaved himself to his feet, excusing himself. Klaare stood with him and walked him to the door. He whispered in her ear, then kissed her cheek. Dan and Julie sat speechless. This was how their year turned from one to the next. It would be two weeks before anyone saw or heard from Tim.

TWENTY-FIVE

Dan tried to start the year off with a positive attitude, in spite of Tim's disappearance. Tim texted to say he had some things to settle, and he would be back as soon as possible. It was a mystery even to Klaare, who was heartsick. In his efforts to feel better, Dan drank blueberry banana smoothies and ate tons of mushrooms squirted with oregano oil and smothered in garlic. His favorite pastime was taking long walks around town or down into the Gorge. The Christmas snow still lingered halfway into January.

The afternoon of January 12 Dan wandered across town, up the hill, and into the cemetery. At the center was an enormous granite obelisk, a monument inscribed with "Wentreck Family" and "Dimitri Wentreck, Born 1901, Died 1982" and "Francesca M. Wentreck, Born 1902, Died 1965." Dan pondered what kind of life they might have lived. How their miserable offspring became the monster he was. He leaned against the monument. From it he could see all of Stony Grove. Covered with snow the town looked fresh. It could be any of the villages he had seen in Europe.

Dan stood in a white field populated by lesser pieces of granite. They stuck up out of the snow in neat rows. Generations had passed, history had blinked, and the time continuum never paused. The bumps in the snow represented nothing significant, it seemed to Dan. Why does anyone bother? All that remained of these people were their names and dates of birth and passing. Lives lived but nothing to tell of them—meaningless to future generations. The wind picked up, Dan felt it in his bones. He had often wondered how the horrid acts of the Nazis ever occurred in the villages he had seen in Europe. Such beautiful places. *Why do people have to be so ugly?*

He started for home, trudging through deep drifts, reading the granite stones. He paused; the wind blurred his vision, but he made out the name McKenzie. Jim and Louise McKenzie. *You remind me of my father*, old John McKenzie had told him . . .

###

"Where have you been?" Julie hugged Dan as he came through the front door.

"I was up at the cemetery."

"The cemetery? Why?" Julie stepped back.

"Shopping, just shopping."

"Not funny, Dan... not funny at all."

"I'm sorry, but I was looking around. Someday we'll need a spot. Maybe in fifty years."

"Dan, I'm afraid of losing you. Promise me you won't joke about it anymore."

Dan went silent, then dropped onto the couch. Julie put on her coat.

"I'm going to the store. Do you need anything?"

Dan shook his head. The cold of winter had everything frozen; even the ghost hadn't been heard from. His walk in the cold had played him out. But even more, when you know health and wellness are pending, when evil is lurking, it feels worse than a straight on confrontation of evil. *Most of my life events have happened around me; now it is happening to me. When the spring thaw comes, it's going to get ugly. We are now in the eye of this storm.* He hadn't looked for another attorney or been back to the doctor's. Tonight was the first scheduled meeting of the New Year for the political action group, but he was in no mood to see anyone. He fell asleep on the couch.

A knock at the front door woke him. Dan eyes opened, but he didn't move; then a second knock put him in motion. It was Tim. Dan opened the door, but neither man spoke at first. Dan stepped aside and motioned him through the doorway.

"Good to see you, my brother. What can I get you to drink?"

"I'll have a mug of the pineapple apple juice I can smell simmering."

They walked into the kitchen. Dan sensed Tim's down mood.

"What's up? You sure disappeared suddenly."

Dan ladled out two mugs and stuck a cinnamon stick in each, handing one to his brother. Tim looked into his cup and stirred.

"The text on New Year's said our breakup had a minor complication, but she said she would take care of it."

"Tim?" Dan couldn't help but translate Tim's depression and look of loss and grief into the worst-case scenario of a man's relationship with a woman terminated.

"She killed my child and I had no say in it. How can you be with someone for three years and not know them? I went to Houston but couldn't find her or contact her for about ten days. When I caught up with her, it was too late." He stared at his feet. "I want to be a dad. I would have taken the child, and she'd have never heard from me again unless she wanted. I would have been a great dad for my kid."

"I'm sorry, Tim. That's horrible."

"I'm well enough off, I could have taken care of things another way. I feel like I took a shot to the gut, and I'm feeling the pain the baby felt. I'm lost, Dan."

"Klaare's been real concerned."

"I hesitate to see her. I left so abruptly. I didn't explain why. Honestly, I don't want to get too involved with anyone right now. I'm still sorting myself out."

"Give yourself time to process all of this."

They walked to the living room.

"How're you feeling? Have you been back to see the doc?" Tim asked.

"Just between you and me, I feel weak. Sometimes I get light-headed. And no, I haven't seen the doctor since I last saw you. I've had my weekly blood tests, and I'm scheduled to see Dr. Cohen next week. Tonight we have our community action gathering. I don't look forward to it. I've got no fight in me. Everything is starting to seem stupid to me. I don't understand people or life."

"Sounds like depression. I'm sorry I told you my troubles."

"It's reality, isn't it? I feel for you. It ain't about me. I'm fine with me. I accept my situation. I feel bad for and about other people. I know what the punch you're talking about feels like. I see it in Julie's eyes. Man, I don't want to leave her alone—and the boys? I've got a lonely feeling in my own gut. I want time to stop, but the days keep on keeping on."

"I've always looked up to you, big brother. You're my hero. I went to college because you told me your way was the hard way. I owe it to you for guiding me to this path I have lived. You joined the service at seventeen and made it work for you. You can beat this."

"The world is designed to take you down. I've fought my whole life. I've watched good people—friends—be taken out. Your life becomes less with each loss, but you go on. The world is never the same; each loss extracts a little bit of sweetness, while you fight the bitterness."

"When Mom and Dad died... well, those feelings I had then seem to have just rushed back to the surface. I feel the same now as I did then. I haven't experienced another close loss until now. Now it seems like my whole world is a loss. You mean a lot to me, Dan. I've thought of you more as a father than a brother. Please, keep up the struggle. There are a lot of us counting on you."

"I know. Thanks. We'll get through this. I have no idea how I managed to make it this far—no, I'm wrong. I made it by the grace of God and because of Julie's prayers."

Dan closed his eyes.

"It's because you are one tough soldier," Tim whispered from across the room.

Dan opened one eye and grinned, just for a moment. "Yeah, I keep forgetting."

Julie came through the front door carrying several bags of groceries. "Tim, I saw your car parked out front. We missed you. Is everything all right?"

"Glad to be back here. I missed my family."

Tim grabbed the bags from Julie's hands, pecked her on the cheek. Julie gave Dan a quick glance, then followed Tim into the kitchen.

"He's down in the dumps," Julie whispered.

"Yes he is. I'll be around as much as I can. He needs to get out."

"I think not having a job is giving him too much time to think."

"I've got the same problem. Maybe we can help each other. Maybe we'll create jobs for ourselves."

"That would be great. You both need to start praying."

"I'm gonna get out of here and let you get ready for your meeting. Love you. Tell Klaare I said hello, and I'll call her as soon as I feel I can do justice by her."

"What's up, Tim?"

"Let's just say, it doesn't have anything to do with the present. I just need to come to terms with my past. Klaare doesn't deserve to be burdened with my baggage. I need to shed as much of it as I can first, although some of it will never be left behind."

Tim walked toward the front door and paused near Dan. "Take care, both of you. Call me if you need anything."

Julie busied herself preparing finger foods for the evening's gathering. She expected a large turnout and wanted everyone to feel welcome.

Dan went to the bedroom to take a nap, in the hopes he would feel better by the evening. He also wanted to be out of the way while Julie cleaned.

Julie struggled with her guilt of putting them in this situation. She also felt frustration with Dan for not attending church with her. The person Dan was becoming scared her. Even though she knew it wasn't deliberate on his part, she wanted him to fight harder. She could feel a tension growing between them.

Julie had been right. The house filled with all the original members and an equal number of new faces. The big surprise was Harry McDonath. Harry brought ten members of the church with him. *We should have rented a hall*, Julie thought.

It was an electrified meeting with angry citizens disappointed in the town council. They wanted the old guard out. Several people voiced their intentions to run for office. Dan never made an appearance. Julie had checked on him an hour before the meeting. He said he would be down, but he had spoken without opening his eyes. Even with the noise of the meeting, he continued to sleep. Julie fought to keep her thoughts on the meeting, her mind distracted by Dan's condition.

Harry and the ten members of the church congregation were the last to leave. They wanted to let Julie know they had a prayer chain in motion for both Dan and the situation with the house. He updated Julie on the progress of the corruption investigation. His source had confided in him that they were moving in, the evidence was mounting. It would only be a matter of time before arrests were made and people lost their jobs. Harry's words lifted a lot of the weight off Julie's shoulders. Her emotional state wasn't up to running the community action group on her own.

"We have waited a long time for this. Tell Dan we're sorry he wasn't well enough to take part in this evening's gathering. We give you and him credit for the changes taking place."

He began to shrug into his coat. "Good night, Julie. I'll see you in church."

"Harry, we haven't done much."

"I'm an old man. I still have my wits, though. I've paid attention to a lot of trends. Do you know anything about economic bubbles?"

"I've heard some things on the news about housing bubbles and such."

"Right—housing, oil, tech stocks... but you know it also applies to people. Denial on what constitutes fair value is the root cause of a bubble. Val is in such a denial. He has an

overinflated sense of his power and influence. He's a big fish in a small pond."

"I don't get it, Harry."

"Well, this little pond is becoming connected to the ocean. Val isn't the big fish anymore. His ego is nothing more than a bubble."

"How do we fit in?"

"Don't kid yourself. A point of a pin will pop a bubble. Stony Grove has reached its time. You know, evil is a destructive force. It does not build or create. It can manipulate the forces of love to accomplish some of these things, but by its very nature it always destroys. It reached such a point, and your presence in Stony Grove has tipped the scales. There are things in motion being played out. It is out of our hands. They say God moves in mysterious ways, and one of those ways is to let things play out. He watches."

"I hadn't thought about it from that perspective. Thanks, Harry. Thanks for coming this evening."

Harry took Julie's hand and held it. "We don't know. We have to have faith. All we can do is choose our sides. It's better to let the enemy destroy himself with his own greed, selfishness, and hatred. Evil always loses. It's just a shame so many good people suffer before it does."

TWENTY-SIX

The next morning Dan woke early. He found the kitchen stacked with dirty dishes and the trash overflowing. Apparently, Julie had gone to bed as soon as everyone had departed. Dan smiled. All indications were of a good turnout.

He started a pot of coffee, then cleaned up. He went about it in stealth mode, trying to avoid waking Julie. He took a handful of supplements and drank half a bottle of blueberry juice, then sat in the dining room to drink his coffee. He couldn't believe how well he felt. With each sip of coffee, he held the cup close to his nose to savor the aroma. He thought about what Tim had said—*You're a tough soldier*—and smiled. Physically, he still felt weak. His strength didn't come from muscle.

Julie walked into the spotless kitchen and poured a cup of coffee before she noticed Dan at the dining room table. She set her coffee down and without a word embraced him. She massaged his back and shoulders.

"I'm sorry I missed the meeting. It looks like you had a good turnout."

"It was wonderful. You were missed. Several people asked about you. Harry McDonath credits you with stimulating the entire town to flow with the changes on the horizon against the old regime. He said to thank you. There are a lot of people praying for you."

"I see... well, I don't plan to let them down. I needed the sleep, I'm feeling a little better. Maybe yesterday was the bottom. How about if we take a ride today?"

“Where to?”

“Let’s go visit your mother. We could take her out for dinner.”

“Are you serious? She would love it.”

“Yeah, no special holiday, just an appreciation day.”

“Dan, you’re the best. I’ll call her. When do you want to leave?”

“We can go whenever you want. Let’s get ready now. We’ll stop at some places along the way. Wake the boys, they’re going too. They need to learn their grandma needs attention as much as they do.”

“Why don’t you wake them while I fix breakfast?”

“No way, we’re eating every meal out today.”

And this is the way the day started for the Winslow family.

###

Val Wentreck arrived at Mayor Whipple’s office at noon. The mayor was out to lunch. Val sat in the overstuffed leather chair smoking a cigar. He rifled through the mayor’s drawers, not searching for any particular thing. It was more for his amusement in violating someone. He found a half bottle of scotch in the lower left-hand drawer along with a water glass. He filled it half full. *How about that? A free lunch*, he thought. He finished the scotch and returned the bottle and glass to the drawer.

The door opened and Joe strode through, then stopped dead in his tracks at the sight of Val occupying his office and his chair. “Val... good to see you.”

“You’re a lousy liar, Joe. Your face tells it all.”

“To what do I owe the pleasure of your visit?”

“Don’t play politician with me, Joe. There was a meeting at the Winslow house last night. The reports are, they had a big turnout. These new people moving in are going to vote my boys out.”

“You don’t know for sure.”

"Shut up, Joe. When you talk, you sound stupid. There's something in the works. Somebody is pushing buttons in Louisville. Big money is investing in student housing that looks like resorts, in college towns. This big money is putting pressure on our friends. Winslow is a pain, but this other stuff is serious. My big out is getting the alley opened up so I can dump my chunk of land to a developer."

"What do you want me to do?"

"I want you to tell me what you know about the Louisville push. I also want to know why you haven't been keeping up to date on it."

"Val, I don't know anything. Honest, it's as big a shock to me as it is to you."

"I heard the university president turned in his resignation this morning. Did you know about it?"

"Dr. Aldrich?"

"Yeah, Ben retired."

"Did he tell you?"

"No, his secretary called. Ben didn't have the guts. He's running scared."

"I thought you two were tight."

"We did business, nothing more. Years and years of business. Retiring won't protect him. I want to know a time frame for all this. You get on the phone and call in some favors. I don't care if you need to drive out to the capitol—I want answers. Find out who we own and start pulling some strings."

"Sure, Val, I know some people to start with. I'll get right on it."

"This isn't going to be good for any of us, but remember—I never lose. I'm going away for a while. When I get back, I want answers."

"Where you heading, Val?"

Val stared at Joe Whipple. Joe Whipple cleared his throat as Val stood up. With great effort Val moved from behind the desk. He leaned on his cane as he approached the mayor.

"I'll destroy this town if I have to. Got it? I'm not pulling any punches. Just for the sport of it, even if it gains me nothing. The Winslow family is going to pay."

"Val, they don't have anything to do with this investigation."

"It doesn't matter. I'm just in a foul mood, and I want to hurt someone."

Val blew cigar smoke in Joe Whipple's face. "I'll be out of town. Make sure everyone knows I'm out of town. I'll be with people who can vouch for me."

"Val, don't do anything crazy."

Val's face turned red, a vein protruding on his forehead.

"Crazy? What I do, I do. Nothing I do is crazy."

Val's look put the fear of Satan himself into Joe Whipple. He had never received a look like that from any man he had ever known. Val almost knocked Joe off his feet as he barged for the door. Joe Whipple feared for his political job and his marriage, and now his life. Val was a man who had never had to deal with external pressure. He had always been the one to create pressure on others. He feared Val would crack under the pressure and ruin everybody's life. Joe had been guilty of some indiscretions, but he thought of himself as a good man. After all, he went to church every Sunday.

Val made his way to his Escalade. It already held his suitcase. He drove to Fred's house, on the way to Hank's. Fred threw his overnight bag into the back of the Escalade and plopped himself in the front passenger seat. "What a day. I hear the Winslow meeting had a big turnout. This guy is causing a lot of trouble, Val."

"It's going to be his trouble, not mine. How much money did you bring?"

"Two grand."

"Two grand? What are you going to do after the first day? That's chump change."

"What did you bring, Val?"

"Guys like me don't bring money. I have an account. They know me, everybody in the joint knows Val Wentreck."

Fred sighed. Val's attitude never changed. He was always the big man. Fred planned to disappear as soon as they hit the casino. He would go his own way. He would have dinner or drinks with Val, but he couldn't keep up with Val's high-roller style. Val loved to rub it in. Hank would just spend the trip drinking. The three of them weren't friends. They were just loners doing the same sad things alongside each other. They had no delusions about it either.

The three men checked in at the hotel to the dismay of the clerk, who couldn't hide her disgust at Val and his crude humor. They hit a few slots on their way to dinner. In the restaurant Val ordered a steak dinner with all the fixings while delivering patronizing remarks to the waitress. Fred and Hank settled for fish sandwiches. They watched as Val wiped grease from his chin, then stretched back, rubbing his stomach.

"Why don't you two go do your thing. I'll be at the high-stakes tables."

"Sure, Val, we'll be in the lounge."

Hank trailed Fred into the lounge. Val lumbered toward the craps table, talking to the pit bosses manning their stations along the way. At the craps table he took up the space of three. People gathered to watch him play.

###

Klaare showered in the bathroom at the far end of the basement. The exhaust fan made a loud whirling sound, the spray of the shower even louder. With the Winslows still on the road and Klaare's apartment dark except for the bathroom, the house on Elm Street looked deserted.

The screen door on Klaare's apartment squeaked open. It rested against a shoulder coated in black cloth. A pair of gloved hands fumbled with a lock jimmy without success. Soon the hand punched into the glass in Klaare's door.

The sound penetrated Klaare's bathroom, for an instant. She thought she heard something, yet it had been so brief and undefined she shrugged it off. *The Winslows must be home.* She continued her shower, rinsing the shampoo from her hair.

A gloved hand reached through the broken glass to unlatch the dead bolt. The door to Klaare's apartment swung open. The man in black stepped in, listening for the sound of an alarm or occupant. Silence. He smiled; this would be a piece of cake. His assigned task was to violate, leave a mark of intrusion, and strike fear. He crept into Klaare's sitting room. From there he could see light around the closed bathroom door. Klaare had turned off the shower, patted dry with a towel and slipped on her robe. The man in black watched the light beneath the door shift. *Movement... someone is in there.* He moved close to the door. Klaare turned on her blow dryer, running a large brush through her hair.

He flung open the bathroom door to a scream.

###

Val's luck didn't work on the craps table. He walked away after losing ten grand. He sat down for a round of poker. He could expound about the nights he pocketed two to three hundred thousand dollars. He never mentioned the nights he lost five hundred thousand. Tonight he stacked four hundred thousand in chips in front of him and looked around the table.

Hank and Fred slouched at the bar.

"How does he do it?"

"Who, Val?"

"Yeah. I know he collects a lot of rent, but he is out of control."

"He runs Access Cards for druggies."

"What?"

"He scans Access Cards. Say you have three hundred on your welfare card. He's got scanners. He scans in the three hundred and gives you a hundred and fifty. You can now take cash and buy your drugs. The taxpayer sends Val three hundred, he doubles his money. He's got places all over the hood."

"Wow, sweet."

###

Dan parked in front of the house, the new normal since the paper alley has been in dispute. He stopped to gaze up at a billion stars, while Julie and the boys headed for the front door. A distant scream broke the silence of the night. The house was dark, save for a patch of light from the basement bathroom. They stopped to listen for another scream or noise to determine where it came from. The second scream sent Dan into a run for Klaare's side-door entrance.

Klaare took her hot curling iron and jammed it into tender flesh of the intruder's neck. His hand grabbed her hand, seemingly ignoring the pain. Klaare's left hand reached for her can of wasp spray; Julie had told her to always have a can with her. "Better than mace, it shoots twenty feet," Julie had said. Klaare sprayed it into the assailant's face, burning his eyes. He let her go and stumbled backward. He heard the entry door bang the wall as Dan burst into the apartment. No time to linger, the intruder rushed toward the noise and crashed into Dan. The impact knocked Dan off balance long enough for the assailant to breach the door and run into the woods toward the Gorge. Dan gave chase but could not continue in his weakened state.

Julie told the boys to wait on the porch as she entered the apartment. She found Klaare slumped against the bathroom wall sobbing. Julie comforted her until Dan reentered the apartment.

"Did he hurt you?" Dan sounded winded.

"No, I burned his neck with my curling iron. All he did was grab my hand. Then I shot wasp spray in his face."

Julie smiled. *Glad you listened to my advice.*

"We better report this."

"No, Dan, don't bother. It will be a waste of time. If she's not hurt, we should just let it go."

"Yes, let's not report this to the authorities," Klaare said.

Dan pondered the event and what the women were saying.

"Well, I'm calling Tim. Have you talked to him since he's come back?"

"No."

"I think it's time. What do you think?"

"I would like to see him... if he wants to see me."

"I'll go up with the boys and call him."

"I'll stay down here while you get dressed, Klaare." Julie dropped onto the couch.

Dan stopped to assess the damage to Klaare's door. He looked at the stakes in the driveway. Plastic danger ribbons fluttered in a light breeze. He didn't know for sure if this new incident had any connection to the alley, but there was a strong possibility. *This alley isn't worth it. They're all dead. Who cares, what does it matter? It's time to end this.*

TWENTY-SEVEN

Dan sat on the front porch enjoying the change of season. The birds were returning from their southern migration. The threat of snow was gone. Crocuses and daffodils bloomed. A warm breeze carried the fragrance of new life. Dan closed his eyes in thought. He had applied for jobs all around town; the hardware store promised to hire him, but they had hired three new people since the promise had been made. He didn't feel up to working anyway. His involvement with the community action group was taxing enough. He had driven down to see Lee on a couple of occasions. Lee's wife had somehow managed to survive the winter.

###

Val's luck seemed to have taken a bad turn. The company insuring his main student rental had refused to renew his policy after conducting an inspection of the premises. The building had at one time been the largest building in town. Constructed in the 1940s, it had never been upgraded to meet new standards. It lacked a sprinkler system, fire and smoke detectors, and proper fire escapes from the upper floors. Without insurance, the building could not be occupied. Several town council members had resigned over the threat of the state's investigations into the university and surrounding community. New council members had been elected in a special election.

The town council began to put pressure on Val. The first thing they did was make the student rental owners responsible for paying for garbage pickup. The building inspector was replaced, and new occupancy permit applications for all rentals were required. Things were changing, but not in a steadily positive manner. The new politicians were quick to develop greedy attitudes as their lust for power and authority grew. They played out their vengeance on Val and pursued the new bigger boys moving in with their large crews to construct student housing.

Val's rental office occupied an old red brick house on the far end of Main Street. He had parked a large moving van there, which never moved. With his name painted on the side, it had been a way to get around a law on sign restrictions. He kept the truck inspected and functional, so there had been little to prevent him from circumventing their sign restriction. This spring he had begun posting signs on the truck, political signs protesting the new council members and their new rules. The wording on the signs seemed like a cry for help. One sign offered a free can of soda and a bag of chips to anyone who would stop in to talk about the political changes taking place in Stony Grove. Dan had even thought about stopping in, but he didn't.

Stony Grove was a small town. Val and Dan encountered each other occasionally, at store entrances or at the gas pumps. Val always stopped, his face frozen in a scowl. The dark circles under his eyes enhanced his psychotic stare. Dan avoided eye contact so as not to give Val the satisfaction of an acknowledgment. He didn't know for sure if his tactic worked.

As the days lengthened and new life blossomed everywhere, Val sat on the edge of his bed, struggling to breathe. He held a Colt .45, flipping it from one hand to the other. He kept it polished and well-oiled and was a deadly shot. His skill with a pistol was one thing his mass had not impacted. These past few weeks, when he visited the game lands to shoot, he didn't even get out of his car. He fired out the window. Fred Black did all the running, posting the targets and then fetching them so Val could admire the pattern of holes tight to the bull's eye. Val's sphere of influence was shrinking. He loaded the Colt.

###

The spring semester had one more week as Julie and Klaare strolled from the university toward home. Klaare voiced her anxiety over her inevitable departure for Estonia. Her visa was good for studies and did not allow her to remain to work and live. She had come to love her adoptive family. Every Sunday she attended church with Julie. She prayed for Dan's health and for peace to come to the town. Most of all, she had fallen in love with Tim. Julie had been brainstorming, trying to figure out a way for her to stay.

The black Escalade slowed as it approached them. The windows' dark tint obscured a view of the driver. The SUV slipped by, its presence bringing a knot to Julie's stomach. Their mood turned somber, and Julie struggled to focus on God and good in the presence of such evil.

Dan rested on the front porch swing, waiting for Julie and Klaare, his eyes closed. He had maintained his diet of probiotics, even having increased his intake of oregano oil, mushrooms, and garlic. Every few weeks his blood test indicated slight improvement, though his symptoms remained. Dr. Cohen decided to write a paper detailing Dan's case, which he planned to present at a seminar in Paris in August. He remarked on Dan's ability to remain steady, even to be improving.

Dan had begun to pray with Julie in the mornings. It was the point in the day where he chose to be positive and thankful for his many blessings. Now he sat in silence offering additional prayers.

Julie and Klaare perked up when they saw Dan waiting for them. They always tried harder to be positive in his presence. Dan's eyes opened when he heard the first step creak beneath Julie's foot.

"Hey, girls. Beautiful day, isn't it?"

"It is," Julie agreed. "You look good."

"Thanks, I feel pretty good." He didn't feel much different than he had in the last several weeks, but he refused to say it.

Julie sat on the porch swing beside him. Klaare smiled and turned toward her side entrance. Tim would be picking her up in about an hour.

"How were your classes?"

"Same old stuff. I hate the game. I think I'm too old to buy into the rhetoric. They teach opinions, not facts. Not much sense in talking about it."

"I was praying when you got here, made me feel better."

"Dan, have you considered getting baptized?"

He didn't answer. They had discussed it before. He had been contemplating it, but he didn't want to do it in his weakened state. He wanted to come to God without looking like he had an ulterior motive. He wanted to do it with strength but knew the day might be far into the future.

"I would feel better if you would do it—you will too."

"It wouldn't hurt, I suppose."

"Oh, Dan!" Julie kissed him on the cheek.

"I'll go to church with you this Sunday. We can talk to your pastor."

"*Our* pastor... he's our pastor. You'll like everyone at the church. They're nice people."

"Maybe we can get a two-for-one deal."

"What do you mean?'

"My brother. He might be ready to do it too."

"Oh, that would be great... what if Klaare... ?"

"I'll bet Klaare will if Tim does."

"Awesome... simply awesome."

###

Lee sat beside his wife's bed, a soup spoon in one hand, steadying a cup of broth with the other. As he held the spoon to her lips, she would pucker and sip. Her eyes never opened, but they did twitch. Her sipping was more of an instinctive response than a conscious effort. Lee dabbed her chin with a napkin. He whispered apologies to her and asked the Lord to forgive him for his weaknesses. Buck lay nearby. It had been a week since he had been to the bait store. He had plenty of bait on hand with an honor pail for money collection. He needed to fetch it and restock the bait supply. He knew her time wasn't far off and didn't want her to die alone. When he began to sob, Buck came to him, placing his paw on his thigh. Lee scratched Buck behind his ear and sniffled.

"She's still with us, boy. I'm just a mess."

Buck let out a whimper, lowering his head to rest his chin on Lee's leg.

###

Pete Peterson sat in his patrol car up on Cemetery Hill. He looked down on Stony Grove, curled his lip, then licked the wrapper on a joint. He twisted the ends, holding it up to admire his handiwork. He dangled it from his lip without lighting it and reached for the report on the passenger seat. He gave the cover page a hard look: "Police Brutality, Excessive Force." Peterson's hand fell hard on the passenger seat, releasing the report. He struck a match and cupped his hands, igniting the end of the joint.

###

Jack Monroe sat in Mayor Whipple's office, the door closed. Whipple had scrambled to save himself and his job. He had made a deal with the State Attorney General to add to the state's evidence, spilling his guts. It had been agreed: no charges would be filed against Whipple, and he could serve out his term in office. He agreed never to run for office again. The evidence Whipple had turned over was still being processed. He had kept accurate documentation of behind-the-scenes meetings with dates, times, and names. Whipple knew Val had the goods on him. He just wanted to be quicker on the draw and nail things down before Val could produce the evidence, ruining his marriage and therefore his financial future and any possibility of a comfortable retirement. It was all risky.

Jack Monroe had never liked Joe Whipple.

"Well, Jack, have you thought about the promotion?"

"I've been thinking on it."

"And? You know we're coming down on Pete, never liked him much."

You would have never guessed it, Jack thought. *Only now that the state has stepped in do you decide you don't like Pete. It's the truth.* Jack studied the mayor's face.

"I'll be honest, Mayor, I never liked much about anything around here, and Pete's ways have caught up to him."

"What are you saying, Jack?"

"I'm saying you're surviving all this, but it doesn't make you clean. I'm saying I don't like politicians. The police force is just Pete and me. You're taking Pete down, but it isn't a noble gesture, and offering me his job is no bargain. I'm not for sale, Joe. I'm looking forward to my day in court. I'm going to tell all I know. I'll figure out my next career move after all is said and done."

"Jack, don't be a fool. Nobody cares if you're straight and noble."

"I do, Mayor. I do."

###

The black Escalade pulled into the fire department lot. Val laid on the horn several times until Hank Davidson appeared from a side door. Val powered down his window.

"Val... how you been?"

"Have you seen Fred around?"

"No. What's up?"

"He doesn't answer his phone and he's not at his house."

Hank leaned against the Escalade looking in at Val. The forty-five rested on his lap.

"Looks like you're going huntin'."

"I wanted to go target shooting. Fred always sets me up and checks my score. You busy?"

"As a matter of fact, we're working on the pumper."

Val gave Hank a hard stare. Everybody was turning on him, bunch of liars. Val grabbed the forty-five with his right hand and stroked it with his left.

"Too busy, huh, Hank? Too bad. Seems like all my old buddies are bailing on me. Seems like I've got one friend left."

"That's not true, Val, we're still friends."

Val narrowed his lips in disgust, shaking his head.

"If you see Fred, tell him I'm looking for him. I'll be over at my office."

"Sure, Val, if I see him, I'll tell him."

Hank backed toward the side, not turning his back on the forty-five. Val gave him a dead man's stare, soulless and cold. Val didn't restart the Escalade for quite some time. He just sat and caressed the pistol.

###

Zane jiggled the lock on his locker. It always took a little extra tugging to open. It released, and he slid it from the latch, opening the metal door. He needed to exchange his English book for his trigonometry book. He felt the presence of someone standing close, too close. A hand brushed the back of his neck, chilling him. Zane shrugged his shoulders and twisted his neck in defiance.

"Hey, Zane, what you been up to?"

It was Liam, Professor Bell's son. He pressed against Zane, whispering in his ear. Zane pushed back, and Liam backed away, his hands raised.

"Leave me alone, Liam."

Liam's face contorted in sarcasm. He lowered his hands. "Just trying to be friendly, dude. I want to invite you to the rave this weekend. It's going to be the biggest blast yet."

"I'm not interested."

"Everyone will be there."

"I won't."

"Mom and Dad won't let you? My old man says you Bible thumpers are a bunch of hypocrites. Loosen up, dude. Don't let your old man run your life."

Zane paused, giving Liam a cold stare. Liam mocked his pose. Zane turned toward his locker, slamming the door and setting the lock. Liam leaned into Zane, whispering his vulgar intents for the girl he had lured to the rave. Zane spun around and pushed Liam backward.

"Hey, man, just having some fun!" Liam chuckled as he spoke.

"No, man, you're the one trying to manipulate everybody. Don't listen to my parents, but listen to you. I have free will. That bothers you, doesn't it? My parents let me think for myself. I make my own choices. You aren't even on the list."

"Your parents have brainwashed you with a fairy-tale book. It's all hogwash."

"Is it? Did you ever read the Bible or try to understand it? You're in the book, Liam. It tells you what your future is."

"Who are you to judge me? You can't condemn me to hell. You don't know."

"Who said anything about hell? You are just starting down a trail of misery for yourself and everyone you infect. Your dad is the one who can't tolerate a differing opinion."

"F-you." Liam gave Zane a shove. Zane grinned and strode down the hall.

###

Val pulled into the game lands, all alone. Fred be damned, he didn't need anyone. As he slogged through the spring mud, the clay caked to the soles of his shoes. Even with his cane he barely maintained his balance. He removed a couple of bottles and cans from a plastic shopping bag and staged them on a board. It began to drizzle. His hair fell flat, and cold rain ran down his face. He cursed it, looking skyward. He would not let it stop him. He waddled back to lean on the Escalade.

He brought the pistol level and fired. A bottle shattered; a metal can flipped, and he hit it three more times. He felt a release of tension. They weren't targets, but people. He mumbled names under his labored breath. They'll be sorry they betrayed him. Backstabbers they were.

He knew he had never had any real finesse. He just always had the upper hand because he had inherited so much. His father had conditioned the community to accept his way, but his father was the one with finesse. Finesse coupled with ruthlessness. Val had inherited his family's ruthless nature, something he struggled to keep in check, even in the best of times. These were not the best of times.

Val reloaded, emptied, and then reloaded again and again. The drizzle had turned to a downpour. Unfazed, he fired away.

TWENTY-EIGHT

Castleton, once a thriving blue-collar mill town, now held the title as the rust belt's buckle. Unemployment sat at 30 percent although those who had dropped off the unemployment rolls were no longer included. Another 50 percent could be classified as underemployed, holding part-time, minimum-wage jobs. The social structure had broken down, although not along economic lines. Everyone was just poor. The social structure of Castleton now consisted of lazy or bad. Up on the hill above town there was an enclave of older wealthy residents living off investments not of a local flavor. One such family was the McKenzies.

Castleton seemed lawless. The police did their best, but the town had reached a hopeless state of depression. Summer heat now kept the streets clear until the sun started to retreat. Monday the state would issue its findings regarding the charges against Peterson.

Pete Peterson devoted much of his off-duty time to a seedy sports bar, the one thriving Castleton enterprise still hanging on. A place where he knew all the regulars, the bartenders, and the owner. He spent a substantial portion of his pay feeding the poker machines. Both of Pete's ex-wives frequented the place. His first taste of alcohol had been near the pool table. For his sixteenth birthday, his old man had bought him a beer.

Pete's old man hustled pool and drank. He had little to do with raising Pete. He never married Pete's mother—or a few other women around town blessed with his children. One thing Pete's father did, though, was look up each of his kids in their teen years to introduce them to pool shooting and drinking. It was best he stayed away from the kids when they were young, as he had a violent temper. Pete's old man died of liver failure before reaching fifty.

Pete had idolized his old man. Nobody could say anything bad about the guy within earshot of Pete, or they would find themselves flat out. When people told Pete he was just like his old man, he considered it a compliment. Criminally selfish, they both associated with the darkest elements in Castleton.

Now Pete slouched at the bar staring up at an old episode of *CSI*. He had reached the point of just sipping his beer, having already downed ten. During commercials, he stared at the golden liquid, poking his finger through the foam. He rarely showed signs of intoxication, having achieved professional status. At the beginning of the evening he had downed several shooters with tavern clients as they passed through on their way home. Whisky amplified Pete's anti-social tendency, freeing his ugliest side, and Pete was known as a man who suppressed his best side even when sober. Tonight he was a ticking time bomb.

He looked across the bar at two strangers. He had never seen them before. *They are in the wrong place.*

"Hey!" Pete called out. The bartender looked Pete's way, but Pete flagged her away to ignore him; he wanted the strangers' attention.

"Hey, you with the big stupid mustache."

The two strangers looked over at Pete. The one with the mustache pointed at himself.

"Are you talking to me?"

"Yes I am, I hate mustaches," Pete sneered.

"Then don't grow one." The strangers chuckled, enough to light Pete's fuse.

"No, I mean I don't like looking at them. I think people who grow them are jerks. You impress me as a jerk."

"Sleep it off, pal. We just stopped in to have a beer. We aren't bothering anyone."

"Wrong, you bother me."

The guy with the mustache took an empty beer bottle from in front of him and secured it between his legs.

"What are you doing?" his friend asked.

"If he comes over here, I'm going to crack this over his head."

The bartender had noticed the stranger's move and walked over to them. She spoke in a soft whisper.

"Listen, I'll give you some advice. This guy is as mean as they come. In his condition, the two of you can probably kick his butt. But when the trouble starts, I'm going to have to call the police to keep someone from getting killed. Just so you know, this is not a fight you are going to win. The guy is a cop, you win with him and you'll have the whole Castleton police force to deal with. You'll wake in the lockup wondering what kind of truck ran you over. Trust me. It would be best if you two just leave."

"Hey, Tina, you sweet on them two?"

"Pete, they're customers and you better watch your mouth."

"I don't need you telling me what to do."

"You're cut off, Pete."

"I don't think so . . ."

"Pete, just cool it." Tina picked up a towel as she walked toward him.

"Hey!" Pete stood up and leaned over to see around Tina to further agitate the strangers.

"See up there? Up on the TV, 'at's me, *CSI*. It's what I do every day. You wanna mess with me?" Pete's words were slurred.

"Stop it, Pete." Tina grabbed Pete's beer. The two strangers downed what was left of their beers and left.

"Ah, Tina, I was just having a little fun. What's the matter?"

"Go home, Pete—you're done."

"This is my home. I was drinking here before you were born." Pete folded his arms on the bar and put his head down.

Tina walked away carrying Pete's last beer. "No, Pete, this isn't your home. I'm going to have Don ban you, permanently."

"Don will fire you before he bans me!"

"Go!" Tina pointed toward the door, but Pete slumped back onto the bar stool, his head on the bar.

Pete slept about an hour, long enough to let him think he could maintain composure. He got up to leave, then walked along the bar saying good night to everyone. He zeroed in on the double doors at the exit after two tries. Pete always took the back roads back to Stony Grove to avoid the state police.

###

Lee sat holding his wife's icy hand. She hadn't done anything but try to breathe for the last four hours. Lee spent time apologizing to her for the wrongs and heartaches he had caused her over the years. He watched her chest rise and fall, with longer periods of stillness in between. He asked God to be kind to her as he swabbed her lips with a wet sponge stick.

Time lagged, yet Lee never looked at the clock. It didn't matter now. Her chest sank, air rushed from her lungs, and she was still. Lee's head dropped as he spoke his last apology. He whispered a prayer for the Lord to take her in and thanked Him for ending her suffering.

Lee walked into the kitchen to clean a week's worth of dishes. His wife always fussed at him to help keep the place clean. A mere cottage of four rooms, the task should have been easy enough. He had never made the effort to upgrade the former hunting camp with electricity, plumbing, or phone. Now he washed all the dirty dishes. He moved about the cottage storing or tossing his clutter as he mumbled more apologies for the way he had always been. Buck watched his master, a curious tilt to his head. By this time of night, the two of them should be asleep on the carpet near the fireplace. When all was set as right as he could make it, Lee returned to his wife's bedside, dropped to his knees, confessed to cleaning up too late, and then wept until near midnight.

"Buck, you're in charge. It's late and powerful dark without no moon. I'm going on down to the bait store to use the phone.

We need to notify the authorities of our misfortune. I'm fearing for you walking on such a dark road, fella. I'll be back as soon as I fetch somethin'."

Lee patted Buck's head and headed for the shed to get the mare. Calling the authorities could wait till morning. He had lied to Buck about that, and he felt guilty for doing so, but he had more pressing matters on his mind. There was something that couldn't wait any longer. He had already been on hold long enough. There was a bottle of unfinished business in the file cabinet down at the bait shop. Something about the heat of this night drove his thirst. He had stashed the bottle a few years back and prided himself in not having touched it all this time. Lee knew not even his best friend Buck would approve of what he had in mind.

Lee decided to bridle up the mare; there was no need or time for a saddle. Down the lane they trotted a little faster than the mare felt comfortable with, but Lee was the boss. It was less than a mile to the bait store if the road was straight, which it was not. Lee knew shortcuts, up over the ridge, though. He could cut the trip in half by taking those.

He left the road at the first turn, climbing an old deer path up through a stand of hemlock. It was nothing special. He used the trail all the time. There weren't even any low-hanging branches to worry about. He crested the ridge and dropped back down toward the road. Where the trail met the road, the bank was steep. Once the mare started down, she couldn't be stopped.

###

Dan and Julie were awakened by a loud thud. Julie grabbed Dan's arm as they sat up. Nothing could be seen in the dim light.

"Zane, Trent... is that you, boys?" Dan said, loud enough for them to hear him if they were in the hallway. Dan got out of bed, opened the bedroom door, and entered the hallway. There was nothing unusual. He peeked into each of the boys' rooms; they were sound asleep. Julie followed him as he checked the entire house, including door locks and windows. He felt a coughing spell coming on, so he took a shot of inhalant. A siren broke the silence of night, the siren from the fire department at the end of the street.

Julie held Dan's arm as they walked out onto the porch. Looking at his cell phone, he saw it was four in the morning. Their faces flashed in the pulsing light strobes of the emergency vehicles rushing past their home. They watched the vehicles disappear down the street. After a moment of silence, they went back inside.

"There must have been an accident." He rubbed Julie's back.

"I'm going back to bed, Dan."

"Sure. I think I'm going to sit up for a while. My chest feels heavy, I think sitting might help."

Julie gave Dan a peck on the cheek, then went up to bed. Dan sat in the living room watching the shadows of tree branches dancing on the walls, projected through the windows by a streetlight. The motion of the shadows was hypnotic and relaxing, allowing his mind to wander. The only facts he could anchor on was the noise that had startled them awake. There appeared to be nothing amiss in the house, and the emergency vehicles had disappeared into the night. *What are you trying to tell me now? Who are you and why did you wake us?* Dan closed his eyes.

Julie woke at about seven feeling out of sorts, but the sun streaming through the window melted her fears. She paused at the base of the stairs to watch Dan sleeping in his easy chair. He appeared to be comfortable and breathing easily. She continued into the kitchen to try to start a pot of coffee without disturbing him. The boys would wake him soon enough. Julie poured her coffee as she heard the front door and shouts of "good-bye" from the boys, who never even noticed their father sleeping in the easy chair. The door slammed, refreshing the faded memory of the night.

Dan entered the kitchen with a groan and a stretch. Julie threw her arms around him, burying her head into his chest. Dan looked toward the bright kitchen window, the sunlight glaring through. His hands moved over Julie's back, massaging all the points feeling stiff in his own. Their body language spoke of eternity, never letting go. Their union was everlasting, a bond of spirits.

"Dan, I can't imagine letting go of you. I can't imagine a life without you."

"Me neither, I love you so much."

"Holding Louise's Bible... this may sound strange, but it's like I can feel her sadness and loneliness as she mourned the loss of Jim. I think they had a bond like ours. I guess I'm being weird, huh?"

"No, you aren't. Last night when I was falling asleep in the easy chair, I had similar thoughts. I was thinking about what kind of man Jim was. People have said he was a lot like me. They were real people, Julie. They had dreams, laughed, cried, and loved each other just like we do."

"I wish we could get a clear picture of this town. It just drives me crazy the way some people feel they have a right to control and interfere with other people's lives."

"Let's concentrate on the good. I think living here has brought us closer together and given us a greater appreciation of things we were beginning to take for granted."

"You are so right."

"Let's blow everybody off today and go for a walk. Let's get some sun and fresh air."

"I'll pack us a lunch. It's supposed to be near eighty today."

Dan poured coffee for himself and Julie before turning on the small television at the end of the kitchen counter. Julie began preparing a light breakfast of fruit and toast. The eight o'clock news came on with local reports.

"Breaking news: Tragedy struck last night on a backcountry road. Police report a vehicle traveling at a high rate of speed struck and killed a local man. His horse also died at the scene. The driver of the vehicle is in critical condition, suffering from massive head injuries. Details will be released as they are made available. Names are being withheld until relatives have been notified."

Dan stood, stunned. He set his coffee on the counter.

"I hope it isn't Lee."

"Why would he be out riding in the dark?"

"I don't know."

"I guess we'll just wait to see like everyone else. We sure can't ask anybody; the people at the fire hall won't even wave to us when we go by, let alone answer any of our questions."

"I wish I hadn't turned the stupid thing on."

"We should give some serious thought to ridding ourselves of TV. Seriously, who needs it?"

"We'll have to talk it over with the boys."

"I don't think so. The boys need to adapt to what we want. We're the adults."

"Let's just go for our walk, Dan. We can't do anything about it anyway. We need a mental health day. Do you feel up to a hike? We'll take it easy, you set the pace."

"I could never say no to you. I'm with you."

Julie hastened to get herself and their lunch ready. She needed a special day. Dan took his supplements, made a jug of green tea, and packed his inhalant. Before he showered, he tried to do some push-ups. A year ago he could crank out forty in a minute. Today he barely did twenty in three minutes. He made up his mind to work his way back up to forty. "Life is great if you don't get weak," his grandfather had always said. Dan had weakened physically, no doubt. He looked out the window toward the Gorge, remembering his first adventure into it, how strong he had felt. His spirit was intact. He could do this.

TWENTY-NINE

Dan looped a backpack over one shoulder as they walked out onto the front porch. The flawless sky burned bright blue. They felt the sun on their skin as they stepped from the shade of the huge tree in the front yard. As they walked down the driveway, Dan pulled Fred Black's metal fence poles out, tossing them onto Fred's lawn. The yellow plastic caution tape spiraled in the wind as the poles bounced. Julie laughed at how childish it all seemed.

"You know, Dan? It doesn't make me mad anymore. It makes me sad. What a pathetic man."

"I feel the same way. These people don't get it. They're blinded by their own greed and selfishness. I bet neither Fred nor Val have walked down into the Gorge lately—smelled it, felt it, experienced it. I can't wait to show you."

Near the garage, Dan pulled out the last fence post, tossing it into the middle of Fred's backyard, a symbolic gesture of release. Julie put her arm around her man as they strolled toward the woods. A cardinal flew past them and landed on a branch near the start of the path. Blood red, it marked their path. As they approached, it flew a little farther into the woods. The path was clear. A new crop of weeds had not yet appeared. The fall die-off lay flat to the ground, pressed down by wind and snow. It was the perfect time of year for a walk in the woods. They walked to where the boulders along the Stony became visible, the point where the waters turned wild.

"See the hemlocks? They run all the way down the Gorge. There are no weeds, just a soft mat of pine needles. I've wanted to show you this for a long time. We'll go over to those boulders and climb down along the rapids. It's like the garden of Eden. This place is magical."

"How do you feel?"

"I feel good. I'm glad I have my inhaler, though."

At the boulders, Dan held Julie's hand as they worked their way down through several crevasses to the bottom of the drop. He paused at a place that looked like what Lee had described, where Harry had been shot. There was no way of knowing. The sound of the rushing waters was melodic; light trickle sounds harmonized with heavy gushing like a symphony. The sun had warmed the boulders. They couldn't resist the urge to rest occasionally, the sun on their faces, warm rock pressed against their backs. As they sat in silence, Dan studied the boulders and rocks below. He looked off toward the ancient stand of hemlock. It also fit Lee's description well. *Could this be the place where Lee and Harry sat the night Harry was shot?* "I never prayed," Lee had said about when he had faced death. He had not prayed to be saved, which was ultimately what saved him, he had said. Evil had seen his potential. Lee had done nothing. He had done nothing... this was his sin. He had saved himself for a life of nothingness by doing nothing. Dan looked over the back side of the boulder at a crevasse. It could have been where Lee's foot had become lodged.

"What are you doing, Dan? Are you looking for something?"

He didn't respond, as he was deep in thought. *Lee, when I catch up with you, we are going to come to this spot. I want you to tell me if this is the rock.* Dan could envision the night of the event, the scared boy facing death, evil chuckling in the dark night. Julie put her hand on his shoulder, causing him to jump.

"What's the matter with you?"

"Oh, I was just thinking about the story of Lee and about how Harry lost his arm." Truth was, it felt like more than just thoughts. It was as if Lee was speaking to him.

"You know, I don't think getting baptized is going to make a hill of beans as to whether I get well or not, at least in a physical sense."

"No, I never thought that either."

"Yeah, I think I get it. If I don't pray, I may well survive but . . ."

"But?" Julie looked puzzled.

"Well, it just might make all the difference either way the coin drops."

"It absolutely will."

"Julie, we left the military, but we're still engaged in war. It's spiritual warfare. Getting baptized will make a statement as to which side I am on. I want the enemy to know I'm a warrior."

Julie remained speechless. Dan didn't say any more either; he sat listening to the Stony rushing past. He felt the warmth of the sun. Julie rubbed his back and shoulders as he watched birds dance in flight. Both appreciated every breath, every thought, and every minor surrounding event. They became one with the Gorge's splendor.

"Come on. Let's go down below the rapids. You won't believe the enchantment of the forest. The emerald moss, the carpet of pine needles, the smells of the earth, the peace and quiet. I am so happy we get to experience all this—it's like a little slice of heaven."

Julie held on to Dan's arm as they made their way down the final grade. They moved slowly, not out of fear or struggling with the terrain; they just wanted to absorb all of it, savor it. The path turned to sand as it followed the gentler flow of the Stony. There were deeper pools separated by short stretches of swift flows over rocky bottoms. They caught sight of a white flickering tail as a deer disappeared into the shadows of hemlock. Dan put his arm around Julie pointing toward a flock of wild turkey moving up a ridge. Julie hugged his arm tighter, not wanting him to let go.

"I'll bet the water is cold."

"I have no doubt."

They went to the creek's edge, squatted, and put their hands in. It chilled them to the bone.

"I know this feeling. It's the same as the water poured on me in the bedroom."

"Yes, I know. I put my hand in this the first time I came down here. I tried to tell you how it felt, but you have to feel it to understand it."

"What a shame such a beautiful place could be the scene of so much evil."

"It would be easy enough to blame the evil on this place. This place is God's house, and yet our town is filled with churches, houses of God. If you just drive through the town, it seems like a lovely enough place, doesn't it? You would never guess the evil lurking there... so sad."

"Doesn't it seem like evil is everywhere?" Julie cupped her hands around a wildflower, sampling its fragrance.

"It is, but so is God—we find whichever we look for."

As they walked, Dan recognized a small tributary he had followed on his first excursion down the Stony. It was a slight diversion, about a quarter-mile walk or so. The tributary came off a sheer face at the Gorge's high wall edge, dropping into an impenetrable forest of laurel, a quarter mile deep and three miles long. The cascade pooled at the base; resting in full sun, it warmed before continuing to the Stony. Walking the creek bed offered the only access, and the rocks were treacherous.

"Let's go up the side creek. You think what you have seen so far is beautiful? Trust me, you haven't seen anything yet. Are you with me?"

"Wherever you want me to go."

"Come on then."

The laurel offered a jungle look. The stream was lined in a tangle of twisted stems and green verdure. They stretched from stone to stone as they made their way upstream. Dan chose the path and Julie followed. They didn't speak. They just listened to the sounds of the forest.

When Dan first glimpsed the tumbling cascade falling into the pool, he grabbed Julie's hand. They slowed to a stroll along the deep pool. Where the water went shallow, only knee high, they took off their shoes and pulled up their pant legs. The water didn't cause an ache in their feet, like when they put their hands in earlier. This water felt inviting. They sat on a rock on the opposite shore dusting wet sand from the bottoms of their feet, enjoying the warmth in a patch of sun. Dan hesitated to put on his socks and shoes. He rolled down his pant legs, which had gotten wet anyway. Julie's pant legs were also wet.

"You know, we might as well go barefoot the rest of the way. Let's just carry our shoes. The rocks on this side creek are slippery, but there are a lot of sandy places to step on. I think we'll be fine."

"You know me, I love going barefoot."

They made their way a little farther up the creek bed. More than once Julie slipped and grabbed Dan for support. Dan used his inhaler once. The laurel forest exuded a sultry ambience. There were no weeds or underbrush below the thick canopy of broad laurel leaves. Large boulders, debris from ancient landslides, mingled with the laurel. Eventually, the narrow ribbon of water brought them to its source, a crystal-clear pool at the base of a sheer stone face towering above them.

Water tumbled from the precipice into the deep pool at the base, its clarity allowing a wide stretch of the bottom to be seen, small fish shimmering near the edge. The pool's dimensions, perhaps thirty by sixty feet, were entirely illuminated by the sun. Huge boulders sloped into the edges of the pool. A fine mist filled the air, creating a rainbow effect.

"Come on, let's sit and listen to the water." Dan held Julie's hand as they made their way onto a boulder about midway toward the falls. At first the stone seemed too hot to the touch, but he spread out towels from their backpack. Containers of food for lunch came out next as well as the green tea. The perfect place for a picnic and his stomach said it was time. Julie retrieved hand wipes from her small pack. After they ate, she lay back looking up at the cascade. Individual droplets sparkled in the sun.

"This is the most perfect day. This will be our secret place. I'm so glad I agreed to come with you. I should have come that first day. I should always go with you. I'm sorry."

"Oh, no you don't—don't start with the sorry stuff. Just enjoy this moment."

They savored their lunch. A bird stopped by, and Julie threw some crumbs its way. Dan tossed nuts to a squirrel. Overhead a hawk circled above the precipice. Not one cloud blemished the sky. They drank green tea, toasting the glory of the day. Dan removed his shirt to absorb the heat of the sun. It felt good on his chest, the warm rock on his back.

"I call this real therapy. It's better than any health spa."

She ran her hand over his chest, stopping to feel him breathe. He was falling asleep. Realizing he had gone into a deep sleep, she stopped caressing his chest, not wanting to disturb him.

She didn't want to think about anything but the here and now. She admired the lush laurel surrounding them, the rock formations, and the clear water. She moved away from Dan, down to where the water touched their boulder. She sat with her feet just touching the water; it was warm, inviting. She watched fish darting below the surface. Little fingerlings approached her feet, kissing them. She let her legs slide deeper in the water without disturbing the fish. Her head dropped back between her shoulders, allowing the warmth of the sun to caress her face. She felt secure, loved, and safe. There was no future here, no past, just this moment.

She pulled her legs out of the water and instantly felt them drying. Cool currents had brushed her legs as she had dangled them in the water, and she wondered if it was colder out from the boulder. She stood and looked around, taking a deep breath, sweet and fresh. She walked back to the towel next to Dan and sat down, gathering her courage. He had been napping twenty minutes. *Long enough.*

Her squeal woke him. He reached for Julie. Or at least where she had been, but she wasn't there. Just a pile of clothing. Dan sat up looking toward the pool. Julie was bobbing up and down in the middle of it. She waved to him to join her.

"What are you doing, are you crazy?"

"I'm doing what you have been bugging me to do for the last twenty years."

"It was just a fantasy."

"No, it's not, it's for real. Come on, I called your bluff."

"I'll say. Isn't it cold?"

"Nah, I'm already used to it. Come on. It's quite pleasant."

Dan stood and quickly prepared to join her. He gave a rebel yell and splashed into the water. She threw her head back and laughed. It was a secret place hidden in the laurel, a place far from evil. They were in a healing light and a healing place. Their thoughts were only for each other.

THIRTY

Dan and Julie walked into the ruins of the old resort as they continued their hike through the Gorge. Both felt energized by their mountain water swim followed by basking in the hot sun to dry before dressing. Now in the shade of the hemlocks, they could smell their own heated flesh as they walked with their arms around each other. Dan showed her the foundations of the old lodge, cabins, and swimming pool. He told her of Lee's speculations and what he knew of its history.

"These ruins represent someone's dream, a broken dream. You know, when I first came into this place, all I could think about were the guys I knew in the service. The guys I laughed with, suffered with, and shared dreams with. The guys I watched get broken, their dreams shattered. Life is tough."

"Dan, I've been there, too, remember?"

"Yeah, I know. It's just all so sad what men can do to each other."

###

The black Escalade stopped in front of the Winslow house. Its dark tinted window sluggishly lowered. Val studied the uprooted posts with yellow caution ribbons strewn across Fred's lawn. He was Val Wentreck, grandson of Dimitri, life was not meant to go this way. He was the last Wentreck. He looked at Fred's house and cursed him. He looked toward the Winslows' house and cursed them. His thoughts had become twisted and tortured, the forty-five resting on his lap. *I'll show everyone.*

He had always been impulsive, but lately he had become almost purely reactive. Looking at the Winslow house, he thought, *You've ruined everything*. Impulse told him to shoot any Winslow he saw.

Trent had plans to meet Uncle Tim at the local diner, but he had a chore list. Zane cleaned an upstairs bathroom while Trent did the kitchen. He was quick about it. He was running late. He finished and started for the front door.

"See ya. I'm heading out to meet Uncle Tim," Trent called to Zane as his hand grabbed the doorknob on the front door.

"Oh, no you don't, hold on a minute!" Zane bounded down the stairs.

"What?"

"You aren't leaving until I inspect the kitchen. I'm in charge. You aren't leaving anything for me to do!"

Outside, Val took his foot off the brake and coasted down the street away from the Winslows—for now.

After Zane carefully scanned the kitchen, Trent announced, "See... spotless!"

"Good job, my brother." Zane grabbed Trent in a headlock. "Say hi to Uncle Tim for me."

"I will... see ya later."

###

Julie put her arms around Dan. They sat on the edge of a foundation stone to rest, sipping water. Butterflies fluttered through rays of sunlight streaming through the pine branches overhead. He had been suppressing his thoughts all day, but in this place he could no longer contain them. In this place of broken dreams and broken men he had to think of Lee.

"Julie, do you think it was Lee they were talking about on the news this morning?"

“You know him, I only know *of* him. Would he be out on his horse in the middle of the night?”

“It’s hard to say. I can’t help thinking of him. Let’s go down to the bait shop. It’s not much farther.” Dan checked the time on his cell phone. “We have plenty of time.”

“We have to face it sometime. I’m going to be praying for him.”

They climbed the bank near the old iron bridge down the road from the bait shop. A Stony Grove patrol car sat in the parking lot. Dan could see someone sat in the driver’s seat but could not make out his face. Julie hesitated.

“Come on, Julie. Let’s see what he can tell us.”

“What if it’s Peterson?”

“Maybe I’ll kick his butt.”

“Oh, Dan, you’re talking stupid. I’m serious.”

“Let’s see, we have a fifty-fifty shot it’s Jack Monroe.”

It was in fact Jack in the patrol car, writing on a clipboard. He placed it on the dash when he saw them and stepped out of the patrol car.

“Jack, how are you doing? We just hiked through the Gorge. We were stopping to visit with Lee.”

“Hi, Julie... Dan.” Jack tipped his hat. “Did you know Lee?”

“I stop down here once in a while to sit on the porch with him.”

“Sorry to tell you but he had a tragic accident last night.”

“Oh no,” Julie put her hand to her mouth.

“Seems his wife must have been suffering badly last night. We speculate he was heading for the bait shop to use the phone. Seems he came down an embankment off a trail onto the road. It was on a straight section, but just after a blind curve. There was a vehicle traveling at a high rate of speed. There weren’t even any skid marks. We figure Lee and the old mare died instantly. I guess it hit him without even slowing down. Peterson was the driver of the vehicle. It’s why I’m not on this case. The State boys will handle everything. I just have to fill out a report for the office.”

“What about Peterson?”

“He’s in bad shape. He hit a couple of trees after he hit Lee. I can’t believe he even survived. I guess his orneriness is what kept him alive. I think he would be better off dead. He has massive brain damage and a broken back. Those are the most serious injuries, but he has a lot of internal injuries as well. Maybe he’ll die before it’s over... which might be best. Initial reports were—and this is off the record—he had left a bar over in Castleton. He liked his booze. I think it was the only thing he liked.”

“How sad.” Julie put her arm around Dan and rested her head against him.

“I have Lee’s dog in the back of the car. He was watching over Lee’s wife. We had a heck of a time calming him down enough to get into the cabin. We found Lee’s wife had also passed away during the night. She had been suffering for quite a while. My wife used to check on her. Did you know her?”

“No, I never met her. Your wife was a friend of Lee’s wife?”

“Well, she was my wife’s great-aunt. She reached out to Lee’s wife a couple of years back, before she took ill. My wife’s grandmother was Lee’s wife’s sister.

“Lee had told me she was ill.”

“She was a sweet lady, a saint if you ask me. She put up with Lee. They were high school sweethearts. When she was young, she was beautiful, could have had her pick. She picked Lee, and she always told my wife she wouldn’t have had it any different, even if she could go back and do it all over again. She said nobody knew Lee like she did. She gave up everything for him.

“She was a God-fearing woman, but she wouldn’t go into town even to go to church. She read the Bible and prayed every day. I know the Lord will do right by her. She and Lee never had any children. My wife said she didn’t want to bring any into this vile world. Kind of sad, but if you knew some of the goings-on around here, you’d start to understand.

“The Haines family wouldn’t have anything to do with her once she married Lee. My wife said her beauty was nothing short of a curse. It was the best thing when her family turned their back on her. My wife never spoke to me about the details of her troubles, and I don't ask. There are a lot of skeletons around, some are best left to rest. Some families in these parts hold on to grudges the way a dog holds on to an old soup bone. It doesn't even matter if the bone has any meat to it. You know what I mean?"

The Haines family... Julie's mind drifted. *Louise was also a Haines, maybe Lee's wife's aunt. Louise held the keys to the undeveloped land at the end of the "paper alley." Land owned by her father and brothers, so... the vengeance wasn't initially just against Dimitri. She hated her brothers just like Lee's wife hated the male side of the Haines family. The letter had hinted at some sort of family trouble. I wonder if Dan is putting all this together. We'll talk later...*

"Yeah, Jack, I know what you mean." Dan noticed something strange about Julie's expression, as if she'd had an epiphany.

"I had to bring my wife over to the cabin to calm old Buck down. She was the only one he would trust. I got her there just in time. The State boys were about to shoot old Buck. I guess he's mine now. The wife says he doesn't have any other family. I've already got a pack of critters. I don't need old Buck, but what are ya going to do? Darndest thing, when I was driving down here, we went through where the accident happened. He just went to whimpering, kind of uncontrollable. It was just like he knew something or maybe he smelled something. Whatever it was, he started scratching at the back door. He wanted out in the worst way. I never saw anything like it."

"Well, if you don't have room, let me know. I would love to have him," Dan said.

Dan and Julie walked to the rear door of the patrol car with Jack. Jack opened the door, and Buck sat with a panting smile as Dan and Julie fussed over him.

"I'll talk to my wife. She's a real animal lover, a vegan for the reason. I go along with her. It's a shame how they raise animals these days, just for slaughter. In a factory farm they have no chance to even gain a spirit."

"Okay, well, let me know, Jack." Dan scratched Buck behind his ear.

"Things are going to start changing around here. You folks hang in there. I'm telling you, the next election is going to be interesting, and did you hear? When the university president resigned, it started a domino effect." Jack opened the driver's door of the squad car.

"Yep, I've been watching."

"Oh yeah, it was said he was resigning to spend time with his family and to write a book. Don't believe it for a second. The heat is on. Times are finally changing."

"You know, Lee knew a lot about the history of this place. It's like a door has slammed shut. We may never know all the details, but I find comfort in truth and knowing it exists whether it is known or not."

"Lee was no dummy. He watched the dealings of a lot of powerful people in these parts. He never made a difference in this world, but if he would have ever talked, a lot of people would have been sweating it. I'm sure his wife knew all the Haines family secrets as well. She probably knew who burned the Stratton resort up in the Gorge. Between the two of them, I'll bet they could have put half the county in prison for a long, long time."

"Did the Haines family have something to do with it?" Julie gave Jack a serious look.

"For the record, I can't say. There's small-town speculation they did. Nobody has any proof of it. So, I guess I can buy into it, unofficially."

"Jack, you have a future in politics." Dan offered Jack his hand, and they shook. Dan felt a cough coming on. He fumbled for his inhaler, unable to retrieve it before the coughing started. It was his worst attack yet. He coughed until he nearly passed out. White flashes surged in his eyes. Julie and Jack both grabbed his arms to hold him steady. Julie searched for his inhaler with her free hand. She held it near Dan's face and prompted him to open his mouth and inhale. Dan continued to struggle, finally catching on to Julie's pleas, then opened his mouth while Julie sprayed. He sucked in and held for a moment. He exhaled with relief. Jack and Julie lowered him to the ground next to the patrol car. Buck jumped out of the open door, sitting and offering Dan his paw.

"Are you going to be all right, partner? Bad cough you have there."

Dan continued to try to regulate his breathing without responding.

"He's doctoring for it. He's going to be fine. It's just going to take some time. I think we might have overdone it today."

"Are you planning to walk back to town?"

"That was the plan."

"Well, the department guidelines say I'm not running a taxi service. They tell me I'm not allowed to give people rides, but this seems like a medical emergency to me. Besides, my boss is in no condition to question what I do. I'm kinda my own boss now. How about if I give you two a lift back to town? If you don't mind riding with old Buck... or I can take you to a hospital if you would prefer."

"Town works. I don't think Dan wants to go to a hospital." Julie gave Dan a smirk.

"No... no hospitals, I'm feeling a lot better. We could probably even walk back."

"No way, you get halfway up the Gorge and have an attack, what is Julie going to do? It would take hours to get you help. No, this is an emergency. I'll drive you two home."

"Thanks, Jack, you're right. I can't risk putting Julie through any more than I already have."

"I'm going to have to go by way of Lee's accident scene. I just need to snap a couple of photos of the key points for our records."

The patrol car cruised slowly into the straightaway where the accident had occurred. Buck began to fret, whimpering. Dan sat up front on the passenger's side while Julie sat in the back with Buck. She tried to comfort him, but he continued to whine.

Jack stopped in the middle of the road and snapped pictures of the shredded trees Peterson had hit; he snapped some photos without getting out. A hundred yards up the road and about 150 feet from the initial contact point, the road was stained a brownish red, the marks covering the width of a whole lane. A smaller stain marked another spot thirty feet away from the contact point. Jack snapped photos, again without leaving the patrol car. Dan and Julie sat silently out of respect as Buck's whines turned into yelps. Buck slouched down on the back seat, his head drooping almost to the floor. Jack pulled away. Silence flooded the ride back to town.

THIRTY-ONE

Weeks after Lee's death, Dan and Julie spent their days organizing voter registrations and meeting with neighbors. Most of council had resigned. Mayor Whipple left office without notice, skipping out on his government deal. His wife had left him, and he just seemed to walk away from everything. Another special election had been scheduled to vote in new officials.

Two of the original members of their community action group and the most vocal had secretly sold their homes to Val to be used as student rentals. Val was trying to undermine the movement by encouraging betrayal. He had even paid above market value for the homes. The sales had made everyone a little suspicious of each other, but they kept meeting and talking the talk. The betrayal had the biggest impact on Julie, for she had thought the two wives were sincere friends.

Their schedule of activities wore on Dan. He hoped the State's investigation would crack the nut without them, but it moved like government does—slowly.

###

Two o'clock in the morning Julie heard a strange noise. She reached for the bedside lamp, flicking it on. Dan was heading for the bedroom door. He wasn't speaking or making a sound.

"Dan, what's the matter? Where are you going?"

Dan turned, his mouth agape, his hands on his throat. He eyes were huge. He couldn't breathe. He staggered into the hallway, then turned back toward the bedroom in a panic. He was losing his ability to think straight. His heart raced as the panic grew. He was going to die if he didn't breathe soon. Julie jumped out of bed and ran to him, but he fell to the floor before she reached him. His throat felt glued shut. *This is it*, was Dan's last thought as he lost consciousness. Julie watched as Dan's eyes rolled back in his head. His fingers curled and stiffened. His whole body grew stiff. Julie started to pound on him and screamed as the boys ran from their rooms.

"Mom!" the boys shouted in unison.

"Zane, call 911, hurry! Hurry! Trent, get a glass of water." She didn't know why she said it other than she wanted Trent out of the way.

Julie shook Dan frantically and watched as his color started to change to purple.

"Oh, please, dear God, don't let this happen." She rocked back and forth.

Suddenly, Dan let out what Julie took to be the death rattle. Air exhausted from his lungs. Then he lay still, and as she watched, he took a small breath. He took a second larger breath, and he continued to breathe, still unconscious.

"Oh, thank you, God, thank you." Julie bent over Dan, kissing his face, his eyes, his nose.

She heard the fire department siren. Zane's call had gone through. Trent ran up the steps with a glass of water, spilling a third of it on the way. Dan opened his eyes, his pupils dilated. He wasn't seeing at the moment. He was only semiconscious. Julie dipped her hand into Trent's water glass and rubbed her wet hand over Dan's face. He shifted his eyes, looking at her briefly, then blinked a couple of times.

"What happened?" he whispered.

"You passed out," she whispered back. "Maybe you should sip some water to moisten your mouth and throat."

Julie held Dan's head and put the glass to his lips. He took small sips at first. Then he drank a mouthful. It felt good going down his throat.

"Yeah, my throat felt dry and stuck. I couldn't breathe in or out."

"I hear sirens."

"Zane called 911."

"I'm not going to a hospital. It's a one-way ride. If you make me go, they'll keep me. They won't feed me right, and I won't have anything to do but lie in bed and wait for them to kill me. I am not going to the hospital. I'll call the doctor in the morning." Dan was emphatic.

The paramedic arrived about two minutes later. Zane ran down the steps to let them in. Dan still lay sprawled out in the upper hallway resting his head on Julie's thigh. She stroked his hair. The paramedics stumbled up the stairs, a stretcher in tow. They stood in the hallway, catching their breath.

"He says he's fine. He doesn't want to go to the hospital."

"Well, we are liable. We need to determine his status before we leave. Do we have your permission? We need to fill out our report. So, what happened?"

Dan and Julie took turns filling in the details for the report as one paramedic wrote and the other took vital signs.

"Heart sounds good, lungs are clear, oxygen levels are normal, eyes are a little dilated. I need to prick your finger and do a quick blood sugar test."

"You guys are pretty thorough. I won't even need to go to the doctor."

"We recommend you do a follow-up. Do you have any heart problems or lung issues?"

"Yes, I'm seeing a doctor about them."

"Do you have asthma?"

"Well, something like it. Julie where's my inhaler?"

Julie helped Dan sit up against the hallway wall as she slid her leg from beneath his head. She retrieved the inhaler and handed it to him.

"I suggest you use the inhaler again before you go back to bed. It's your call if you don't want us to take you to a hospital. I don't see anything life-threatening in your vitals, but please follow up with a doctor. You may have sleep apnea, which can cause heart damage over an extended period."

"Sleep apnea is where you stop breathing in your sleep, right?"

"Yes."

"That isn't what happened. I was awake and couldn't breathe."

"Tell the doctor. He may want to do a sleep monitoring test to see if you need a CPAP."

"Thanks, will do." *No way*, Dan thought, *that's not what happened, but I don't feel like arguing*.

###

Dan awoke the next morning to Julie's voice on the phone downstairs. She was talking to the pastor about baptism. He threw on some work clothes. Last night's incident seemed like a dream. He felt fine. There was no aftereffect. He descended the stairs as Julie hung up the phone.

"I'm going to call Dr. Cohen to find out how my last blood samples looked. Who were you talking to?"

"The pastor, he's stopping by to talk with you about your baptism. He'll prepare everything, and we'll do it after next Sunday's service. He said he already has two other people scheduled."

"Great, I wonder who else?"

"He didn't say. There's fresh coffee for you. Would you like anything to eat?"

"No... I'll be right in. Let me call the doctor first. I want to catch him before he starts his office hours."

Julie went into the kitchen but stopped near the doorway to listen to Dan's call. Her heart resonated with last night's scare.

"Hello, Dr. Cohen, this is Dan Winslow." There was silence as Dan listened.

"Yes, I wondered about my numbers... sorry, can you repeat that?"

Julie struggled to hear, but there was only a long period of silence. She wished she could hear both sides of the conversation. She feared Dan wouldn't be honest with her about the report. She would just have to trust him.

"I did have an incident last night. It was as if my windpipe had been glued shut. I couldn't breathe in or out. I finally passed out."

"Yes... right... no, I'm fine now. There are no after effects... Sure, I can come in. No problem. Thanks, Dr. Cohen, I will."

Julie rushed to the center of the kitchen, grabbing a dishcloth as an excuse for being there. Dan walked in to get some coffee.

"Well, what did the doctor have to say?"

"He said my numbers are up. They're not normal, but he said I'm definitely getting better."

Julie gave Dan a skeptical stare.

"My immune system seems to be recovering. He doesn't understand my episode last night, so he wants to see me. He said it might have been a one-time fluke or may indicate something new going on. He doesn't think it was connected to my condition, though."

"Well, it all sounds wonderful... if you're leveling with me."

"Honest, Julie, it's what he said. Matter of fact, I think I want something to eat."

Julie gave Dan a hug. She wanted it to be true.

###

Val woke around ten. He had paced his house until four in the morning. He ate a half dozen of scrambled eggs with half a pound of cheddar dumped on a plate, then threw a pound of bacon into the skillet. He usually ate standing near the stove. Bacon grease splattered, stinging his hand. The annoyance threw him into a rage. He grabbed the skillet handle, tossing it toward the sink. Bacon pieces and bacon grease splashed across the counter. As he cursed, his heart began racing, to the point he felt a burn across his chest. Pausing, he caught his breath and started picking up the scattered bacon, eating it as he went.

Breakfast finished, he sat at the dining room table spinning his Colt. 45 with his index finger. Whenever it stopped spinning, he would grab it, pointing it at different objects in the room. The game went on as he mulled over all the nice things he had done for ungrateful people and how many people had turned their backs on him. He opened a bottle of Irish whiskey. "Only drink the best," he had once been told. He poured a water glass full.

THIRTY-TWO

Julie's research into the church records consumed her one day of the week that wasn't filled with classes and caring for her mom's needs. She enjoyed the dark coolness of the church's library. Tome after dusty tome gave her insight into the historical significance of the town's founding. Pastor Kirk pointed her toward the 1800–1850 section of the library. "You'll find food for thought there."

As she scanned the handwritten scrawl, the final entry caught her attention: "Revolutionary War Land grant, 600 acres, along Stony Gorge and including the marsh, owned by Brooks family of Brookston, now recorded at the new courthouse as property of the Haines family." Why would that be? She flipped back through the book. For 1845, one entry said, "An overnight fire has completely destroyed the county courthouse. Authorities are investigating." Her heart raced as she perused through the book, finding no more information about the courthouse fire.

Studying birth records of the time period, she discovered a record of birth in 1840, a son, Josiah Brooks, born to Matthew and Julianna Brooks of Brookston. The attending midwife was Agnes Haines. Julie recognized Julianna's name from other birth records she had studied during her genealogy search. Doing the math, she realized Julianna would have been fifty and Matthew nearing sixty when Josiah was born. Possible, but not likely they'd be having a baby that late in life. Her search continued, as she found notes scrawled in the margins of the old books. She noted "Hettie, house slave of Brooks family, passed 14 September

1840." This was one day after the birth of Josiah, on the same property. Coincidence? She double-checked the birth records. Seems Matthew and Julianna had only stillbirths, other than Josiah.

As Julie took notes, she tried to make sense of it all. Why would the Brooks family simply allow 600 acres to be recorded as someone else's? Why would a baby's birth be recorded as belonging to the family, when it seems more likely he was born to the slave girl, who then died during childbirth? She couldn't wait to discuss it all with Dan. She reshelved the books and reported to Pastor Kirk's study to tell him she was leaving.

He looked up at her knock on the door frame. "Did you find anything to help you there?"

Her head was spinning, trying to make sense of what she'd found. "I think I need some time to piece it all together."

He smiled. "Take your time. We're glad you're making use of our resources. Next time I suggest you look in the 1940s section."

Something in his gaze made her anxious to discover more. "I'll just go check it out right now." And with that she returned to the library, seeking details about the 1940s.

The pastor of the church during the 1940s had much neater handwriting, making the research task simpler. She wondered where Pastor Kirk was trying to lead her. It didn't take long for her to find the connection he must have been hinting at: "A daughter, Sue Ellen, born 21 June 1941, to Janet (nee Brooks) and Henry Parker." Her own mother's birth! She checked her grandparents' birth, marriage, and death records. Why had she never noticed this before? Her grandparents married on November 22, 1940. Her mother was a seven-month preemie? She didn't remember hearing that story.

This time as she stopped to bid Pastor Kirk good-bye, she studied his eyes. "Do you know something about my mother's birth?"

He motioned for her to sit down. "I've read through all of the old church records. I never share what I piece together from them, but I think it's time a few wrongs are righted in this town."

She just stared at him, feeling weak. "I'm not sure what to make of it all. I feel like my brain has disconnected. Maybe I'm in a little bit of shock."

He rose from behind his desk and went to sit beside her, patting her arm. "I'm sure you'll make sense of it, in time. My suggestion is to pray about it. Do you mind if I pray with you?"

She nodded and closed her eyes, her head spinning.

"Father, we thank you for your great creation, your great plan of salvation. We praise you for your mighty loving-kindness. Please grant discernment for this young lady and her family, and bring her comfort and wisdom in this time of upheaval. Thank you for the promises of your Word, especially Psalm 54. In Jesus's name we pray, amen."

When he finished, Julie realized she was teary-eyed. "Thank you so much, Pastor. I need to get home and see my husband. This is all a little much."

He walked her to her car and made sure she set off without mishap. "I'll be stopping by later, to talk with Dan about his baptism." As she drove slowly toward home, she tried not to think of all of her findings until she could lay it all out on the dining room table, study it with Dan, and piece everything together.

She arrived home to find Dan preparing dinner, with places set on the screened porch. She went to him and hugged him close for a prolonged hug. He pulled back to look at her. "Hey, I'll cook more often if that's what it gets me!"

She pulled him to the table to spread out the research notes. She pointed out all the pertinent information she had unearthed today. With his arm around her waist, he began, "Here's what I make of it. Your mother was conceived before your grandparents married. That happens. A hundred years earlier, Josiah was born to the slave girl but probably passed as white. Your great-great-great-grandfather Matthew was likely his biological father. They had no other children and saw this as their chance to have an heir.

The Haines midwife knew the truth of who the mother was, so the Haines family had reason to try to alter some of the courthouse records after the fire while the Brooks family had reason to just let it go. The Haines family gained land while the Brooks family kept their secret. Of course, the land was never legally sold to the Haines, so they knew they had to keep the Brooks family secret, or they'd lose it."

Julie shook her head. "Don't you see? If the Haines family didn't actually own the land, they can't have legally sold it to the Wentreck family. That land belongs to the Brooks family."

They looked at each other a long moment before Dan broke the silence. "The paper alley is a moot point."

She grinned. "Prayers always achieve way above and beyond what we could ever imagine."

They called the boys for dinner, a joyous celebration. Zane looked from one to the other. "What's got into you two?"

They smiled at him. Dan diverted the conversation. "The episode last night was a fluke. The air was dry, I was breathing through my mouth, and my throat dried out. Like the day my vision went haywire; never happened again, did it?" Dan felt better than he had in months, and his improving numbers had boosted his morale.

Zane straightened his shoulders. "I hope you're right."

"I think I'll give Tim a call. Maybe we men can all do something together. After Pastor Kirk visits, let's go bowling or something."

Julie helped to clear the table, then grabbed her car keys. "I just remembered, I promised to take Klaare to the mall."

The Escalade cruised down Elm as Julie pulled away from the curb with Klaare. Julie didn't see it until she looked in the rearview mirror, as it came up behind them quickly. Her heart pounded as she realized Val's face showed clearly in her mirror; he was that close.

At the intersection, Julie turned left toward the mall. Val turned right. She let out a breath she didn't realize she'd been holding.

###

An investigator from the State Attorney General's office sat in Mayor Whipple's office pulling one folder after another from a stack. He read through the folders, took notes, and snapped photos.

The door from the hallway burst open, the doorknob puncturing the drywall. Val filled the gap. His eyes peered out of sunken flesh, and he looked pasty, his breath labored.

The shocked investigator rolled his chair back until he hit the wall. Val raised the forty-five. Val's own hand brought the piece to his temple, but evil pulled the trigger. Blood, flesh, and gray matter sprayed the mayor's door. Val stood for just a moment; his eyes bulged from the energy of the impact. He collapsed into a pile on the floor.

Good had not triumphed over evil. Evil simply had no more use for Val; he had become irrelevant. Evil now had a new game to play and new players to play with. The only thing changing was the cast. Eventually, the new council would pass, enforce, and abuse laws for personal gain. Such is the way of man in his quest to make things about him, in his quest to prove he is the way instead of God. The new men would become just like the old; it is human nature, the nature of self.

###

Julie turned away from her computer to stare at Dan. "You are so not going to believe this."

She didn't know whether to laugh, cry, or throw up. "My DNA results indicate that I'm not closely related to some of my cousins from my mom's side of the family. However, I am related to Harry's daughter Tricia."

###

The real estate office was cool and dimly lit as Julie entered. Harry looked up and smiled. She smiled back and flopped down in the chair across the desk from him. "I'm sorry to give you a shock, but I think this is a happy surprise. Does the name Janet Brooks mean anything to you?

Harry's face grew soft. "I loved her, but lost her... how do you know that name?"

"She was my grandmother."

He slumped in the chair. "Was?"

"Yes, sorry to tell you, she passed several years ago."

His voice shook. "Why are you telling me this?"

"My research has led me to believe that my mother, Sue Ellen, is your biological daughter."

Harry's face lost all color. "What?!"

"She was born 21 June 1941. My grandparents married in November of 1940. When did you stop seeing her?"

"Her parents suddenly forbade us to be together. That was the fall of 1940. I never knew why . . ."

"Seems they are the ones who missed out. Don't you see, Harry, you're my grandpa!"

Harry slowly rose to his feet and came around the desk. Julie stood to give him a hug. "To have gained you as my grandpa is a huge bonus in my life."

###

Jack Monroe left his car in the shade of Elm Street while he hurried to the Winslows' front door. Seems he'd stopped here a lot lately—this time it was a different type of mission. He didn't notice Dan napping on the porch swing until his foot hit the top step. Dan cracked one eye open. As he sat up, he patted the swing next to him. "Have a seat, Jack. I'll fetch you a lemonade."

Jack motioned for Dan to get up and follow him. As they walked the few steps to the car, Jack looked sideways at Dan. "You won't be the one fetching now." He opened the passenger door, and out ambled Buck, who made straight for Dan. He dropped to his knees to give Buck a proper hug.

Jack grinned down at them. "My wife said you need Buck more than we do."

Dan felt like they were finally home. "Please visit anytime you'd like and bring your family."

###

Sunday the church was filled. Harry was the official greeter in the vestibule, passing out programs. Talk of Val's sudden departure had been subdued. It seemed no one engaged in speculation. Most were stunned; some felt sorry for him.

Dan, Julie, and the boys had paused to hug Harry, then found a place in the pews about halfway down the aisle. Tim and Klaare came in separately and walked closer to the front, smiling at Dan, Julie, and the boys as they passed. They had never said they would be attending.

Pastor Kirk opened the service with a reading from Psalm 145, after which the choir sang "Come, Thou Almighty King." Pastor Kirk gave the invocation, and the congregation sang "More about Jesus." Praises and prayer requests were offered by the congregation. Many praises came forth: Brad's successful heart surgery, Walt's new job, Mary's daughter's new baby, Tom finding the Lord, and on and on.

The first prayer request was for the Lord to have mercy on Val Wentreck. The congregation requested prayers for our nation, our troops, our police, Lisa's cancer, May's diabetes, Frank's broken leg, and as Klaare once again asked for prayers for Dan Winslow's health, she turned to give Dan a smile.

Pastor Kirk led the choir in "Take Time to Be Holy" joined in by the congregation, after which he broke into prayer, repeating all the requests and adding a few of his own. He acknowledged all unspoken prayers. After worship in tithes and offerings, Pastor Kirk led the choir in "He Touched Me," and then it was the time of greeting. Dan had been anticipating this moment. He wanted to talk to Tim. He left the pew, smiling, shaking hands as he made his way to Tim and Klaare.

"Tim... what's going on, my brother?" Dan held out his hand as he put his arm around Klaare.

Tim smiled a devilish smile. "Klaare and I are getting baptized today, thought this would be the right place."

"You? So am I."

"Yeah, surprise, my man. Julie and Klaare wanted it to be a family thing."

Dan threw his arms around Tim and Klaare both, as he choked back tears. Julie came up behind Dan and rubbed his back.

He managed to say, "You have no idea what this means to me . . ."

Klaare kissed Dan's cheek as tears leaked from her eyes. The organist started to play, the time of greeting over, and they returned to their seats to sing "Gentle Shepherd."

Pastor Kirk was on fire giving his message he'd titled "Angels—God's Special Agents, Part 6—and Hell's Angels," focusing on verses in Matthew 12 and 25.

"We are engaged in spiritual warfare. There are fallen angels, called demons, at war against God. Pastors and ministers no longer want to address this issue. Our nation is under attack, and we need to return to identifying the enemy. You cannot win against your enemy until you identify who it is. Satan is a fallen angel. He is not God's equal, but he has followers—fellow fallen angels who toy with humanity. They create chaos and confusion. They cannot win, they will not win, but along the way they destroy much. If Satan has an equal, it is the archangel Michael, not God. In Revelation 12 Satan swept one third of the angels to Earth with him. These are the enemy warriors. We must become warriors for Christ. Angels are not and never have been human. They are more powerful than any human. Demons, according to Mark 6, are unclean evil spirits, but we must realize they are rational beings... they believe in God. They know him but they defy him." The entire congregation sat spellbound as Pastor Kirk looked and talked the part of a warrior. He stepped to the side of the pulpit.

"There is a difference between demon possession and demon influence. Search yourselves, have you seen these things in our community? You know and I know, we all have. There have been many casualties in this war. This war is a continuum... man passes laws to deal with these things, but the laws become twisted and the keepers of the law perverted." He stepped back into the pulpit. "Only accepting Jesus Christ in your heart creates a lasting change. Only then is a battle won. You cannot defeat the enemy through government action because even the best government is eventually lost to the enemy. Demons are powerful, but remember they are also without hope. This fact is also what makes them most dangerous. In Mathew 25 they are described as forever doomed to everlasting punishment. Once doomed, they have no reason to repent, so they double down on their terror. We must resist everything Satan offers. I offer you James 4 and 1 Peter 5, which tell us to run from any connection with the occult. Remember, demons are strongly associated with both idolatry and immorality, so flee. I also offer you 1 Corinthians 6, and 2 Timothy 2."

Pastor Kirk read the passages, then summed up with by suggesting the human mind is Satan's target. "You must resolve to commit to win against spiritual warfare. This is truly war, and you cannot sit by while others fight the fight. We must unite. Our battles cannot be won by lukewarm warriors. We must be passionate or we will be lost."

Pastor Kirk quoted several Bible verses pertaining to the dangers the enemy and the need to resist and lean into God for strength.

"Following the service everyone is welcome to join us at the social hall where we will be performing three full-immersion baptisms. I get so excited when young people, middle-aged people, and older people come to the Lord and ask to be baptized. Today we have three wonderful people celebrating a new life committed to the Lord. Please stay to witness. Harry will lead you all in a hymn while I head over to prepare for the baptisms, then you can all follow."

Harry walked to the lectern to lead the congregation in closing with "Faith Is the Victory."

The entire congregation proceeded to the social hall where Pastor Kirk stood waiting in the portable baptismal pool. Dan, Tim, and Klaare had left the church with him and were changing into their baptismal attire: sweatshirts and shorts. Dan would be the first to join Pastor Kirk in the pool. As Pastor Kirk began to talk, Dan entered the baptismal pool.

"This is Dan Winslow, and he comes today to be baptized into Christ. Over the past few weeks, I have gotten to know Dan. He has a strong faith and spirit. It is my pleasure to help him demonstrate to the community of God and to God his belief in spiritual birth." Pastor Kirk offered his hand to Dan.

Dan took it as he approached.

"Dan, please repeat after me the words of the good confession. I invite your church family to repeat them with you."

Dan faced the congregation. Pastor spoke directly to Dan in a low tone, for his ears only.

"I ask you to speak clearly and boldly, Dan." Dan gave Pastor Kirk a nod.

"I believe Jesus is the Christ, the Son of the Living God, my Lord and Savior." Pastor Kirk paused as Dan repeated each phrase.

"Dan, I now baptize you in the name of the Father, and of the Son, and of the Holy Spirit, for the forgiveness of your sins and the gift of the Holy Spirit."

Pastor Kirk positioned Dan and immersed him. Dan emerged chilled and smiling. The water felt much like the Stony and the midnight dousing in the bedroom, yet this time he was refreshed and without fear. His spirit was alive with joy, and the congregation applauded.

"Dan, if you would like, please address the congregation with a few words."

"Thank you, Pastor Kirk."

Dan gathered his thoughts. He looked at Julie and his two sons as he began to speak.

"I've known the fear of physical death. I have witnessed it on the faces of others and felt it in my own heart. I came here with a stronger sense of fear, a fear of my spiritual death."

Dan looked around at the faces of the congregation. "I have been witness to the physical death of many. In its face those who had healthy spirits and strong beliefs fared far better than those who did not. I witnessed their courage. I have also witnessed physically healthy men walk around with a dead spirit, a spirit that had received no new birth. It is a far worse fate than physical death."

Dan could feel his throat tighten. He did not want to appear weepy. He contained it, even as grief for his friends who had passed rolled in his heart.

"I have always been a believer, but sadly, I always clothed my spirit in camo. I realize I must welcome the Holy Spirit to live with me in order to truly live. I want to dress my spirit in the uniform of a warrior. I want my weapon to be the light of Love. Maybe there is such a thing as a light saber for Christ; if not, I will try to forge one. I have been a physical soldier for over twenty years... it is time for me to rise up as a spiritual warrior." Dan paused for a moment to reflect.

"I place my sins in full view of the Lord and ask his forgiveness. I have caved in my weakness and will in the future, I am sure. I accept the offer of Jesus Christ to be saved from myself. I stand here with the promise to be a warrior in the name of Love, in the name of God." Dan and Pastor Kirk grabbed each other's hand, then hugged.

"I hold myself out as an example to my sons. They have God's gift of free will, and it is my hope they will choose this path. It will be by their choice, though, not mine."

Dan left the baptismal pool, wrapping himself in a towel. Klaare was next to be baptized followed by Tim. Zane and Trent both hugged Dan after the service. Dan turned to Tim.

"Well, do you and Klaare have any more surprises in store for us?"

"Like what?"

"Like future plans?"

"Klaare just invited me to go back to Estonia with her. An adventure. Whatcha think?"

"Good move." Dan put his arms around Tim and Klaare, and soon Julie joined in along with the boys.

THE END

EPILOGUE

We never discovered the cause of the mysterious events in our house. We moved away from Elm Street as soon as Trent and Zane were grown. Living in the country had always been our dream, so we built our dream house and now enjoy beautiful views of trees and hills and our pond. We took up gardening to support our healthy diet. Dan's illness has been held at bay through peaceful living. We still love to hike through the Gorge. Our newly discovered family is a source of support and joy.

ABOUT THE AUTHORS

Bill and Dale Ann have hiked and motorcycled through much of North America, Europe, and the Caribbean islands. Their works include several short stories and novel-length fiction creations. Their true story *Instead, by Grace: from dark to light* was published in 2021. When not writing, their other pursuits include homesteading and bicycling.

Please visit braveknightwriters.com
We'd love to hear from you!

Reviews on your online book review platform of choice much appreciated.

Made in the USA
Columbia, SC
07 May 2026

82434295R10163